Eagles

Two miles north, Ryan climbed two hundred feet, slowed down to three hundred knots and did a hundred and eighty degree turn back to the convoy, through a criss-cross of gunfire.

Coming up to it, he pulled hard back and then pressed the pickle button.

It was like aiming darts at a dartboard – only these were a lethal mixture of deadly ordnance. The stand-off bombs streaked forward, landing exactly on target as neatly as a player throwing a double sixteen.

Now climbing vertically, Ryan wheeled round to watch.

Seconds later, the flash momentarily blinded Ames's eyes. Even high above the explosion, the metal sides of the bomber vibrated.

Flames and smoke billowed upwards.

It was like nothing Ames had ever seen or could have imagined. He felt exhilarated, horrified, triumphant. It was like hovering over an erupting volcano of your own making. A volcano tossing up not melted rock, but fragments of lorries, guns, cars, people. None of it seemed real. Just the power. It was like having fused inside his body both God and the Devil.

by the same author

The Blood Brothers
Call Me Captain
Cone of Silence
Electric Train
Excellency
The Gun Garden
The Heart of the Storm
Milk and Honey: Travails with a Donkey
The Proving Flight
The Siren Song
Sword of Honour
The Take Off
The Temple Tree
Village of Stars
The White Sea-Bird
The Wind off the Sea
The Stick

non-fiction
The Human Factor in Aircraft Accidents
The Water Jump: The Story of Transatlantic Flight
Strange Encounters
The Complete Skytraveller

with Betty Beaty
Wings of the Morning

Eagles

DAVID BEATY

Methuen London

First published in Great Britain 1990
by Methuen London
Michelin House, 81 Fulham Road, London SW3 6RB

A CIP catalogue record for this book
is available from the British Library

ISBN 0 413 63330 6

Printed in Great Britain
by Richard Clay Ltd, Bungay, Suffolk

For our dear daughters –
Sue, Carole and Karen

Contents

Book One

16 December
The Court Martial

The Assembly Hall in the United States Air Force Base at Haddington, Cambridgeshire, England, was stacked with empty chairs.

Of the cheap wooden folding variety, these chairs were being carried away from the walls by a man and a woman. Both were wearing identical khaki and green battle dress uniforms with revolvers on their leather belts. Both were American airmen, for sex in the USAF is not differentiated on duty.

As one by one, they moved the chairs and placed them in various parts of the Hall, gradually a pattern began to emerge.

First, six chairs were taken up to a dais and arranged three at each end of a rectangular oak table. Then an altogether more imposing chair with a high straight back was placed in the centre, directly under the Stars and Stripes, its flagpole slotted into the wall and angled so that the flag hung free.

On the main floor opposite was placed a single chair behind a tiny table. To the right was a larger table behind which went a further five chairs. To the left, the male airman placed a single chair behind another tiny table on which the female airman placed a Bible.

On the far wall to the left was the biggest table, behind which were arranged two dozen chairs in four rows.

The two airmen worked in silence till the pattern of chairs was complete. Then the male airman went to the door beside which was a pile of white cards.

Watched by the female airman, he began to position them on the various tables.

On the table on the dais, he put six cards bearing the names of four USAF captains and two majors. A longer card on which was printed COLONEL A. J. STANDISH, PRESIDENT, was placed in the centre.

On the biggest table, he placed a card saying JUDGE ADVOCATE. Then on the smaller table, he put DEFENSE COUNSEL.

On the two tiny tables, he put nothing. The one card he had left was the biggest, printed in large letters, COURT MARTIAL IN PROGRESS. This he took out of the Hall and pinned to the outside of the door.

The pattern was complete. The airmen's work was done.

The woman sat down on the chair behind the tiny table with no Bible on it. The man sat beside her at the table marked DEFENSE COUNSEL and produced a packet of *Philip Morris*.

'Have one?'

'Thanks.'

He lit her cigarette. Then his own.

'I'd die,' said the woman. 'I'd die if I had to sit here for real!'

The man put his head back and blew a cloud of blue smoke towards the ceiling. 'Guess you're right.'

'Whaddayer mean?'

'The guy who sits here for real.'

'Will die?'

'Sure. That's the hot shit. They'll hose the bastard.'

'Jeezus!' The woman's eyes went wide. 'They wouldn't!'

'Why wouldn't they?'

'Not in the USAF.'

'Why not in the USAF, for chrissake?' He mimicked her tone. 'Why's the USAF so goddamned different? It's murder, huh? Coupla thousand men and women in US death cells right now, waiting. An' for what? For the pill, the gas, the rope, the electric chair. They killed. So they get hosed. That's right! That's the law! That's justice! Whasso different about this case? C'mon, Airman, you tell me! Whasso different here?'

Book Two

1 September–18 November
The Flying Operations

One

One thing was certain. Captain Rod Ryan, nicknamed Hotrod, wanted this assignment to the Sixth Tactical Fighter Squadron at Haddington, England so badly he could walk away from his new bride without a backward glance.

The date was 1 September – the day it all started. The sun was just past its zenith in a warm, clear sky over Nellis Airbase from where the two F-115 fighter-bombers in their charcoal lizard camouflage were now taking off, shaking the low dun-coloured hills and vibrating the tarmac under the feet of the two civilian watchers. Four black funeral feathers trailed their exhausts as they climbed. The afterburners glowed briefly like tiny orange suns. Then the aircraft banked and turned.

The suns were extinguished as the pilots throttled back. Now the aircraft became black darts hurtling north-east for what Samantha Ryan, the young woman watcher, regarded as the back of beyond, and her father regarded as a step up the ladder for his son-in-law – and, maybe, for him.

'My son-in-law's right there on the front line. Constant readiness.' That would sound good – the sort of talk they liked on the Hill.

'Did you see that, Sam honey?' the Senator put a stout arm round his daughter's delicate shoulders and spoke in the indulgent tone of a loving father who always gave his only daughter the best and most expensive. 'Your husband's gotten the edge on Scott already!'

She shrugged off his arm. A faraway look came into her wide baby-blue eyes, but she made no comment.

It wasn't true, anyway. The two F-115s were flying for the moment side by side as briefed, in loose formation on Visual Flight Rules. The Nevada desert fell away as they began to climb steeply up into the sky – and into a certain Air Force history.

In the cockpit of Firefly One, Rod Ryan – black-haired, black-browed, with what women found beguilingly Irish blue eyes – glanced out of the small side window as if suddenly remembering he had left his nineteen-year-old wife behind. But when he screwed his head round again, all he said to his weapons system operator was, 'What time the tanker, Milt?'

Milton Ames was a youngster but a clever one – pale and gangling, with rabbity front teeth and a big technical brain, but to Ryan, no discernible personality, no conversation, no get-up-and-go. Just electronic mad. An electronic freak. Ryan suspected he was a virgin, and you didn't come across many of those in the USAF. What the boffins would call an extinct species. It was Ryan's oft-repeated joke that Ames would never lose his virginity till he found an electronic whore. But as Ryan was the best bombing pilot it was right that he should be teamed up with the best wizzo. Whether Ames was a virgin or not, Ryan was broad-minded – and you could say that again.

The wizzos did a pilot's course as part of their training, so they could take over in an emergency. For better or worse, as in marriage, each depended on the other for their safety.

Air commanders and wizzos had what they called a 'Contract' between them. This was a worked out code of behaviour, what they would do in all sorts of circumstances, a mutual trust in each other, a silent unbreakable bond. Certainly Ames had an understanding with Ryan, but it was the understanding of experts in different fields. Inclined to be inarticulate, the wizzo was shy of his AC.

In fact, he was shy of everybody. Now he consulted the faces on the instrument panel – his only friends.

'17.06.'

Ryan settled back in his seat and just for the hell of it asked Ames what he thought he was doing, for chrissake, kissing Samantha like that.

Ames, poor sucker, rose like always to the bait. He looked scandalised. 'But she kissed us all!'

'You more'n the others, Milt! More even than Jonny Scott. And that's gotta be bad! Jeezus, she's not the squadron mascot!'

Ames had heard that Samantha was known as the squadron something, and the word wasn't mascot. She and her parents lived in a grand mansion close to Nellis. Father was an electronic magnate and also Senator on the Armed Services Committee. He took a real fatherly interest in the squadron, asked them to champagne parties and barbecues. Samantha, a dainty little overdressed blonde, was always there, and it seemed to Ames in his ignorance that she came on hot for Jonathan Scott, whose head he could just see cameoed in sunlight, half a dozen winglengths away. The next thing Ames knew, they were all invited to a wedding – and it was Hotrod Ryan who was the lucky man.

Suddenly Ryan could keep a straight face no longer. He burst out laughing.

'Only kiddin', Milt.' He reached over and punched his wizzo lightly on the shoulder. 'She's kinda pretty though, huh?'

'Sure is.' Ames said automatically. 'You're a lucky guy!'

Ryan smiled in self-congratulation. Quite apart from Samantha, he was in an odd mood. If he hadn't known better, Ames would have thought that his aircraft commander was into chemicals. But Ryan was the sort of jock who got high on his own adrenalin. Apart from women, he lived and breathed flying. Before they'd taken off from Nellis, he'd walked round Firefly One, admiring the newly painted yellow and green stripes on its high tail that denoted they would now be attached to the Sixth Tactical Fighter Squadron. He'd run his hand lovingly over the skin of the aircraft, and taking out that famous knife of his from its sheath, he had flipped out a minute pebble in the tread of the port tyre, like the aircraft was some animal to which he was giving the final grooming.

The knife, as everyone on Nellis knew, came from the survival pack of Ryan's father, a Nam war hero. Sent home with his personal effects, Ryan always carried it as his talisman, wearing it on the left hip of his custom-made green flight suit. It was a vicious little object that had cut Ryan Senior out of crashed aircraft, had slit Commie throats, had had more heroic adventures than Batman, and would have won the Nam war single-handed if Hotrod's father had lived long enough.

But he hadn't. He'd crashed in a blaze of glory when Rod was six. He'd left his son the knife and the fight. His son had grown to be a real balls-to-the-wall jock. And a real success with the women.

Ames had no famous father to compare with either Ryan's or Samantha's. His father was a janitor in a downtown New York apartment. A humble kindly man, almost superstitiously disturbed by what he saw as his son's dizzy rise. His gift to his son when he passed out of Squadron Flying School, shamefacedly proffered and shamefacedly accepted, had been a silver St Christopher. Ames wore it round his neck along with his dog-tags. Just a lucky mascot, like Ryan's long-bladed knife. Clamped inside an egg-shell arsenal, not very powerful magic.

Whistling through his teeth, pleased with his sassing of Ames, Ryan called up Firefly Two, spoke into his mike.

'Hi, Jonny!'

Ames thought he was going to sass him about Samantha, which might have been dangerous. But all Ryan said was, 'Wanna bet we'll hit the tanker before you?'

'Negative, Firefly One.'

Inside the cockpit, Jonathan Scott exchanged a smile with his big black wizzo. 'No dice!'

Scott was a tall, fair-haired Bostonian with the relaxed voice and manner of a man who has never had to yell for what he wanted. If the crew in Firefly One was technically the best, Firefly Two's was the most harmonious and steady. Whoever had picked the four crewmen for Special Assignment was not as bone-headed as Top Brass was always reckoned to be. Someone in the Pentagon knew their ass from their afterburner.

Glenn Robinson, Born-again Christian, was a top inter-services athlete. Unflappable. Loyal. Accurate. Courageous. Devoted to his aircraft commander, he saw the USAF's role as peacemaking; now more than ever, with *Glasnost* and a wounded Russian bear out there. Holding the civilised world together. It had been his idea to name the aircraft the *Peacemaker* and have a dove as the nose art. But none of the ground crew or aircrew had liked the idea, and tactfully Scott had suggested they leave out the 'e' and make it *Pacemaker* with an athlete like Glenn on the cone. Ryan's aircraft was called the *Probe* – maybe named after the end of a tanker's boom, maybe not.

'Chickenshit!' Ryan called over his radio.

'What I'll lay is you'll sneak in first somehow.'

'You bet your sweet life I will!'

But it was all good-humoured. Eventually, the tanker's beacon came up on Ryan's radar. Ten minutes later, he made the connection. There was a female boomer manning the probe. That made Ryan's day, or rather night, for it was now quite dark. He did a quick lock-on and a swift suck, accompanied by a stream of smartass talk to the poor sergeant boomer. Ryan just loved the probe and suck analogy. He swore he could see her face in the tail light of the Stratotanker above them, and she was blushing.

Certainly Ames was. He had old-fashioned ideas about women. He bet to himself she'd be real glad to get Scott next in the queue.

Then they were uncoupled, and were streaking in and out of huge *cumulo-nimbus* castles.

'You gotta treat an aircraft like a woman, Milt. And vice-versa. Smooth her along. Make her take you where you wanna go. Not where she wants to go. Gentle but firm.' He stared down admiringly at his own hand on the throttles. 'Only one thing's as good as fucking and that's flying! An' now you and me are gonna do real flying! Front-line flying!'

Christ, Ames thought, the way Ryan batted everyone's ears with the Sixth TFS's front-line status, you'd have reckoned Haddington, England, was just across Red Square from the Kremlin. No wonder Samantha didn't plan to come over yet awhile!

It didn't make the Special Assignment that much more attractive to him. He turned his eyes away from Ryan, and glanced down at the cloud-carpet below. Caught in the sunlight, he could see the two aircraft shadows racing forward, ringed in full rainbow circles. That sight of the Brocken Sceptre – the name itself was bad enough – always chilled him. As if they were already dead and gathered in – little black crosses, little cloud haloes to mark their going.

He reached out and pulled down the green shades on the windscreen. Back went his eyes to the familiar faces of the friendly instruments. He began to wonder what it would really be like in England, if the Brits all spoke like he'd heard on TV soaps, if they liked Yanks or if they'd gone soft on Gorbachev, if the four of them really were on an important assignment, or if they were just going to beef up a slack squadron.

Two-thirds of the way over they refuelled again, and Ryan's mood changed. There was no girl boomer, so no fun.

But that wasn't it. It was as if the tentacles of Europe and England, the purposefulness of the front line had come out ahead of the first squiggle on the radar screen to grab them.

Ryan suddenly turned to Ames. 'D'you believe in anything, Milt?'

Ames had never heard Ryan talk on any subject but women and flying, so the question threw him. 'Like what?'

'Like anything.'

'Like Glenn, d'you mean?'

'Jesus, no! Not that crap!'

But he couldn't explain what crap he did mean. And anyway, as it wasn't electronics, Ames couldn't understand. Ryan wasn't sure he understood himself. Just a gut feeling of something coming round. Something waiting for you.

'Life's crazy, Milt!'

Ames looked at his AC nervously. 'Sure is.'

The first scribble came on the radar and that was the heel of Ireland, and Ryan didn't even salute his Irish heritage.

'I'll tell you something that'll make you reckon it crazier still.'

Ames trembled to think what in God's name might be coming. Ryan was maybe going to explain his gung-ho mood, and Ames wasn't sure he wanted to hear it. He waited in fidgety silence as he stared at the queer glowing pig-snout that announced the coast of Wales.

'The wing commander at Haddington,' Ryan said in a deadpan voice, 'was my father's squadron commander in Nam. Whaddya say to that, Milt?'

All in all, Ames was relieved.

'Like you said, life's crazy,' he said.

'Is that all you can say, you stupid bastard? My father was a hero.'

'We all know that, sir.'

'Got the Medal of Honour. Highest USAF award.'

'We all know that, too.'

'Craddock knew he was the best. We're gonna make sure Craddock gets no less from me.'

Ryan leaned forward. Their radar showed the Cornish coast as clear as crystal. The next moment, the wizzo's ears were deafened. Firefly One began shaking. On the machmeter, the needle shot past Mach .6, Mach .8, Mach .9 till behind them the whole universe echoed to a gigantic thunderclap as the F-115 went through the sound barrier.

'Jeezus . . . Rod . . . where's the fire?'

Over the radio, Scott's voice, dimmed by distance, as laconic as ever but edged with anger at this breach of flying discipline.

Ryan didn't answer. He stared ahead through the windscreen as Firefly One shot over a sliver of sand and began flying in a cloudless sky over a chequerboard of English fields.

'New ETA?'

'07.33.'

The answer seemed to please Ryan. He spoke into the RT.

'Haddington Tower, Firefly One. Permission to cancel Instrument Flight Rules.'

They were at Flight Level 300 – thirty thousand feet. Their present speed made it like sitting astride one of their own rockets.

'Firefly One . . . cleared CAVU.'

Back went the throttles. The speed dropped. But steeper and steeper down went the nose.

In the roaring disquiet, Ames consulted his friends on the instrument panel as to what the hell Ryan was up to now.

They were as nervous as he was. The altimeter unwound like crazy. The machmeter clicked dementedly.

Ryan was going to fly into Haddington in a blaze of glory. Nervously, Ames touched his St Christopher and prayed that, unlike his dad, Ryan pulled out before they actually hit the ground.

Two

Even before she opened her eyes, Maxine Craddock put out her hand and explored that empty other half of the king-sized bed where her husband ought to have been.

She squinted at the clock on the bedside table.

Seven-fifteen on a cold British summer morning. Caspar up and gone with that mysterious quietness he had probably learned, God help him, in Vietnam. In her moments of self-doubt, which grew with the years, she wondered if he ever slipped as silently out of other rooms, and then was immediately ashamed. She trusted her husband, didn't she, more than any man she had ever known? If maybe only for the reason he'd never had the time for other women. Colonel Caspar Craddock, the workaholic, the Commander of the Ninth Tactical Fighter Wing at the USAF Base at Haddington, the sort of man that the NATO front line rested upon.

Every morning when she was awake in time, and when he was not attending on some bunch of generals at Mildenhall, Ramstein or Brussels, Maxine watched a metamorphosis: her husband returning from the bathroom. Tall, broad-shouldered, slightly bull-necked with a rugged unremarkable face, brown hair wet from the shower, donning his uniform – the strong, warm, known, occasionally loving body changing like an accelerated chrysalis into the tight-lipped keen-eyed beribboned Colonel, hardly known to her at all.

This morning, not even that.

This morning, a discreet tap on the bedroom door, followed by the silvery well groomed head and thin profile of a sprightly elderly man in a white monkey-jacket and formal grey-striped trousers. Jarman, the Craddock servant, locally employed. A treasure, as the Brits would say. To Maxine, an evocation of childhood and more certain days in the warm soft South of God's own country.

'Good morning, madam.'

Jarman entered as quietly as her husband had left. He didn't actually whip out a thermometer, but his shielded grey eyes took the psychological temperature.

'I trust you slept well?'

He was aware (for of what that went on in this house was he unaware?) of tension last night. The Colonel was uptight about something on the Base, and to make matters worse, Miss Sharon, the Colonel's step-daughter, one of those wild free-thinking American students, had telephoned from Berkeley. That always upset Mrs Craddock. She wanted her daughter over here with her. But that wouldn't do. Jarman pursed his lips and shook his head to himself as he scanned Maxine's beautiful haggard face.

'Just fine! Slept like a babe!'

'The Colonel said to bring your tea at seven-fifteen.' Jarman poured fussily from the silver pot he had acquired for his employers and proffered the china cup with a flourish.

'Thank you, Jarman. What time did he leave?'

'Twenty minutes ago, madam.' Jarman smiled primly. 'It's Monday. Wing Commander's Inspection.'

'Don't I know it!'

'And he has a busy day after that.'

'Always has, Jarman! Always has!'

'Shall I draw the curtains, madam?'

'Yes, do that.'

Jarman enjoyed the view from this bedroom window. The Commander's large solid house was set apart from all the other married quarters on the only slight rise within this Fenland airbase. There were no flower beds, because Americans didn't seem to go in for that particular frivolity. But beyond was a splendid view of the Headquarters building, and the white flagpole in front of it, where morning and night, the flags of the two nations were raised and furled – Colonel Craddock's Stars and Stripes and the small RAF pennant of Squadron Leader Naylor, the RAF liaison officer, which symbolised the Base's landlords, the British. Just to stand there made Jarman feel ten feet tall. After a lifetime of buttling here he was, at the best, most important assignment of all. At the hub of real power.

He had given up his post with a Scottish duke to look after his elderly mother at Haddington. In the sad hiatus after she died last year, Jarman liked to think of himself as having been head-hunted by Squadron Leader Naylor. It had worked well. He never looked at that flagpole without flattering himself that his perceptions, his tact, his skills, helped to keep those soon-to-be-raised flags together.

'Breakfast is ready, madam.' Jarman turned to go. 'And your first appointment is at nine o'clock.'

Maxine grimaced. 'Damn!'

Twenty minutes later, dressed elegantly as always, this morning in a lettuce-green linen that flattered her huge hazel eyes and red-brown wavy hair, she paused for a moment, hand upraised at her dressing-table, to watch the morning ceremony.

Caspar was there, of course, a figure diminished by distance, but towering above the men on either side of him – dear kind Evan Walton, his vice-commander, and on the other side, Steven Naylor, plump and jolly on too much Yankee food and too many dining-in nights, the titular head of the Base, the liaison officer, but really the football between two sides that didn't trust each other over much. It never failed to amuse Maxine to see the little blue pennant, a small pointed triangle with its RAF roundel, rushing to the top of the pole as the bugler sounded 'Reveille', to be then dwarfed by the big spread of the Stars and Stripes. Then the cold British wind flapping them both together regardless as the band played 'God Save the Queen', followed by the 'Star Spangled Banner'. It still gave Maxine an almost erotic pleasure to watch her husband, even from a long way away. Like that, she could fall in love with him a little again. She could make a circle of her thumb and forefinger and encompass the distant him. Hold him. The him that for the past ten years had grown inexorably further away from her. The man, turning as he climbed the magic ladder, into the monster Air Force machine.

Last night he had been further away than ever. It hadn't just been Sharon. Sharon, the adorable five year old when Caspar and she were married, had also changed, espousing all the, to Caspar, forbidden ideas – CND, student protest, Yanks out of wherever they were in. Impossible to have her over here in this house, a kind of Yankee Fifth Columnist amongst the Brits.

The smell of hot British toast and good American coffee came wafting up the staircase. Jarman's way of prompting madam. Maxine clipped on her wrist watch, and walked across the landing, past the door of the never-used bedroom that was ostensibly for Sharon.

Downstairs, Jarman, never one to waste a moment, was rubbing up the silver cups and trophies that crammed every shelf and cranny of the dining room sideboard. All of them Caspar's but one – not just bombing and navigation and air race trophies, but swimming and baseball and golf. For here was the all-round American male. The only one that was hers was a small mounted medal for drama at Vassar. She had meant to be an actress. But then at twenty, she had met and married her first husband – a vivid, voluble and persuasive producer – experienced a swift and bitter awakening from naïve girlhood, given birth to Sharon, divorced her husband by disenchanted mutual consent and, four years later, fallen in love with her first husband's true opposite, Caspar Craddock, a granite rock of a man who, placing her at once on the pedestal she had yearned for, had seemingly left her there.

Stowing away his duster, unpeeling his rubber gloves, Jarman busied himself serving breakfast. Yes, the Colonel had eaten a hearty breakfast. And yes, he had left the list of her day's engagements. He had seemed in fine form, absorbed as always, but in good spirits. Jarman's small bland lips curved in an indulgent smile, demanding that Maxine smile back, playing the charade of Happy Families.

'Did he say when he'd be back?' Maxine squinted at the list of her engagements. 'He's not, I guess, going to drop in on our senior wives' coffee party?'

'No, madam. No to both questions.'

'Did he mention dinner?'

'No, madam. But I took the liberty of so doing. He said for it to be something cold. He had no idea what time he'd be home.'

Now why should that strike some dull heavy chord inside herself? Why did the day suddenly stretch out in aching loneliness, that most awesome loneliness, the one surrounded by chatter and meaningless business – the wives' coffee party; judging the bonny baby competition at the crèche; attending junior school assembly; tennis with Squadron Leader Naylor's wife, Elspeth, who carried the *Entente Cordiale* too far and always let Maxine win; presenting the prize at the inter-section quiz. The Colonel's wife, fluttering on her rounds – smiled at, deferred to, friendless.

Then the waiting for Caspar. And so to bed.

And there the worst loneliness of all. At forty, she was at the height of her beauty – a few extra lines on her sculpted face, but good bone structure. The most attractive woman on the Base, Caspar had once said in a moment of tenderness, rare these days, a dozen times more attractive than Sharon. Most importantly, the only woman he, Caspar, had ever loved. So he had said when they married thirteen years ago, and she believed him. Still believed him, though there were some very attractive women on the Base, trim girl officers in their twenties who treated Caspar like God.

But even they weren't really the point. For steadily, year by year, his affections, as they say in divorce court language, had been alienated. Not so far as she knew by another woman. But by the Air Force. He lived by the Air Force, thought Air Force, slept and dreamed Air Force. And last night he had withdrawn even further from her, because something to do with the Air Force was bugging him. He couldn't talk to her any more. The man inside the uniform was shrinking to a withered nut inside an impenetrable calcified shell.

As Jarman set the coffee-pot in front of her, and tried to engage her in discussion as to what the Colonel might favour for this evening's cold collation, she felt a childish longing to smash that shell, to draw her husband's attention to herself, to hit jolly Mrs Naylor over the head with her tennis racquet, to declare all babies uniformly ugly, to have an affair with Evan Walton, who adored her, to scream – or anything.

Instead, the screaming was done for her. Used to low flying, this was something more immediate, more terrifying, more threatening than ever she had heard. An aircraft, an F-115 by the shriek of it, hurtling only feet above the quivering, quaking roof-top.

Jarman, pale-faced and open-mouthed, threw up his hands in horror. As they held their breaths for the seemingly inevitable crash, the glasses on the cabinet chimed together, the dishes danced, the floor shook, and Caspar's most prized cup for Best-Run Base, toppled forward on to the floor.

No crash came. Amazingly the aircraft pulled out. Jarman, ever indulgent towards the strange doings of Yankee airmen, smiled, shrugged and swooped to pick up the cup.

'No harm done, madam.'

In his finicky way, he pulled out a duster and polished the cup again, before carefully replacing it.

'I quite thought—' He turned his hooded grey eyes skywards but didn't say what he thought. 'But all's well that ends well, eh, madam?'

He invited her to smile. But she couldn't. She had a disturbing feeling that all was not well, and this was the beginning – not the end.

Three

Still as a statue, Colonel Craddock stood outside the Base hospital as the F-115 screamed overhead, so low that automatically his three companions ducked and then shamefacedly straightened.

Not so the Colonel. He remained rigid, hand upraised to the gilded peak of his cap, shading his narrowed eyes, his mouth grim, watching the F-115 tilt vertically to port, slide inches above the ground between the Maintenance hangar and the Avionics section, wheel round on to the Approach, then put undercarriage and flaps down for a perfect landing.

Uncertainly, the other three – Lieutenant-Colonel Diefenbaker, Lieutenant-Colonel Evan Walton and Squadron Leader Naylor, the RAF Commander – glanced up at his outraged face.

'Christ-on-a-crutch!' Diefenbaker exploded. 'Talk about cutting the heads off the daisies!'

The Colonel dropped his hand to his side, and looked sharply at the Squadron Commander of the Sixth TFS. 'None of ours is airborne?'

'None, sir,' Diefenbaker agreed eagerly. 'Guess it's one of the new guys.'

'Making his entrance,' Walton suggested pacifically, and was immediately shot down.

'It'll be his exit too,' Craddock retorted, eyeing the other three as if it had been their fault.

High above their heads, a second F-115 appeared, made a copybook circuit and a softly-softly touchdown. As if to make amends for the first performance, Diefenbaker observed, 'Cat pissing on glass!'

Prudently, Naylor said nothing about either landing. Though the backlash of those first few screeching seconds would surely land on his desk, he knew when to keep his mouth shut.

But the Colonel correctly read his pained expression. 'Apologise to whoever complains, Steve,' he said. 'Tell them it won't happen again. They have my word for it.' He turned to Diefenbaker. 'Find out which pilot it was. Tell him this is England, not the Nevada desert. And tell all four crew men I'll see them in my office—' he glanced at his wrist watch, 'one hour from now.'

Diefenbaker saluted smartly. 'Sir!'

'Thank you, gentlemen. All in all, a good inspection.'

Which was less praise than was due, Diefenbaker thought, as they all three saluted the Colonel and dismissed. The bombing up of the practice F-115 had been four seconds less than on the last inspection, but still ten seconds short of the Colonel's target. There had been a trail of spilled oil on the concrete floor of Hush House, and one of the fitters was using a non-issue ratchet which the Colonel had snagged him for. A cook in the Mess Hall had sores on his hand, and the Colonel, whose eyes missed nothing, had sent him packing to the hospital. But all in all, a bloody good inspection.

Colonel Craddock, now bounding up the three steps to the Base hospital, would have agreed. Pushing open the hospital's revolving entrance doors, he was momentarily brought up sharp against the flickering reflection of himself in the glass panels.

Not given to looking at himself in mirrors, this unavoidable reflection always startled him. The tall immaculate officer, hat set dead straight over straight knitted brows, short thick nose, the upper lip, long and puggy, the chunky chin slightly fleshing, the sharp grey eyes glaring at him like a hostile stranger.

Then the unwanted vision spun away. He was in the rubber-floored, white-painted hall, the sergeant behind the Reception counter jumping up to greet him. An officer emerged from the corridor, saluted him smartly – and the unfriendly stranger was among sychophantic friends.

Colonel Bates, medical officer in charge of the hospital, threw open the door of his office to welcome him inside. A thin clever doctor with wispy white hair half an inch too long for Craddock's liking, he was within a year of retirement and couldn't wait. But as they walked the corridors, the wards, the laboratories, the X-ray and physio departments, Craddock found little to fault.

Then at eight twenty-one, he released Colonel Bates and looking at his watch to make sure how much of that precious hour was left, he tapped on a door marked Major H. Mansell, Aerospace Medicine.

Entering that office was something like entering cool shade after relentless heat. The sensation was possibly not so much due to the white paint, the tall green plants and relaxing club chairs as it was to the occupant.

A slim girl, her fair hair parted neatly in the centre, rose from behind the desk to greet him. That desk was in front of the window, which always gave her the advantage. He felt himself respectfully but minutely studied.

'Hello, sir.' She had a soft, quiet voice to go with the quiet composed face.

'Hello, Helen.' He smiled across the desk at her. 'How are things?'

'OK, I guess.'

They each motioned the other simultaneously to sit down and laughed. It was the first time, he thought ruefully, that he had laughed that morning. He settled himself comfortably in one of the club chairs. He felt like Bunyan's Christian, momentarily taking off his load and dropping it beside the psychiatrist's couch.

'Coffee, sir?'

'That would be great.'

Before she turned to get the coffee out of a little machine on the far corner of the filing cabinet, she handed him her weekly report and he began flipping through it.

One of her responsibilities was Base Morale. The USAF in its wisdom recognised that it could not transport three thousand of its personnel, together with wives and children, dump them in a foreign land, keep them in varying states of Battle Readiness and expect no problems. A high barbed wire fence, ostensibly to keep terrorists and unwanted visitors out, kept the Americans in. The Cage, the inmates called it. And what the fence didn't do, a psychological barrier did, so that a proportion of the Americans never even left the Base.

The Airbase had the usual human quota of fights, crimes, broken marriages, drunkenness, drug abuse, absenteeism, sickness and plain unhappiness. But all boiled together, as it were, in a pressure cooker.

It was one of Major Mansell's jobs to minimise the steam.

She put the coffee cup at the Colonel's elbow, and watched his face.

This was the moment when life as it was caught up with life as Craddock, the good Air Force officer, wanted it to be. He never liked the breakdown of the week's medical statistics. There in black and white, in unimpassioned reports and inescapable figures was the fact that people didn't always behave like loyal officers and patriotic enlisted men. He himself found no difficulty in putting the Air Force first. If necessary, before wife, family, friends and certainly himself. He could not understand why they were unable to do the same.

Combat fatigue, he could understand. Just. But marital abuse, sexual assaults, VD, theft, drug abuse – he tapped those items, shaking his head.

'Why? Why do they do it, Helen?' He looked up at her.

'Very often it's drug abuse among the families . . . teenagers.'

'Still the same question, why?'

She shrugged. Odd, he thought, that he found her difficult to talk to, even on subjects he could not have brought himself to discuss with his own wife.

'I guess,' she suggested slowly, 'they are looking for something better, something they're missing.'

'They're looked after like fighting cocks, Helen.'

'But maybe they miss the fighting.'

He said nothing for several seconds. Then, 'I want it better, Helen.' But he spoke gently. Not in the tone he had used to Zweig in the hangar or the supplies officer.

'So do I, sir. Though short of the Second Coming, I can't see how.'

He tutted mildly at her irreverence, but smiled. That was something he liked in Helen, a certain astringency mixed with that pleasing calm.

'People are people, sir. No one's perfect. Everyone's got their problems. Their weaknesses and their vices. So take a whole bunch of them—'

'Not just any bunch though, Helen,' he interrupted. 'Above average. Better physique. Better every way.'

'Guess you're right, sir. Exactly. Younger. More virile. Better fed. More sexually active. More under stress. Living dangerously. Trained, some of them, to be killers. Slap them down in a base like this. It's a cooking-pot for hang-ups.'

He stared at her pale almost prim face with its matter-of-fact expression oddly at variance with her disconcerting blue eyes. The Ice Maiden the jocks called her, but he doubted they were right.

'Do you have a hang-up, Helen?'

He shouldn't have asked her that question. Helen Mansell was a very private person. Married three years ago to a young pilot and widowed six months later. He had no right to pry.

She looked surprised at his introduction of the personal note, but not offended, even pleased. She answered him lightly. 'But of course, sir! That's why I chose psychiatry!'

She paused, waiting for him to go on, as he knew now he would go on. It was as if, metaphorically, he reached for that load beside his chair to spill it out, sort it through under her matter-of-fact gaze.

'Did you see that smartass beat up the Base?'

She shook her head. 'I heard it though! Thought he was going right in. D'you know who it was?'

He hesitated. 'No. But I'll soon find out.' He thrust out his jaw.

She smiled at his toughness. That sternly repressed, softly feminine part of her revelled in it, both admired and took comfort from his masculinity. 'You bet you will!'

He smiled back, then said, 'One of the new guys.'

'Oh, of course! They're arriving today.' She tipped back on her chair, opened a drawer of the filing cabinet. 'I have their medical documentation. Captains Scott and Ryan, isn't it? And Wizzos Robinson and Ames?'

'Correct, Helen.'

'So which are the bad boys?'

'I don't know.' He thought for a moment before going on. 'But I kinda hope it isn't Ryan.'

'You know him?'

He shook his head slowly. 'Knew his father. Way back. Twenty years ago. Jeezus, twenty-one!' He shook his head at the passage of time. Metaphorically again, he fingered his load, as to how much, now he had begun, he could spill out even to her. How much in fact there was to tell?

'So in Vietnam?'

'Yeah.'

She folded her hands on the desk and looked down at them.

'He got the Medal of Honour.'

'A hero?'

He drained his coffee cup and put it down with finality like the ending of a chapter hardly begun. 'You could say that.'

'And the son's following his father's footsteps?'

Craddock frowned. And now on an apparently different subject, speaking in general terms, he said, 'Tell me, Helen, in all these aircrew psychological analyses, has anyone ever examined heredity?'

'Heredity? Oh, sure. There's the Dodds and Steiger study. There's—'

'I don't want the detail. Just tell me the conclusions.'

She shrugged her shoulders and spread her hands apologetically. 'Psychiatry isn't like that, sir.'

'Don't I know it!'

'The conclusions were indefinite.'

'Always are!'

He gave her an affectionate, exasperated smile. 'You psychiatrists are great fence sitters.'

'That's where most of mankind sits.'

'Guess so. And a goddamned uncomfortable perch it is, too.' He frowned reminiscently. 'Only play I saw Maxine in . . . I shall always remember it. Something called *Ghosts*.'

'By Ibsen?'

'Was that his name? Yes. Anyway, that was about heredity.'

'Physiological heredity. Not psychological.'

'Ah, so not relevant.'

'Not really, sir.' She had over-simplified, but for some reason it was the right answer.

The Colonel looked at his watch. 'Thanks for the coffee, Helen. Time I dealt with those young men.'

'Talking of them, sir,' Helen followed him to the door. She smiled up at him teasingly. 'I'm backing the other horse.'

Craddock turned and raised his brows in humorous question.

'Jonathan Scott's not the smartass type. I knew a Jonathan Scott at Princeton. Years ago. But I guess it's the same guy.'

The Colonel made no comment. He replaced his cap dead centre, saluted her and left.

The same unfriendly stranger stared at him from the revolving doors, his expression if anything sterner.

He always walked the third of a mile from the Base hospital to his office. That way he could in isolation digest the inspection and whatever discussion he had had with Bates and Helen. From which, if he were honest, which he was, he should delete the name Bates. Bates and he had little to say to one another. The discussion with Helen was the highlight, the most prized half hour of one whole week's work.

Not that he was in any way sexually attracted to her. Jesus

forbid! But mentally perhaps. Psychologically perhaps. Character-wise certainly. He trusted her more than any other person. The very fact that she wore the same uniform as himself underlined that trust, underlined her probity.

He felt no disloyalty in talking to her as he would not talk to Maxine. He didn't desire Helen. She was just part of his team. Their relationship was mutual respect and loyalty.

He valued her opinion. She was probably right about the culprit being Ryan. Absentmindedly, he returned the salutes of two female airmen in Battle Dress Uniform (BDUs), smiled frugally at a group of children whacking a baseball in the school playground. But Christ, he hoped she was right about heredity and that Ryan wasn't his father's ghost. One Ryan per lifetime was enough.

He crossed from the road named Cheshire after some forgotten British airman – or was it after some county? – into one marked Dowding. Dowding was full of pizza parlours and bowling alleys and duty free shops, for set in the flat British marshlands, this was a good American township no matter what they called the roads, side by side with the grim curves of the hardened aircraft shelters, the blast-proof Operations and the green grassy mounds of the bomb-dumps.

His memory flitted back dangerously to other grassy mounds in Vietnam. Jesus! He scowled so hard at a saluting young officer that he almost flattened himself against the wall of the Stores block.

The Colonel dragged his mind back from the past. Maybe that was why he remembered *Ghosts*. His own personal ghost . . .

No! He clamped his mind rigidly shut, concentrating on the rest of the day's work ahead. He pushed open the door of Base HQ, strode down the corridor, rapped on the glass window of his secretary's office.

'I'm back, Martha!'

She followed him into his office – a tall, good-looking black lieutenant with an unfailing smile and a slow, honeyed voice. 'Sir, Captains Ryan and Scott and Lieutenants Ames and Robinson are waiting in the outer office.'

She nodded towards the four personal files on his desk.

'Let 'em wait.'

On top of the first file was a note from Diefenbaker. It read, 'Re low-flying incident at 07.50. Aircraft TJ 324. Aircraft Commander Captain Roderick Ryan.'

Craddock grimaced to himself. In his heart of hearts, he had known it would be Ryan. And Helen had been right about her friend Captain Scott. He was vaguely irritated on both counts.

He jumped up and opened the hatch that connected to his vice-commander's office.

Evan Walton leapt to his feet. 'Sir?'

'Any complaints on the low flying?'

Walton pulled a rueful face. 'Plenty,' he sighed. 'Including one from the local police and one from Lady Haddington.'

'Is Steve coping?'

'He's taking it on the chin, sir.'

They exchanged brief smiles at Squadron Leader Naylor's favourite remark and the whole uneasy situation – the Squadron Leader's boy-with-his-thumb-in-the-dyke attempts to stem British criticism in his endearing, irritating British way.

'Damn Ryan!' Craddock said under his breath. And to Evan Walton, 'Damned if I enjoy lacing a welcome with a bawling out!' He slammed the hatch shut and sat down behind his desk and drew Ryan's file towards him.

Ryan, Roderick Michael, MR – the US initials that stood for Mission Ready, meaning in immediate combat shape.

Was he like the man he was named after – Mission Too Ready?

The fingers of Craddock's left hand moved up and down drumming the expensive green leather top of his desk as though it were a piano keyboard, a habit which Maxine called 'counting his worry beads'.

Parents: Lieutenant Rory Michael Ryan, Medal of Honour, deceased. Kathleen Ryan (née Corken). No other siblings. Born 23 March, 1962.

Six years before it had happened.

Craddock's fingers stopped their drumming. Leaning his elbows on the desk, he covered his face with his hands.

'Colonel Craddock will see you now.' The tall black lieutenant's voice was still honeyed, her smile wide, but there was a frosty gleam in the big brown eyes that told them that her master was annoyed.

Ryan jumped to his feet, eager to be the first to march in. He was curious to see Colonel Craddock's expression when he first saw him. His mother used to tell him he was the image of his father. She had lived just long enough to see him in the same uniform.

But apart from the formal welcoming smile, Colonel Craddock's expression was unreadable. Not by the slightest flicker of a muscle did he betray the profound shock of Ryan's appearance. It was as if he'd fallen through a crack in time, and here was Rory Ryan, back and alive. Alive and to be dealt with. Truthfully this time. The whole truth and nothing but the truth.

Jesus! For a moment, it was as if he saw a flickering of images as when a movie film flaps free of the sprocket in a projector. Heard those godawful sounds. Smelled the flames.

None of this showed as unhurriedly the Colonel rose and extended a hand to each crewman in turn. 'Welcome, gentlemen, to Haddington and the Sixth TFS.'

He waved them to the four chairs already neatly assembled on the other side of his desk, smiled while they surreptitiously studied his office and him. All four pairs of eyes rested on the large silver-framed photograph of Maxine, and who could blame them?

He was doing the same with them, of course. Studying them. Only he didn't have to be surreptitious. He went into his well-known briefing about Haddington's front-line status and constant War Readiness, for the USAF was not fooled into thinking peace had broken out. He saw their young eyes brighten with his own remembered eagerness. Bewitched by flying all of them. Had to be. And maybe bewitched by killing, too. Or the thought of it.

Craddock shifted his gaze from Ryan's flushed face to Scott. The real professional officer, Craddock would have said – steady-eyed, meeting his probing stare without flinching. A young man comfortable inside himself. Helen's friend. Now why should he suddenly remind himself of that, he wondered, as he rattled off the USAFE (United States Air Force in Europe) hierarchy of command.

'And now to our geographical situation.' Craddock let his eyes rest on Robinson's big black attentive face and interrupted himself – 'Where you from, Glenn?' It was all in his documents, of course, along with the fact that he was a Born-again Christian and inter-services champion runner, but every good monologue should be self-interrupted.

'Greenmail, Alabama, sir.'

'Know it well. Did a Flag exercise there in '84. Fine country. You'll find some similarity – not a lot, but some – with Haddington, England. Folks don't differ all that much. They have their own ways of doing things.'

'Guess they just want us to look after them while they do them,' Ryan chipped in.

Craddock ignored him. 'While you're on British soil, you're ambassadors of your country. You will behave at all times with respect to your hosts. While you're in the air, you'll fly by the rules. Your aircraft and ordnance make you the most powerful creatures that ever were. Remember that. Remember you fly an instrument of destruction, not a toy!'

Craddock got to his feet. 'Captain Scott, Lieutenant Robinson, dismiss. Captain Ryan and Lieutenant Ames will remain.'

As Robinson followed Scott out of the office, his big hand momentarily descended on Ames's shoulder, squeezing it with painful reassurance.

Noticing the gesture, for the first time Craddock studied the somewhat nondescript youngster. Ames had a way of melting into the background. Craddock couldn't make up his mind whether he was the perfect foil for Ryan, or the worst. He made a mental note to discuss him with Helen.

Then he was face to face with Ryan and the inescapable past.

Because of the circumstances, he had already decided how he was going to deal with this incident. He would treat it as a mistaken and dangerous example of youthful exuberance. This time. This time only – and make goddamned sure Ryan never did it again. Ryan would no doubt apologise. Turn on the charm, polish the apples like his father.

For five uninterrupted minutes, Craddock had the face off Ryan, threw at him every regulation in the book. In the end, Ames's pale face looked as if it had been roasted on a spit.

But Ryan's expression hadn't changed.

'What I can't figure out, Ryan, is why? Why do anything so goddamned stupid when you're here on such an important mission?'

Ryan didn't answer. Ames turned to look at him as if imploring some defence – for both their sakes.

But he couldn't give one. If Craddock didn't understand what he'd been trying to show him, then Christ help them all! The war's still on, he was trying to say. Your generation had Nam. We got the Russkies. Same old Commie bastards! But it's our turn now. And I'm your man!

But Colonel Caspar Craddock had parked his ass too long in the Commander's chair and forgotten about real balls-to-the-wall flying. Sure he had to be MR – Mission Ready – all the commanders had to be. But he couldn't have flown like he had done to save his fat ass. No wonder his father had died if that's what his commander was like then!

Craddock allowed the silence to continue. Outside, voices shouted, a truck changed gear, high overhead an aircraft screamed – sounds that underlined the uneasy quiet.

When Ryan realised that the silence was going to be allowed to continue till he made some answer, he said sulkily, 'Guess it was just an announcement of my arrival.'

'An ego trip?' The Colonel raised his brows. 'We don't go in for those here. You should have grown out of them by now.'

And this time it was Ryan who flushed scarlet. Not with embarrassment, but rage.

The Colonel closed the files in front of him, pushing them to one side to indicate that official business was now over. Speaking in a man-to-man tone, he said, 'I knew your father, Rod. We served together in Vietnam.'

'Yes, sir. So I understand.'

'He was—' Craddock searched his vocabulary for the right word. And if possible, a truthful one, while Ryan waited for the paeon of praise. —'a gifted pilot,' Craddock finished slowly.

'And a brave one, sir. A hero. The best.'

Craddock was spared saying yea or nay. The scrambler line from General Vosper in Ramstein buzzed. Craddock dismissed the two of them.

At the door, Ryan turned. The chickenshit Colonel had been real tight-assed in praise of his father. But he'd show him! 'I promise you, sir, I'll be just as good!'

Four

Scott and Robinson had checked in at the Single Officers' Quarters, had their comfortable anonymous flats assigned, dumped their bags, showered, changed, and found the Open Mess bar by the time Ryan came in, followed by a shadowy Ames.

Ryan had recovered his cool and, like always, made an entrance. He shoved open the glass doors into the bar – legs apart, shoulders back, contentious blue eyes raking round the clumps of lunchtime drinkers, waiting for the applause.

None came. The bar was three-quarters empty. Scott and Robinson stood alone at the polished oak counter. The corporal barman was unhooking a glass tankard. A couple of aircrew were sunk in armchairs, reading newspapers. A group of four were playing crap. One of the players lifted a hand and said 'Hi!'

With heavy sarcasm, Ryan thanked him for the enthusiastic welcome and straddled a barstool. Still standing, Ames hovered behind him.

To the crap players, Ryan threw over his shoulder, 'Rod Ryan. Posted from Nellis. Special Assignment.'

The crap players looked unimpressed. 'You don't say!'

Ryan turned to Scott. 'What you buying us, Jonny?'

'Glenn and I have ordered.' He was still sore at Ryan's beat-up. Sure the Colonel hadn't included them in the bawling out, but it had been a damfool thing for Ryan to do, and some of the shit had inevitably stuck to him as well.

With a derisory smile, Ryan watched the barman pour a Budweiser for Scott and a low calorie Coke for Robinson. Then looking at his wizzo, he pretended to recoil. 'Jeezus, Milt, you look like you could do with a brandy!'

'After that gig of yours,' Scott drawled in his slow rich-boy accent, 'I'm not surprised.'

'Surprised nothing! You're jealous, Jonny! You couldn't've flown like that to save your ass!' He ordered a brandy and a rye on the rocks. 'Jealous,' he repeated. 'And not just of my flying!'

Ames looked owlishly from one to the other. But instead of Scott getting sore and asking Ryan what the hell he meant – as if everyone didn't know he meant Samantha – Scott just threw back his head and laughed.

And that really made Ryan mad.

So that called for Glenn to put his peacemaking oar in. He raised his glass of Coke to toast their new base.

'Shit to that!' Ryan retorted. 'This goddamned base needs beefing up!'

'You're just sore Craddock hacked you,' Scott said.

'Hacked me nothing! He doesn't appreciate good men.'

'I reckoned he was OK.'

'You would, Jonny! He's your type. Fly by the Book.'

Hastily, the peacemaker intervened again. 'Let's drink to our Special Assignment, then!'

'What is our Special Assignment?' Ames muttered, but no one appeared to hear.

'OK, Glenn,' Ryan conceded. 'To waxing Commie bastards anywhere!'

He threw back his head, downed his drink in one, climbed off the stool and left.

The other three could hear him thumping down the corridor, hammering at the door of the Mess Secretary, demanding if anyone was at home or did the siesta time start at noon on this goddamned British front-line base.

'Guess he's missing his new wife,' Glenn suggested charitably.

'Missing something,' Ames murmured into his glass, looking from Scott's face to Glenn's as if he'd like to say a helluva lot more, but daren't.

Scott's face had assumed a deliberately discouraging expression. Arguing with Ryan, pilot to pilot, man to man was one thing. Listening to bellyaches from crew was another. Maybe Ryan was right. Maybe he was jealous of the man's flying. But goddammit, not jealous of his fluffy little girl wife.

But while Scott frowned, Glenn eyed Ames kindly and with the speculative eager interest of the amateur counsellor. Though all Glenn's counselling led eventually to an appropriate Bible text and an invitation to follow his example and be born again, Glenn did a good job of mopping up some of the frustrations and tensions.

Now he put his big warm hand on Ames's shoulder. 'Wanna talk about it?'

Ames nodded.

The two wizzos shifted further round the bar, out of earshot of the others.

'Can't figure out what the hell got into him, Glenn! Bang! Suddenly! Just like that! Hammer down, going for knots! Did he flip his lid or somep'n? Oh, he's flown knife-edge! Often. You know that. Ground-hugging, late pull-outs, corkscrews, loops. But spot on . . . precision stuff, just right for evasive low-level. Never fazed me. But this, Glenn . . . ! Reckoned we'd be comin' in, tits up. Sure did!'

'Got to remember, Milt.'

'Remember what?'

'An' make allowances.'

'Allowances?'

'Recalled from his honeymoon.' Glenn shook his head. 'Eleven hours tied up in an F-115. Then he must be trying to figure . . . like the four of us are . . . what's goin' on. Why are we here?' He got up and took Ames's glass. 'I'll get you another brandy.'

Over at the bar, Scott listened to the indistinct murmur of their voices with affectionate amusement, as his wizzo edged closer to What the Good Book Says. He downed another drink, was about to go into lunch when the glass doors opened behind him.

He turned idly, casually. Then his attention stiffened. He felt a shock of immediate and painful recognition.

A slim, fair-haired officer was walking in with a male sergeant a pace behind her. The hair was different, smooth now and severely parted as if the better to frame the regular features and the most unfrivolous penetrating blue eyes. The cheeks had lost their teenage roundness, but there was something quite unmistakable in the way she held her head, the purposeful yet graceful way she moved, the unconscious sway of her slender hips.

She recognised him. Fleetingly, the blue eyes showed a pleasurable surprise, then wariness, then the old armour was riveted back in place. Typically, she left him to speak first.

When she was only a couple of paces away, he smiled as if unsure. 'Hello, Helen. It is Helen, isn't it?'

'Hello, Jonathan. Yes.'

For the first time, he saw the medical symbols on the lapels of the jacket and the major's oak leaf. For some reason, both discomfited him. Clumsily he asked, 'Helen . . . what?'

She flushed. 'Mansell.'

'You're married?'

'I was.' A pause. 'How about you, Jonathan?'

He shook his head. 'Not guilty.'

'You surprise me,' she said drily, hostilely almost.

The conversation appeared about to stop dead. Then, 'Have a drink, Major? Or should I call you ma'am? How does one address a senior female officer?'

'Try Helen. And no, thank you. I'm on duty.' She turned to the sergeant. 'This is Sergeant Delaney, i/c Base hygiene. Captain Scott. We were together at Princeton, Sergeant. Sergeant Delaney and I are about to inspect the Mess bars and kitchens.'

The corporal already had the counter raised and an obsequious expression on his face. The bar was filling up. A group of men in BDUs pushed past, greeting her, one of them whispering something in her ear. Somehow the tables had been turned on him. Helen, the humble little preppie, now the senior officer, very much at home.

'Have one when you've finished your round,' Scott persisted.

She hesitated. 'One-thirty? Will you still be around?'

'If you say so, ma'am.'

She smiled at his unusual humility and nodded – so presumably she was saying so.

Ryan on his own was saying out loud – but only to his motorcycle – every expletive known to Air Force man. The bike wasn't the culprit – a brand new Suzuki, delivered by the weekly Hercules with his other baggage.

The culprit was Colonel Craddock and maybe himself for misjudging the man. Like every good red-blooded jock, Ryan had had his sights for months on a front-line base. Samantha, unlike some young wives, was all in favour of him coming over. For the first time in his life he had a real Irish trefoil of good luck. First, cutting in on Scott and marrying Samantha, second her father being a rich senator, third being posted on Special Assignment to a base commanded by Colonel Craddock.

And though even before they left Nellis, the brightness of his luck had dimmed – the honeymoon had been a disaster and he had been relieved to be recalled; the senator was an interfering bastard;

Samantha a spoiled sexy brat – all that was nothing to the chilly welcome from Caspar Craddock. Christ, couldn't the man appreciate an entrance, the real knife-edge of flying? Jeezus, what a man to command a front-line base! No wonder the Commies had it all their own way! He just hoped the Special Assignment didn't turn out to be a fart as well.

As Ryan roared towards the main guard-house, he had no clear idea where he was going. He wanted to blow his lid, to beat up this toy-sized countryside that Craddock's attitude had already soured.

At the gate, he burned to a stop. A black military policeman in immaculate blancoed webbing and outsize white gloves was conducting the orchestra of in- and out-going traffic like a cross between an acrobat and a drum majorette.

At any other time, Ryan might have been amused. Today the policeman's graceful antics were all part of the Craddock circus. His careful rolling-eyed examination of Ryan's ID plastic, his exaggerated quivering salute, his smiling, 'Mind how you go, Captain! They drive on the wrong side of the road here, sir,' all irritated Ryan.

He didn't bother to return the corporal's salute. Crouched over the handlebars, he exploded out of the entrance like a stunt-man out of a cannon. Not giving a damn what side of the road the British tried to drive on, he headed towards a weak and watery circle in the cloud that might be the British version of the sun, and gunned the engine.

The sensation was good. He felt better. The road was as straight as a runway and almost as empty. The greens and yellows of the countryside whipped past on either side like stiffened ribbons. He could feel the front wheel of the Suzuki trying to become airborne.

Till suddenly the British road played a nasty on him. It bent sharp to the right at an almost ninety degree angle.

He negotiated it safely of course. His reflexes were as good on the ground as in the air, and he stayed aboard. But he was at some incredible speed, and on what the Brits would call the wrong side of the road. And in his path was an old-fashioned clapped-out vehicle which had to be on its way to the nearest motor museum.

He made contact. Hard crunching contact. By misfortune, he caught the vehicle on its front offside wheel. The tyre burst. The wreck collapsed on to its knees. Then just as Ryan killed his engine and dismounted to offer whatever was called for – apologies, but not too many because the bloody thing was better off the road than on – the driver's door was opened.

Out jumped not some old greybeard to match the car, but a woman – young, curvy, and reasonably pretty.

Always with women, no matter where he met them, Ryan did a quick sex inventory. This one came out somewhere in the middle. Say six to Samantha's nine point nine. Four or five years older than Samantha, neat ankles, not bad legs, rosy country-girl face, good figure of the comfier sort, dressed in a dark blue uniform that fitted her high breasted figure like a second skin.

But she mighty soon dropped to the bottom of the Ryan rating. Off the clock, in fact. That round face was a hellcat's. Those bright eyes didn't shine, they glittered. The flush was not country health, but rage. She was trembling. Not with fear or shock, which goddammit, he had the right muscular arms to deal with. But with speechless fury.

She soon found her speech. An angry clipped English voice demanded what the hell he thought he was doing driving at that speed on the wrong side of the road. The expletives sounded awful in the English ladylike diction.

'Sorry, ma'am,' Ryan drawled, trying the ingenuous Yankee boy act. 'Didn't figure I was!'

'Didn't figure you were!' She repeated with crushing scorn, pointing at the insignia on his leather jacket and turning her eyes skywards. 'And you're in charge up there? In one of those?'

He continued with the ingenuous boyish smile. 'So help me!'

'Not so help *you*! So help *us*!'

It was a bad start. Irrecoverable. He had a mind to abort the proceedings there and then by getting out his wallet and plastic. He began to say he'd pay for the damage, or the USAF would. And fast.

But she didn't give him the chance.

'I was on my way to a confinement,' she announced, not so angry now, but crisp and businesslike as if she really was upset and not putting it on to make him eat crow.

'A confinement?' he repeated stupidly, his mind somehow rotating round confinements to camp and such military connotations.

'A confinement. A birth. A baby.'

'Jesus. Jee – zus!'

'Hopefully, not.' She gave him a wintery smile. 'But whoever he is, Jesus or not, he's early . . . or she is, and I've got to get there.'

She dived back into the wreck and pulled out a leather bag of the kind doctors used to take around in old B-movies he'd seen as a child.

'I'm the District Nurse,' she explained over her shoulder. 'That means I'm the local midwife too. You'll have to push my car to the side of the road, and take me on your bike.'

No argument. Just that.

They exchanged names formally as they mounted the Suzuki. Sister Harriet Harper. Captain Rod Ryan. No one could say it was the beginning of a friendship. It was an unlikely alliance born of necessity.

He tried a mild compliment as he stowed her bag. 'You're young to be in charge of . . .' he wasn't quite sure what she was in charge of. 'All this!'

'You're young to be in charge of all *that*!' She pointed upwards and added sharply, 'And you can do much more damage.'

So on that happy note, the race to be at the birth began.

'Fast as you can!' she ordered as the engine fired.

For someone who had complained about his speed, that was rich.

'Then hold tight, Sister! Bloody tight!'

It was miles and miles. The only words she spoke were 'Faster!' or 'Left here!' or 'Right there!' accompanied by a thump on his shoulder and a pointing finger.

During the last bumpy half mile, he did have a moment to think about just what he had let himself in for. A birth. His stomach turned. Less than two weeks into marriage, no one could call him a family man. No brothers, no sisters, no father. A mother who loved him but who died before he'd ever had the money to make things easier for her. Girls, of course, he knew all about girls. Every shape and size and race. He was an expert. But pregnant women turned him right off. And as for the bloody messy act of birth . . .

At the thought of it, he squeezed harder on the accelerator, and got another thump, this time centre spine.

'Slow down! It's just at the bottom of the lane! You'll see the thatch in a moment!'

He saw it, this side of a sheet of inland water. A drooping grey brown walrus of a thatched roof, above a white-washed cottage now covered in mildew. The last fifty yards were a minefield of broken bricks and old railway sleepers.

'For drainage,' Sister Harper said, as he stopped and she saw him surveying them balefully. 'That's why I wanted you to slow down.'

She hopped off the bike, seized her bag and ran in through the gate, permanently ajar on its sagging hinges.

Immediately, the cottage door opened. Sister was ushered in. He saw her disappear up a wooden staircase, steep as Jacob's ladder.

Unsure of his role, Ryan stepped into the cottage, which smelled of dry rot and fish and overcooked cabbage. In a strange loud local accent, he heard a man's voice ask, 'What's that Yank doing with you, Sister?'

Not what you imagine, Ryan thought. He heard her reply, 'My car broke down. He gave me a lift.'

On the strength of that, in a moment a stout woman bustled downstairs. She wiped her hands, nervously rather than because they were wet, on a clean white apron. Her cheeks had high red spots and her eyes were bright, as if preparing for tears.

She smiled abstractedly. 'You'd like a cup of tea, sir . . . that I know.'

Ryan would have liked a bourbon. But he allowed himself to be ushered into a parlour that looked as if it hadn't changed in a century. There was a sofa covered in imitation leather, and above the mantelpiece, a large stuffed trout.

The tea was brought by yet another member of the family, a boy of eleven or twelve with round bright suspicious eyes behind round spectacles. He wore oilskin trousers, and black rubber boots with fingernails to match.

'Mum's gone back upstairs with Jennie. She's frightened, is Jennie.'

She wasn't the only one, Ryan thought, sipping the fawn unstimulating fluid. 'Who are you?'

'Billie. Jennie's brother. You bin over here long?'

'I flew in this morning.'

It seemed a decade ago. But the answer appeared to please the boy. 'You don't know our Jennie then?'

'No.'

'Never met her?'

'No.'

'Mum don't like Yanks. Dad don't either.'

'How about you, Billie?'

Billie shook his head slowly in family solidarity. But then added, 'You're all right.'

And then the air was shattered with the most ear-splitting screams. Ryan put down the cup and saucer hastily before he spilled more of the liquid. They both turned their eyes nervously to the ceiling.

'Come on. One last push!' Harriet spoke deliberately sharply – so sharply that her order penetrated the mildewed ceiling of the parlour below. 'Push! Push! Push! Harder, Jennie! Harder! It'll soon be over!'

But how? She felt young Jennie's will-power ebbing out from under her fingers. Tears were already coursing down her mother's face. A whiff of death and defeat and decay in the bedroom. After months of fumbling inexpert attempts to get rid of the baby, after more months of trying to conceal Jennie's pregnancy, nobody except Harriet wanted a live baby anyway.

'Push, Jennie! You're not trying!'

It was a dry birth, which didn't help – the waters gone before Harriet arrived. Jennie was young, seventeen, but already giving up. The only tenacity she seemed capable of had been keeping quiet about her condition and keeping the father's name secret. Forever, she said. A Yank, bound to be, her parents said. There were more Yanks than anyone ever let on. They went around in civvies so you didn't know. Mrs Dann had even gone so far as to predict a black baby.

'Jennie! We're nearly there! The head's coming! Push!'

Jennie gave another terrible scream, and as if that was the last push she was capable of, flopped loose and flabby like part of the mattress.

But Harriet had the baby – slippery, bloody, but alive.

It was a moment that never failed to move her profoundly. As she cleaned the crumpled face, she bent down, 'You've got a son, Jennie!'

Jennie opened an eye and smiled. The baby was the reddish colour of most new-born babies, with a little fat nose like Jennie's and no negroid features other than a halo of soft black hair.

Suddenly the gloom of Jennie's pregnancy gave way to the magic euphoria of birth. Mrs Dann hugged her grandson, and Mr Dann disappeared downstairs to return with a bottle of homemade elderberry wine. Dusty as an age-encrusted port, it had a terrible potency.

Harriet had left her glassful till Jennie was made comfortable and the baby washed. She had almost forgotten about the American waiting down below, or, maybe he wasn't waiting. Maybe, if she knew Americans, having delivered her he had now vanished. She didn't greatly care. She floated downstairs in a euphoria compounded in equal parts of the spiritual uplift of a new life created and the powerful physical uplift of Mr Dann's elderberry wine.

In the parlour she found Ryan had also been invited to wet the baby's head. He had knocked the drink back with gratitude after listening to the performance above, and had held out his glass for more. He, too, was caught up in the euphoria.

He put his arms round Harriet and hugged her. She was a nice armful and cuddly. She returned his kiss with the enthusiasm of the occasion.

Picking their way over the rough road to the motorcycle, he kept his arm round her, expounding on the ordeal it had been for a non-family man like himself.

'Worse than anything up in the air . . . so help me!'

'You're not married then?'

'Hell, no!'

He was after all, hardly married. Right then, he didn't feel married at all. Just a bit emotional, a bit drunk, a bit lonesome. The nurse was a warm mixture of motherliness and sex. He expounded on the loneliness of a Yank just arrived over in a f – he nearly said foreign, but substituted friendly, yet unknown, country; his need for kindly female company.

For a moment, Harriet remembered that she didn't like Yanks and didn't approve of Yankee airbases in her country. But the euphoria of the birth still swaddled them. They still walked on air.

Mounting the bike, she put her arms tightly round him and they went bumping up the narrow road into the now dark night, lit distantly by the weird phosphorescent ellipse of the Base that never slept.

Five

'Hi, Milt!'

Dressed in singlet and shorts, Glenn Robinson stopped running down the steps of the Officers' Open Mess to drop a friendly hand on his fellow wizzo's shoulder. 'Where you bin hidin' yourself?'

Always pale, Ames's pallor was emphasised today by dark shadows under his eyes. Glenn looked at him more closely.

'Hey, what you bin up to? You look shagged!'

Ames made a small rueful grimace. Ever since they had arrived twelve days ago, they had been flying every day but one, orientating themselves with the British Isles geography, carrying out day low-level bombing exercises on a multiplicity of practice targets from the Wash to the Hebrides, night navigation trips, combat air patrols, practice interceptions, manoeuvring in card and St Andrew's Cross formations, making mock attacks on ship targets.

The one day they hadn't flown was last Wednesday when a mock terrorist attack was suddenly sprung on the Base. As everyone knew, there had been lately enough terrorist attacks on Uncle Sam's person and property to justify an exercise of that nature just about every day of the week. The exercise had been really thorough. All personnel had been engaged on it – even those in hospital.

Male and female airmen in BDUs with revolvers and live ammunition in their holsters had been tearing around. Gun carriers had had a field day, smoke bombs and flares and fireworks had been let off. Net result – congratulations to all personnel from Colonel Craddock, all sixty 'terrorists' had been killed or captured, and twenty-three telephone calls of complaint from the village of Haddington, just beyond the barbed wire, had been received by Squadron Leader Naylor.

Today had been the first time that Robinson, a dedicated long distance runner, had been able to fit in the circuit three times round the perimeter track that he'd promised himself to do every day.

'Come an' join me, Milt! Get those leg muscles working! Get those lungs expanding!' He thumped his chest and began running on the spot. 'Best tonic in the world, man!'

Ames looked doubtful. Whenever he was on the ground, he made himself scarce. On the Sixth TFS, he was already known as the Invisible Man.

'No gear.'

'I'll lend you some.'

'Wouldn't fit.'

'Excuses, excuses.' However hard Robinson tried he couldn't winkle that guy's nose out of a technical manual. 'Slip on some pumps and come as you are!'

But Ames was already disappearing through the Mess doors. 'Tomorrow, Glenn.'

Glenn never gave up on anyone. 'Keep you to it!'

He pointed severely at Ames, then sprang down the remaining steps to the ground.

Puzzling guy, he was thinking. Clever at his job. The best, but a loner – and lonely. Tied up inside. Unable to communicate. Like there was some great knot in there, waiting for a kindly hand to untie it. A man if ever he'd seen one (and he'd seen many) just waiting for the loving words of Jesus. Mind, flying with Ryan couldn't exactly encourage a man like Ames to communicate. The best pilot maybe. But not the best aircraft commander. An arrogant big-mouth in Glenn's opinion.

Robinson fell into his running rhythm and clicked his stop-watch.

His feet making a measured regular time on the tarmac, he passed the school, where a trio of cheeky children shouted a jeering accompaniment. He waved to them magnanimously. Then the big brick building with plain glass windows and an enormous wooden cross in the grassy sward in front – the multi-denominational church where services of varying faiths were held all through Saturday and Sunday, one after the other with appropriate changes of altar, books, priests and vestments, finally ending with the Revivalists. He would invite Ames to accompany him there next Sunday, maybe share a pizza afterwards at the handily placed pizza parlour, challenge him at the bowling alley, take him in hand at the gymnasium.

Muscles gave you strength. And confidence. His own leg muscles felt slack after being cooped up flying so long for so many days, but he forced his own pace – past the baseball pitches, the veterinary section which cared for family pets, the restaurants, the post-office, the PX stores, the gas station with its pumps priced in dollars, as with everything else on sale.

Robinson viewed the scene with satisfaction. Except for the cold wind flipping the flags, and the grey rain falling from the sky, it could have been Main Street of Greenmail, Alabama, where his father farmed fifty acres, and where he had been brought up.

This was America. His land, the land of democracy which he was dedicated to protect. For forty-five years, there had been no World War, due, he was certain, to the American capability. That Russia was the enemy, he had not the slightest doubt. His training had clearly demonstrated it. And though he viewed the misguided, misinformed Russian people with compassion and sorrow, they were still part of the Evil Empire of the Anti-Christ. Unlike Ryan, he had no hatred for them. He prayed for them. That the Lord would one day make the bastards see sense – but not, maybe, till Glenn Robinson's Air Force career was over.

As he ran, the hymn tunes that he had sung so fervently last Sunday resonated in his head. He passed the Armament Store and Soft and Hard Ops, the green mounds of the nuclear bomb-dump, passed Hush House which did little to dampen the noise of a Pratt and Whitney jet being run up to 25,500 lb thrust, and arms going like pistons, began topping the slight incline to the south of the field.

Trucks, tankers and bomb trolleys were continually passing him, though he paid little attention to them. Then a taxiing F-115 driven by Grunter Gruber caught him up. Gruber was a short, ugly black-haired jock. You always knew you'd got him in formation from his G-releasing grunts over the RT, but with a pair of flying hands as delicate as a concert pianist's.

Buzz Barlow, his wizzo – a real solid Ace-of-Gauges – pressed his bright farmer's boy face against the window and cheerfully gave Glenn a rude two-fingered salute.

In return, Glenn gave him a wide seraphic smile.

Now he was running down on the other side of the airfield. From here, he could see the spire of Haddington church, soaring above the pattern of thatch and red-tiled roofs, and beyond that the neat small fields of a foreign land. He must visit there. Those decayed old churches needed the revival spirit of the New World, he was thinking as he rounded the Hard Hangars. Here all the important maintenance work was done because the hangars resisted nuclear attack, and they mustn't let the Commies find them napping.

All at once he was brought to a standstill by a huge roll of newly laid barbed wire, guarded at the only entrance by a grown-up version of a toy sentry box.

'Lawdy Lawd!' Robinson stopped swinging his arms and threw them up above his head in exasperation. 'What's goin' on?'

Out of the sentry box, with the snappy clockwork precision of his grandmother's little alpine weather-house, popped a small figure in a BDU. Carefully arranged locks of gold brown hair peeped becomingly from under a steel helmet. The powdered lipsticked face beneath was the prettiest he had ever seen on any young woman anywhere, let alone a sentry.

And this cute little figure carried the most enormous rifle, with a great shining bayonet on the end.

'Beg pardon . . .' Immediately both astonished and bemused, Robinson pointed to the wire. 'But this . . .?'

The bayonet pointed threateningly at his solar-plexus. 'What you doin' here, mister?' The voice was as pretty as the face but the tone as steely as her bayonet.

'Me? I live here, ma'am.'

'Then show me your ID plastic, mister!' The bayonet was thrust forward till the point was actually touching the cotton of his sweat shirt.

He indicated his running gear. 'Now where would I put my plastic?'

'Name?'

'Glenn Robinson. What's yours?'

'Della Lewis.'

'Della . . . that's nice! Suits you!' Gently, he put his big thumb on the blade and turned it away.

'Rank and muster?'

'Lieutenant. Wizzo.'

She looked abashed and disappointed. 'Sorry, sir . . . I wouldn't have . . .' She blushed. 'I didn't know . . . I . . .'

'Course you didn't know.' A gentle forgiving hand began firmly pushing aside her and her rifle. But with dignity, she shifted herself and her weapon back into the middle of the pathway.

'Not this way, sir.'

'But why, Della? C'mon, why?'

'Orders, sir. Something goin' on in the hangar. No one past this point.'

'Well, then—' He smiled and shrugged. 'OK, I give up. But I guess I'm allowed to stay and talk, huh?'

'Guess so, sir. Just a little while.'

'Been here long, Della?'

'Four hours, sir.'

'I mean on the Base.'

'Three months.' She paused. 'And you, sir . . . you're new?'

'Now how did you figure that out, Della?'

'Guess I'd've noticed you,' she said, and then blushed.

'Della, you're real nice! And you're right. Got here last week.'

She stared at him hungrily. 'How was it back home?'

'Fine! Just fine!' He saw her eyes fill with tears. 'You homesick, Della?'

She hung her helmeted head and nodded.

'But it's a fine country out there. Mighty pretty!' He pointed to the Haddington roofs. 'Eh?'

She shook her head. 'I dunno, sir.'

'Don't know, Della?'

'I've never been out of the Cage, sir.'

'Never been out? Why in the world not?'

'I just feel better inside. Safer, I guess.'

'Whatever are you scared of out there, Della girl?'

If she answered, he didn't hear her. For the doors of the hard hangar behind her had suddenly opened. Robinson saw the Chief Electronics Maintenance Officer and the two Master Sergeant radar technicians who had been servicing Firefly One.

Under the weird acid-blue lights, they were working on their F-115. Gone was the charcoal lizard camouflage. Instead the whole aircraft had been painted with the new radar-resistant black paint he had previously seen only on the secret Stealth aircraft.

The nose cone was off. They were fitting a radar of a type he had never seen before. And under the fuselage was an outsize metal rack.

For what?

Jeez, there it was! On the bomb-trolley beside the aircraft. A thin silver lozenge like a sky torpedo.

And that he *had* seen before.

The latest stand-off bomb, a guided weapon that could wax the target from any distance.

As Robinson stood stock still watching them at work, a shiver ran down his spine. Bits of the jigsaw began coming together in his mind. New secret equipment was first given to the top crews. Now he knew. It was just like the centring of the cross-hairs of a bomb-sight on a target.

This was why they were there.

Something was on. Something big. Maybe even something For Real.

Six

'Cas . . . Cas Craddock . . . that you? God, man, you sound far away! Point is . . . can you hear me?'

Colonel Craddock smiled wryly to himself as General Vosper's voice boomed over the direct scrambler line from Ramstein, the Headquarters of the United States Air Force in Europe.

It was eight-thirty on the morning of 14 September. The tension was tightening.

'Yes, General. I hear you.'

'Got the presents I sent you? Course you did! That's fine! Boys making use of them?'

'You bet, sir! Night flying for the last three nights.'

'That's the stuff! Keep 'em at it!'

'The Brits will bellyache.'

'Tell me something new!' he snorted. 'Cas, we got our eyes on the Sixth TFS. Just between you and me, Cas, the wind's blowing up.'

There was a new element in the General's always hearty voice. An excitement rigidly suppressed, but audible.

'Sir?'

'It's gonna happen, Cas.' The tone sank momentarily to a growl. 'It's gotta happen.'

'When, sir?'

The General gave a short sharp bark of laughter. His tone returned to a jovial boom. 'Can't tell you that, Cas. An' you know better'n to ask. But now, way that son-of-a-bitch is getting his tail out of line – sooner than later.'

'Has there been another incident?'

'An hour back. One of Akhbar's motherfuckers let off a bomb at our base at Crotoni.'

'Any casualties?'

'Six.' There was a pause. 'Now hear me, Cas. We're going into the next phase now. I got you the two best crew in the Air Force. Select two more and fly the asses off 'em.'

Craddock thought that was the end of the conversation, but the General went on. 'Now you remember three things, Cas! Keep those four crew flying! Keep tight security! And keep the Brits happy!'

'Jesus!'

The General laughed. 'Oh, and Cas . . . might just drop in one day and see how you're doin'. Maybe that lovely wife of yours . . . Maud . . . Millicent . . .'

'Maxine.'

'Yeah, Maxine, would fix me dinner one night, huh?'

'She'd be delighted,' Craddock said heartily and raised his brows apologetically at Maxine's photograph as the General hung up.

So something more than dinner was really cooking. The sixty-four dollar question was what? And the next question was how? How in God's name did you keep tighter security, do more night flying and at the same time keep your friendly/unfriendly hosts, the British, happy?

A word immediately sprang to Squadron Leader Naylor's lips. Sometimes, Craddock thought, the man had been born with it there.

'How, sir?' he asked in his respectful British tone when Craddock got him on the line. 'It's not just putting a quart into a pint pot, it's putting three of them. With this increased night flying, there've been squawks. If we start moving everyone from the perimeter fence, there'll be more. And how can we push out the hospitality boat . . . and that's the way to oil the wheels . . . with tighter security?'

It was one of Naylor's favourite maxims that there was a lot of international mileage in a bottle of champagne and a plate of smoked salmon.

Craddock allowed him to trot it out now.

'At the same time, sir, if we're going to have a state of security alert, you don't want too many strangers around. Would you be thinking of cancelling the Saturday night Liberty buses?'

These were the buses sent out every Saturday night to garner the young womanhood of surrounding towns and villages for the airmen's weekly dance. A security risk if anything was blowing up, but vital for morale.

'It would cause a lot of heartache if they were cancelled, sir.'

'Bellyache, more like. But we'll have to see. Do what you can, Steve. You know your own countrymen. And,' he added sternly, 'we're here to help them.'

Just for a moment, those stern words echoed hollowly in his own ears. He was suddenly shot through with a memory of Vietnam. His own astonishment as a young man, twenty odd years ago, that Yanks weren't all that welcome in Vietnam. And hard on that memory, newsreels of Russian soldiers, astonished at their hostile reception in Czechoslovakia and Afghanistan. Then the memories flickered away and were gone.

'Speak to the Anglo-American Society, Steve. That's what they're there for.'

Docilely, for he was by nature amiable, Naylor said, 'Will do,' and waited till Colonel Craddock had said, 'See you, Steve,' and hung up.

He did not see fit to mention that in fact half of the Committee of the Anglo-American Society was at that moment in his waiting room.

Being the third Thursday of the month, this was what the Squadron Leader called his 'surgery' and a not inept description was it either. For at this time came a regular representation of those blinded, deafened, but not struck dumb by the presence of the Yanks. The sick of the palsy of Yankee occupation – as they in their ignorance liked to call it.

There were, of course, as always another group of Britons opposing their own countrymen in a very enthusiastic pro-American lobby.

Whittaker's Garage at the southern end of the village green had a yard stacked high with huge crashed American cars – their late owners neither used to narrow twisting country lanes nor to driving on the 'wrong' side of the road – and there was always a brisk trade in small British cars to replace them. Even though the airmen bought their 'gas' in dollars at cheap American prices on the Base, there was always a queue of their cars waiting for checks and repairs.

The tiny antique shop next to the village pump had a sideline in 'distressing' wood and metal into an early old age to sell as genuine Georgian, and three more rivals had sprung up in competition within the Parish boundaries. The American wives were avid for antiques, just as their husbands were hotfoot on the trail of ancestors they were sure had formed part of that band of East Anglian pilgrims who in 1620 had made their way to Southampton, from there to sail across the Atlantic in the *Mayflower*.

Insurance salesmen, tax accountants, pubs, hotels all loved Americans. Estate agents were always very obliging at letting accommodation and selling houses at inflated prices. Taxis did a roaring trade. Sweet shops displaying 'homemade humbugs' could be sure of big business. Two turkey farms and an enterprising pumpkin grower cashed in heavily at Thanksgiving. Golf clubs welcomed American sportsmen and made them feel immediately at home. In a cute little one-bedroomed cottage beside the mill on the stream that trickled through Haddington, lived Mrs Pippa Smith, who ran a thriving 'Kissogram' business at fifty dollars a time – distance no object, costumes ranging from Schoolgirl through French Maid to the Leather Outfit that the Yanks liked best, with which went a complimentary whip at no extra charge.

And in addition there were the English girls who arrived on the courtesy buses for their Saturday night dance with nothing but their sweet smiles, and returned loaded with cigarettes, perfume, tights, chocolates and chewing gum.

And lastly, there was the Member of Parliament for the area, a stockbroker to whom the anti-lobby wrote frequently, always receiving a courteous acknowledgement together with the NATO handout in reply.

Unfortunately for Naylor, this sizeable section of the British community kept a very low profile. They would nod enigmatically when the subject of the Yanks came up, not saying a word, only listening to the sweet sound of dollar bills slipping into their tills. Aware of the vicissitudes of international politics, while not looking forward to the day (God forbid!) when the Yanks were withdrawn, they nevertheless prudently recognised that the time might come when they were dependent only on the goodwill of the anti-Americans.

So Naylor could depend on little outside support. But as he was wont to tell Colonel Craddock, he could take it on the chin. He was a short jolly man of forty-two, with a round unlined rosy face and a genuinely charming smile. He was a conscientious general duties RAF officer, happy in his work. He loved his wife and he loved the Air Force, and he was kind to children, animals and Yanks. What Jarman did in the Craddock household, he did on a much larger scale on the Base as a whole and its environs. He did his very best to explain the Yanks to a disbelieving world. And vice-versa.

Now he got up from his desk, and opened the hatch that separated him from his secretary, Celia Bentall. She was an executive class civil servant from the Ministry of Defence – smart, efficient, tight-lipped and fiftyish. To Mrs Naylor's delight, she was the only woman in her husband's employ, though he had a little army of two hundred Ministry of Defence police whose duties were to keep the British and the terrorists out. So far, thank God, not a single terrorist. But Lord, did they get the British!

'We've really got the VIPs today, haven't we, Celia?' Steven Naylor jerked his head towards his waiting room. 'Think you could rustle up six cups of coffee? And some biccies?'

Then he put his most disarming smile in place, and went to open the door of the lions' den.

Kipling was right, of course. It was the female of the species, the lioness, that he most dreaded.

'Lady Haddington! How very nice to see you!' He took the withered, long-fingered hand of the tall old lady who stood ramrod straight, eyeing him speculatively.

'Such a pleasant surprise,' he gabbled.

'Neither,' she contradicted crisply. 'Neither a surprise, nor pleasant.' Then her still strangely beautiful face softened. 'But not your fault, Steven.'

She moved impatiently towards the door to his office.

A big beefy man with grey bristly sideburns lumbered after her. Naylor shook his hand vigorously. 'Councillor Muggeridge, good of you to spare the time. Busy farmer like you, very good indeed. Rector! Don't let me forget, sir, the Base has some offerings for your Harvest Festival.'

A tall thin professorial type who ran the bird sanctuary, remarked that he didn't think Harvest displays of bombs and bullets was quite Christian.

Naylor laughed heartily. 'Oh, that's not our only harvest. No, indeed. The sergeants grow sweetcorn at the back of their Mess and the young officers' wives are marvellous on pot plants. But I think it's the cakebake that's coming your way, Rector.'

He turned to greet the last occupant of the waiting room – Sister Harper, a friend and foe in almost equal but quite comfortable parts.

'Hello, Harriet! Patients not sleeping?'

'Hello, Steven. You can say that again. But who is?'

She gave him a sweet, almost sympathetic smile. But when he spread his hands to include them all and suggested, as they no doubt came about a single purpose, that he see them together, she whispered, 'D'you mind if I stay on afterwards and say my particular piece?'

'Harriet, that would be my pleasure!'

He shepherded them all into his office. It was an impressive place, as large as Craddock's and in the Colonel's opinion, better furnished. Naylor had, of course, the advantage of history. When he sat at his desk, above his head he had the guardianship of the lion and the unicorn and the plaque of the Royal Air Force inscribed *Per Ardua ad Astra*, only it was the Americans these days who were getting to the stars and the RAF who had the *Ardua*. But no matter – on his left was the RAF flag and immediately on his right, even now squinting disapproval at the assembled company, a magnificent State portrait of Her Majesty the Queen. In between these big guns were scattered the minor artillery of framed pictures of VIP visits to the Base – senators and congressmen, usually with General Vosper dancing attendance, and with Steven himself smiling and shaking hands.

'Now before we begin,' Naylor rubbed his hands together cheerfully, 'coffee! I'm sure you're all dying for a cup. I know I am!' He smiled at them all as Ms Bentall came in with a tray. 'Oh, and choccie biccies, Celia! You are spoiling us!'

Seated in the middle, Lady Haddington accepted the cup, waved away the biscuits and said sternly, 'Steven, I'm sure you're busy. Shall we get straight down to business?'

He was used to her taking charge, of course. Her family had been taking charge hereabouts for centuries. She had lost two sons in the RAF in the Second World War. Her response to their deaths had been to give a Spitfire which she called *Haddington's Reply*. She was devoted to the RAF, supported Naylor because he was a serving officer and though she wouldn't accept chairmanship of the Anglo-American Society, had agreed to deputise for her one surviving son, the present Lord Haddington, who had accepted it with alacrity – but was never present. If Naylor had to summarise her attitude, he supposed it would be that the Yanks are here, and though the RAF would do the job a great deal better, they must be treated politely.

'Shall I be spokeswoman?' Lady Haddington put down her cup

and glanced around just long enough to accept the immediate nods of her companions. 'Very well then. Steven, item one,' she held up her index finger. 'This dramatically increased night flying, now right over the village instead of doing their noise-abatement turn. Our villagers simply can't get a wink of sleep, especially the children and the elderly. The planes go screaming right over the old peoples' home. Why, Steven, *why*?'

'Operational necessity.'

'But why, Steven . . . when the Cold War seems to be over?'

'I've had three cows abort,' Councillor Muggeridge chipped in, 'in the past five days. You can't tell me, lad, that's coincidence.'

'The Brent geese have virtually abandoned their feeding grounds,' Mr Priestley said portentously, 'and—'

Steven Naylor cut him short, spreading his hands munificently. 'Lady Haddington, gentlemen, I am the bearer of good news! The night flying is soon to finish! The pilots are simply trying out a new safety technique.'

'Their safety or ours? Not my cows', that's for sure!'

'Oh, for *all* our safety, Councillor.' Steven smiled. 'Their safety is our safety. And vice-versa.' He would never go so far as to use General Vosper's well-known ace of trumps: if the Brits bellyache about our aircraft, tell 'em they're lucky the planes don't have Red Stars on their wings. 'I'm sorry about the cows, sir. But sometimes these things happen, don't they?'

'Not to my cows, no, that they don't!'

'And I have observed,' Mr Priestley said, 'that they are carrying a new sort of bomb.'

'Just practice,' Naylor assured him.

'But for *what*?' Mr Priestley persisted.

Only Lady Haddington's desire to get on permitted a change of subject.

Item two – low-flying by day. Villagers practically having their heads chopped off in the High Street, lessons at the Primary School suspended. This was a real free-for-all. Even the Rector, regardless of Harvest Festival goodies, waxed lyrical: the tiles on the twelfth-century church spire dislodged, a funeral service interrupted, stained glass cracked in the west window. Horses bolting with young child riders, and those cows that didn't abort, breaking their legs in a mad stampede. Then there was all this lorry traffic, extra this week, they'd swear. And the perennial favourite, prices forced up by the overpaid Yanks.

By noon, Steven Naylor was sweating but still smiling. He had heard them out and made promises according to their several needs. He would take their complaints right up to the top. He would talk to General Vosper himself, who was a real Anglophile.

Meantime, happier topics. The Base would be hosting a big dance, a big children's party, a big football match. Yes, he did mean English football. The Yanks were anxious to learn, and he knew Councillor Muggeridge had been a county player in his time.

'And some time, sir,' he addressed Mr Priestley, 'I wonder if you would give a talk about the birds in your sanctuary. There are some very interested men and women on the Base who would love to hear more about it.' At twelve-thirty, he opened the hospitality cupboard and handed out brimming glasses of excellent sherry.

'And now you've got *me*,' Harriet Harper smiled apologetically, as the others took their cordial farewells. 'Think you can bear it?'

Steven Naylor stretched his arms above his head and sighed with massive relief. 'Of course I can! Been looking forward to it. After that, some light relief!'

She sat herself down on the chair immediately opposite him.

'Don't bank on it.'

She clasped her hands together. Then she told him about Jennie's baby and how Jennie wouldn't name the father. Till now, that is.

'Don't tell me!' Naylor struck his forehead several times with the palm of his hand. 'He's a Yank!'

'Yes.'

'Ye gods, that's all I wanted! *That is all*!' The lines of his face seemed to dissolve. 'And you know his name?'

Harriet shook her head. 'I know he's a flyer.'

Naylor ran his hand distractedly through his hair. 'A pilot?'

A wizzo, she thought. Something like that.

'Something like that!' Naylor echoed desperately. 'Christ, your Jennie's really done it! They're going to be furious! The powers-that-be are going to be as mad as hell!'

'And what about her, for God's sake?' Harriet jumped to her feet. 'And the baby! I don't give a damn about your powers-that-be! They shouldn't be here in the first place! And it takes two to make a baby!'

She walked to the door.

'I'm sorry.' Naylor spread his hands and shrugged in disarming apology. 'It's been a rough morning. Very rough! And this baby has just appeared at a very bad psychological moment.'

'They often do.'

'The Yanks are a bit keyed up at the moment. The Colonel's got a lot on his mind. But leave it with me. I'll be in touch. I'll make sure things work out all right!'

It was ten days before Squadron Leader Naylor gained an audience with Colonel Craddock. Nowadays, as he grumbled to his wife, it was like gaining an audience with the Pope. In the intervening period, rumours and poops had been rife. The Forces simply didn't believe in the so-called 'democratisation' of the eastern block. There was bound to be trouble, instead of peace on earth – to hear the aircrew talking in the bar, you'd have thought the Third World War was imminent, and even that wasn't soon enough for some of them. The Commies worked behind the scenes. There had been another atrocity – terrorists trained by General Ahmed Akhbar of Hammadaz with Soviet-supplied weapons had exploded a bomb on an American civil aircraft, killing nine, including USAF wives and children.

What exactly was imminent, Naylor had no idea, and frankly he didn't *want* to know either. Harriet Harper's piece of information was quite enough for him to handle at the moment. Sister had, at his instigation, extracted the name of the father from Jennie – and it hadn't made his task any easier. With the uncanny instinct of naughty young girls, she had chosen to sin with one of the USAF's most valuable crew members.

But as the Colonel's PA showed him into Craddock's office, none of his worries showed on that smiling rosy face. In contrast, most of Caspar Craddock's showed on his. In the past week, to Maxine's dismay, he had slept for an average of only three hours a night, after watching the four chosen crews fly their night bombing exercises.

The task of choosing those crews hadn't been all that difficult. Inevitably Ryan and Scott had been two. Diefenbaker had naturally insisted that he should be one – which was right – and both he and Craddock had agreed on Captain Gruber for the fourth, not so much because Gruber was a most consistently good AC, but because his wizzo, Lieutenant Buzz Barlow, was a real hot shot. Before the two top crews had been posted in, Barlow was the

Squadron Bombing Leader, and it was clear that in whatever was brewing up, accurate bombing would be the first priority.

But that was as far as the agreement had gone. When the names of the four crews selected, plus the one stand-in, Kowalski, had been pinned up on the squadron offices board, a howl had gone up from the unlucky ones like hungry wolves deprived of a kill. They'd handled it, Craddock and Dief and Helen, but it had taken time and patience. As Helen pointed out, the boys were hyped up for action. They smelled it in the air. Then they were told they couldn't have it, but someone else could. Always supposing of course that action really did come of it.

'Yes, Steve? Just what can I do for you?'

Naylor gave his best salute and his most ingenuous smile and said, 'I think, sir, that in this instance, the boot might be on the other foot. It might just be this time what I can do for you.'

He had decided on this mode of approach after much careful thought. With the Yanks, you had to be bold. Never apologise for your countrymen. Nor for your seventeen-year-old countrywomen.

'That's good news,' Craddock said drily. 'What? What can you do for me?'

Naylor immediately fell into his patter about cementing good relations with the British. The Anglo-American dance.

'Lady Haddington, sir, was most enthusiastic. She would love to have Mrs Craddock call and discuss a date.'

Wearily, Craddock scribbled on a notepad. 'I'll get Maxine to do that. What else?'

What else, was football and baseball and talks on birds. Craddock raised his brows derisively. 'You figure that will help, do you, Steve?'

'Oh, yes, sir! You see a number of these people are potential trouble-makers. So we get them involved in activities. That's a good old RAF custom.'

'Well, I guess I'll have to take your word for it.' Colonel Craddock shifted his bottom on his seat as if to indicate the audience was over. 'Is that it, Steve? Is that all you wanted to talk to me about?'

'There's just one other matter, sir.' The atmosphere was not as Naylor had hoped it would be, and he cleared his throat nervously. 'A matter of some delicacy.'

Craddock's brows shot together over his nose. In a tone of weary confidentiality, he said, 'I never like to hear that.'

'Hear what, sir?'

'A matter of some delicacy. Always means it's gonna be something I don't like.'

Naylor's normal bounciness deserted him. He felt and looked deflated.

'Well, go on, Steve! Shoot it out!'

Out it came without the finesse with which he had hoped to present it. 'Sir, a girl in Haddington has had a baby.'

The Colonel closed his eyes for a moment. Then he asked unhelpfully, 'So what's new?' And before Steven could bring himself to answer, Craddock answered himself. 'No, Steve. Guess you don't have to tell me. I know exactly. The father is a Yank. Or the girl says the father is a Yank.'

'Oh, he is, sir!'

The Colonel regarded him sternly. 'You were there?'

Naylor looked hurt but said nothing. And in kinder tone the Colonel went on, 'How come you're so sure?'

'Sister Harper delivered the baby. She's sure.'

'How is she so sure?'

'She knows the girl. She knows the family.' Naylor paused, then with determination added boldly, 'I think it's very important this is handled right, sir.'

The Colonel looked at him slowly and witheringly. 'Are you reckoning it might not be?'

'No, sir.'

'Sure glad to hear that.'

'But I am reckoning it'll be tricky. Now the girl's spilled the beans, it'll get all round the village. If the man just gets shipped off home like Parkes was, the whole village will be furious. They're a clannish lot these East Anglian types. On the other hand, if he marries her, that would be perfectly splendid! We could give them quite a wedding. The village would love it!'

'Steve! For chrissake! That's carrying PR too goddamned far. This girl's maybe just wanting to get her claws into a Yank. Grab herself a meal ticket. She could be like the broads that come to the Saturday night dances. The father could be anybody. She's maybe had dozens. I'm not going to lumber one of my men with a marriage he doesn't want so you can have an Anglo-American circus!'

Naylor protested. 'That isn't what I meant, sir.'

'Sounded like it to me.' The Colonel thrust out his lower lip. 'So what's this stupid son-of-a-bitch's name?'

'Barlow, sir. Lieutenant Barlow.'

'*Wh-a-t?*'

The Colonel extended that agonised word to three syllables. He put his hands to his head, his fingers extended over his skull, as if forcibly to contain his half-blown mind. 'Say that again! No! Don't! Give me another name! For chrissake!' Then he blew out his breath in a long gasp. 'Barlow! Christ-on-a-crutch, Barlow!'

He got to his feet and waved Steve out of his office like someone shooing away a squawking hen.

'Thank you, Steve! That's all!'

In some disarray, Naylor saluted and backed to the door. With his hand on the knob, the Colonel called to him, 'And Steve, next time you have something you can do for me, forget it! Do you hear? For chrissake, forget it!'

Within twenty minutes, Craddock had the putative father in. He had been located in Ops, genning up on the night's bombing exercise. A man of twenty-seven with what the ordinary observer would have regarded as a healthy open countenance, under close-cropped curly brown hair. He had a wide humorous mouth, a cheerful, can-do manner, this despite the fact that after marrying at twenty-one, apparently happily, his wife had left him because she couldn't stand Service life.

As Barlow came in and saluted, Craddock had no doubt that he would shortly be wiping that smile off the young man's face.

'Any idea why I've sent for you?'

The wizzo wrinkled his brows. His clear hazel eyes looked puzzled. 'No, sir.'

'Try to guess!'

'Sir?'

'Go over what you've been up to recently.'

'Is it my night bombing, sir?'

A spasm twisted the Colonel's face. 'Not exactly.'

'I bin AA . . . Above Average, sir. All except the first night. Major Diefenbaker said—'

'It's not about your night bombing. It's about your private life.'

'Sir?'

'You're divorced?'

'Yes, sir. I've not seen Lorraine for four years.'

'But you have seen girls over here?'

'Only one, sir.'

'One too many.'

And then Craddock told him.

A variety of expressions crossed the wizzo's face; anxiety and surprise and disbelief and embarrassment to begin with, followed by a host of such contradictory emotions that Craddock, student of men though he was, gave up trying to interpret them.

When he'd finished, Barlow did have the grace to apologise in a low strangled tone of voice. 'Sorry about this, sir. Real sorry!'

'We're *all* sorry.'

Barlow blew his nose vigorously, and then said, 'So Jennie's had a baby? Actually had it?'

'Yes.'

'Are they OK? The baby and her?'

'According to the District Nurse, I understand they're both well.'

'Is it a boy or a girl?'

Craddock caught his breath. It seemed a goddamned frivolous question. What the hell did it matter?

'I don't know,' he answered shortly. 'I didn't enquire.'

Then he went on to outline what he called the options open to Barlow in the circumstances. Beginning with option one, that the baby was not his and he should vigorously deny paternity. He could be repatriated, would certainly be immediately repatriated. The Air Force was an understanding employer. Then a second option – if he wasn't sure, the girl could be asked to undergo tests. Rigorous tests.

At that point, he paused at the sight of Barlow's distressed face.

'D'you want to say something, Barlow?'

'Yes, sir. It *is* mine, sir. I didn't know she was pregnant. But it figures. The time's right, if you know what I mean, sir?'

'Yes, I know. Go on.'

'We had a godawful row. And I thought she'd just done a Lorraine on me. But I've always wanted her. An' I want to marry her. Her folks'll be mad at first. They don't like Yanks. But they'll get used to it.' He swallowed hard. 'I'd like to apply sir, formally sir, for your permission to marry.'

When the door finally closed behind Barlow, Craddock heard above the brisk rap of the wizzo's retreating feet, the sound of the 'Wedding March' cheerfully whistled.

I am getting out of touch, he thought, getting old. These youngsters are amazing me much too often.

Seven

Krk-krk-krk.

Sitting together in their lounge, drinking coffee after a late Sunday lunch, the Craddocks listened to the soft pad of Jarman's feet as he went to answer the telephone.

'If that's General Vosper on the line,' Maxine called through the closed door, 'tell him to damned well get off it!'

During the last two weeks, they had hardly had a moment to themselves. In direct contradiction to Naylor's assurance to Haddington villagers, training on the new radar bomb-sight in the four black-painted F-115s continued day and night. And Vosper was continually on the scrambler, demanding to know progress.

It was, in fact, going well. The whole squadron knew something big was up – though nobody, not even Craddock, knew exactly what.

The lounge door opened. 'It's not General Vosper himself on the line, madam,' Jarman announced. 'It's the airfield controller. To let the Colonel know that General Vosper is approaching in his helicopter.'

Craddock left immediately.

He was on the tarmac when the chopper dropped to the ground with the godalmighty thud that told him the General himself was at the controls.

General Vosper was at his most genial. Instead of returning Craddock's salute, as he got out of the helicopter, he slapped him on the back and called him, 'old friend'.

This was the man who had selected his base for such an important secret operation, hinting at a General's star after its successful execution – a stocky red-faced Texan with bright eyes as hard as diamonds. Beside him stood a tall, pale flagpole of an aide-de-camp.

'Wanna see everything, Cas! Wanna meet the guys! Wanna talk to 'em! Wanna see 'em in action!'

'In action, sir?'

'You gotta training detail tonight?'

'Every night, sir. They take off at 20.00 hours at maximum all-up weight.'

'And loving it, eh?'

'They are. The Haddington villagers aren't.'

'Cas, they're goddamned lucky those birds don't have Red Stars on their wings!' The General snorted. 'Tonight, they'll have my helicopter added to the orchestra.' He looked at his watch. 'Now let's get started!'

First stop – the Simulator section. The General watched intently as a night refuelling proceeded. Or rather, didn't proceed, as the pilot couldn't manage manoeuvring under the tanker and holding station on the green of the traffic light guiding system.

'He's very new,' Craddock explained. 'The four-crew team have night refuelling wrapped up.'

'Better have,' Vosper said cryptically. 'They're sure gonna need it.'

So whatever else the operation might be, Craddock thought, it's somewhere far away.

'What's next, Cas?'

The second stop – the curved hard hangars where the Chief Radar Officer explained the intricacies of the new bomb-sight.

'A combination of radar, television, laser beams, computers and infra-red,' he told Vosper. 'The big step forward is the magnification of the image. In this thing,' he tapped the big Head-Up Display in front of the wizzo's position, 'all the pilot has to do is to centre the cross-hairs on the bomb-sight. Each cross has a little light on the top which indicates target direction. When the pilot has the target in the centre of the cross-hairs, all the lights will illuminate, and the radar soon slews automatically to align with the target and lock-on. And you can spot the joins in railroad tracks at five miles.'

'What about EW?'

'The lot, sir! Every electronic warfare device we got. Cockpit mounted threat indicator. The latest radar jammer. This missile detection system releases decoys in response to the signals from heat-seeking missiles.'

'And for night attack?'

Craddock looked at the General sharply.

'Thermal camera for night-firing. Hot night-sights for total darkness. Infra-red locking and guiding.'

'Great! Now what about surprise? Does that anti-radar paint give protection?'

'Some, sir. They'll still have to have the jammers on. Not easy for the wizzos to identify a small target.'

'That's what their training's for.' Vosper turned to Craddock. 'Now I wanna see the cookies.'

Third stop – Armament Section. Laser target fixing and guided stand-off missiles called smart bombs would be used 'in anger', if necessary, along with iron bombs, old-fashioned but with tremendous penetration.

'For dropping on the target boats in training,' the Chief Armament Officer explained, 'we use these eleven pounders. Scares the shit out of the sailors when they hit the armoured decks.'

'Which they do?' the General asked.

'Which they do often,' the Armament Officer replied.

Fourth stop – Maintenance hangars where the General examined minutely the complicated fusing mechanisms. The computers had calculated the fixing of the target, the exact position of drop, the guidance system, whereby the wizzo could monitor the missile's track and correct where necessary.

Fifth stop – Sixth Tactical Fighter Squadron Crew Room. By now, the General was bursting with confidence and bonhomie. Though he talked to everyone on the squadron, he spent most of his time with Diefenbaker, Scott, Ryan and Gruber, who were already in their flying gear.

Diefenbaker took him through what he would see from his helicopter. Four target boats would be in the Wash – each producing slightly different echoes on the aircraft radar. The object was to select the right echo – small and very difficult to see through the jamming – lock-on, drop, guide and hit. There would be three exercises – radar bomb-sight, pilot release, formation bombing.

'You guys going to hack that mission?'

Led by Ryan, they assured him in chorus that they were.

'You better! 'Cos I'll be watching!' The General looked at his watch. 'Jesus . . . *tempus fugit*, eh? You guys'll be wanting to start up.'

'Shall we have a bite before we go up, sir?' Craddock asked.

'No, no, Cas. Wanna see the take-off. When d'you reckon we'll be down?'

'Exercise'll take a couple of hours. Debriefing a couple more.'

'After which I'll take that rain check your gorgeous Maud . . . Millicent . . .'

'Maxine.'

'. . . gave me. Be tickled pink to see the lovely lady again, Cas! Give her a call and say we'll be at your place—' again the General looked at his watch —''bout midnight, eh?'

Gingerly Craddock strapped himself down in the helicopter next to Vosper. Behind in the jump seat sat the aide-de-camp, paler than ever. Generals were not noted for their flying ability, and Vosper's was notorious.

They watched the four F-115s – nose-to-tail, white indentification lights flashing, green anti-collision lights, navigation lights steady – grunt their way to the end of the flarepath and take off into a blustery wind, trailing scarlet fangs from their afterburners.

Then Vosper started up. With a jerk, they left the ground, shot up vertically into the sky and followed the Christmas tree of lights in the direction of the Wash.

The rest of the sky was pitch-black.

'Don't think we're going to see much, sir,' Craddock warned.

'Enough,' the General replied. 'And the guys get a kick from knowing I'm here.'

'They're not the only ones,' Craddock thought as the helicopter bucked violently to port.

They arrived over the Wash to a flurry of instructions from the controller of the bombing range. There was no sign of the F-115s, though the voices of all four aircraft commanders came booming through the RT into their ears. There was no sign either of the target boats, till Craddock pointed out four white snakes far below them on what presumably was the dark water of the Wash.

The babble on the RT reached a crescendo. Next moment, low on the water, a huge lighted brooch of red, white and green flashed towards the wriggling target boat washes. Craddock could just make out the silhouette of an F-115.

'Pilot release, sir.'

Eagerly, Vosper pressed his snub nose against the windscreen. The chopper rocked to the right, but already the lights had disappeared into the night.

It was like that for the next hour. Over the radio, orders to Firefly One, Firefly Two, Firefly Three and Firefly Four were interspersed with interim results from target boats and the range controller. Now and again, they caught sight of lights moving very fast, low down on the water, and the helicopter began bumping up and down and sideways as Vosper tried to get a better view.

Looking over his shoulder, in the slight light from the instruments, Craddock saw the aide-de-camp was being decorously sick into the handkerchief spread neatly over his knees.

The continuous stream over the radio gradually dried up. The lights disappeared. The white snakes gradually became smaller.

Even Vosper realised the exercise was over. 'Let's head for home, eh, Cas?'

'Good idea, sir.'

From the jump seat came a sound half way between a sob and a cheer, as Vosper turned the helicopter unsteadily south.

But the General pronounced the exercise 'very impressive'. Not even almost going through the tarmac with his landing could dent the optimism with which he was looking forward to the debriefing.

The bombing results confirmed the most optimistic of Craddock's hopes. Videotapes from the aircraft cameras showed pinpoint bombing of the highest order. From the trailer complex with its set of five dish antennae, the range controller confirmed this assessment – in spite of the jamming signals, simulated surface-to-air missiles and anti-aircraft guns they had thrown up against the F-115s.

Apart from one incident in the formation bombing exercise, over which Scott accused Ryan of cutting right in and forcing him to skid port so that Hotrod could position himself to score the bulls-eye, the exercise had gone like clockwork. All aircraft had correctly identified the right target – no mean feat in the gusting darkness. Ryan had scored direct hits on all three runs – formation, bomb-sight, pilot release. Scott, Diefenbaker and Gruber had only one each, but their misses had been very close.

General Vosper was going round slapping everybody on the back. He had a special word to say to the wizzos – Lynch, Robinson, Ames and Barlow.

'With guys like this, Cas,' he declared delightedly, 'I feel real good!'

But his special pleasure was reserved for Ryan. And Ryan, like his father, knew when to move right in on a softened target.

'Thank you, sir,' he murmured in a new, modest tone. 'Guess waxing that target, getting it right, meant more to me than most.'

With beguiling diffidence, he brought out the famous Vietnam knife. 'My father's, sir,' he told the General affectingly, and followed that up with his father's story – shortened of course, but vividly dramatised.

To an observer, it looked like Ryan was putting the knife at Vosper's personal disposal. It must have looked like that to the General.

Leading him over to Craddock, he said, 'We gotta hear more from this jock, Cas. And to think his hero father served under you, Cas! Guess that means a lot to you. Makes him one of the family.' He looked at his watch. 'And say, it's already half after twelve. I just know the lovely Maude . . . Millicent . . .'

'Maxine.'

'. . . won't mind laying an extra place for Rod at our little dinner, eh, Cas?'

The three of them – Scott, Robinson and Ames – foregathered in the Open Mess, accepting their buddies' drinks and congratulations with becoming modesty.

Ames, who shared the victor's crown, showed no emotion. Inwardly, he felt his skill-confidence rise to an all-time high, but he was still uneasy about Ryan, and a bit sore, too, about not being included in the Vosper-Craddock invitation. He wouldn't have wanted to dine at the Craddocks', but he would like to have been asked. More even than Glenn Robinson, he'd come up the hard way. He'd never had the time or money to learn to be a good mixer, so maybe he felt the unintended slight more than Glenn, who always handed it on to the Lord with Christian resignation, or Scott who had the easy, laconic confidence of one born into a well-off family endowed with a natural skill and a life in which everything seemed to fall into place.

And after all, in the final analysis, the bombing was down to the wizzo. The pilot just took them to the target.

'Some are called, but few are chosen,' Glenn said with vague cheerfulness to Ames as they raised their glasses.

The point of the text was not clear to Scott either, but he said, 'Amen to that, brother,' to please his wizzo. 'Both you guys did a bloody good job, Glenn, Milt. It was just that Ryan had the flying edge on me.'

And a bloody dangerous edge at that, he wanted to say – but didn't. They'd been level scoring till the formation drop. Then, damn Ryan, he'd managed to come so close, he'd forced him that fraction out. But he wasn't going to criticise Ryan to the wizzos, so he buttoned up his mouth and said nothing.

'No one's got the flying edge on you, Jonny,' Glenn pronounced loyally.

'I wasn't fishing, Glenn. That's the truth of it. Both you and Milt were great. I was just stating a fact.'

A voice in his ear asked drily, 'Still stating facts, Captain?'

Helen Mansell had threaded her way through the crowded bar. She had a half empty glass which she raised.

'Congratulations! All of you! I hear the General was impressed.'

'Sure was.' Scott nodded sagaciously.

'Where are Grunter and Buzz?'

'Gone to bed like good boys.'

'And where's the star of the show?'

'Right now basking in the sun that shines out of the General's you-know-what,' Scott winked at her. 'He's dining *en famille* at the Craddocks'.'

'Kinda late, isn't it?'

'Special invitation by the General.'

'My, my!' Helen looked humorously impressed. Then her smile faded. She looked intently at Scott, her blue eyes disturbingly penetrating. He felt his unspoken criticism of Ryan, his jealousy of his success maybe, clear for her to read.

He felt his anger increase. Only now it was less against Ryan than against her for being so damned perceptive. For still being the goddamned studious little preppie, only this time not meekly accepting his favours – not even wanting them.

She didn't suggest they talk. Nothing as crude as that. But somehow, Helen and Scott drifted over to a table by the window. This time, she said, the drinks were on her.

She bought them both a double bourbon – obviously a tongue loosener.

And he talked. He didn't mean to, but she was good to talk to. And she asked all the right questions. They began reminiscing again about Princeton. She had a remarkable memory. She told him a bit about what had happened to her meantime. The pilot she'd married. The flying accident that killed him. Formation flying.

What Scott couldn't say to the wizzos, he could say to her. He didn't have to explain the whys and wherefores of F-115 bombing tactics, and it was good to get what he thought of Ryan's flying off his chest.

But though the talk left him feeling relieved and relaxed – as the good little psychiatrist no doubt meant it to – it left him also feeling very dissatisfied.

For throughout the hour or so, she seemed to have been totally unaware of him as a man, which he wasn't used to, while ironically he had become increasingly painfully aware of her as a woman.

He wondered if she knew, and if this was her way of repaying him for being such a smartass at Princeton, all those years ago.

The following morning, Maxine Craddock drove out of the main gate of Haddington Airbase at ten-thirty, in good time for her coffee appointment with Lady Haddington, when arrangements for the Anglo-American dance were to be discussed.

She was not in a mood to discuss anything. But keeping the Brits sweet had been one of the General's themes at the uncomfortable dinner last night, and Maxine's efforts scored points for Cas.

She was used to playing the good wives' game to Caspar's superiors. But she found it came harder with Vosper than anyone so far. Bull-necked, with a square fleshy face and small greedy eyes, he was a man she mistrusted.

An officer turned politician. A man with a mission. Himself.

The whole thing had begun badly. What sort of time was one in the morning for a meal? She'd asked Cas that when he phoned. 'The time the General wants it,' he'd answered in his quiet, deadly commander-to-insubordinate-subordinate voice. Then the last minute extra place to be set and the young man it was set for. Rod Ryan, Ace of the the Base. The high flyer with a chip on his shoulder.

The food had been Maxine's best – which was saying a lot – impeccably served by Jarman. A bit of wisecracking on Jarman from the General.

'How long you been here, Cas? Four months? An' gettin' more British than the British!'

This was followed by the little homily about British public opinion, the USAF keeping a low but friendly profile, now more important than ever with, well . . . a thick red finger to the side of a thick red nose and a reddened eye winking in Caspar's direction.

Classified information. Best not say. Even good American walls have ears.

Apart from that, the dinner table was dominated by this young black-haired pilot with the insolent sexy mouth and the dark blue Irish eyes.

He'd talked flying tactics, Flag exercises, night ground-terrain following sorties, and how he'd won the John P. Hallowman Bombing trophy in '87. He'd also let fall that his father-in-law was Senator Seegar. The General knew him. Ed Seegar was a buddy of the Air Secretary. It sure was a small world. They toasted Ryan's marriage in Caspar's best burgundy. Their glasses were recharged while in silence they remembered Ryan's father.

Over Maxine's elaborate grand-marnier, pineapple and whipped chocolate sweet, at the General's invitation, Ryan had described the bombing practice which had so delighted Vosper. At one point, her flower arrangement had become the target, the silver cream pitcher and the crystal shoved aside by Vosper to give the pilot more room to mime his bombing run.

And as his flattened hand had zoomed down and almost but not quite brushed the expensive hot-house rose petals of the flower arrangement, his sensuous lips had curled back, his narrowed eyes had glittered, his profile had sharpened to that of a killer.

The General had watched that momentary transformation and his smile had broadened. 'That's great! That's the sort of flying we want, Cas!'

'In my opinion,' Caspar said levelly, addressing Ryan, 'in the formation, as wingman, you cut in sharp on your leader.'

The General wouldn't have it. He'd laughed, genially enough, and slapped Caspar across the shoulders. 'Times change, Cas! You and me . . . we're the old men! It's the youngsters now!'

Maxine had seen the almost childish look of vindictive triumph that Ryan shot towards Caspar. A look wasted on Caspar, his eyes were lowered, he was listening to something the General was whispering in his ear.

You have an enemy, Cas, she thought. But Caspar said nothing. People could hate him, love him, want him, reject him, but he sailed on. Nothing penetrated the Air Force uniform.

Suddenly Maxine realised that in her introspection, she had taken the righthand turning out of the camp instead of the left. The righthand road to Haddington, as Caspar had so often warned her, was one always to be avoided at that time in the morning.

And hard on the heels of that thought, the reason for it. She saw the tent, a small ramshackle affair on the green grassy verge of the road. Out from it with disconcerting suddenness, stepped the figure of a woman in a fawn dress and leather sandals. She carried a soft mat which she unrolled on the tarmac right in the centre of the road, and fell unhesitatingly to her knees. Then she folded her hands in prayer. Though Caspar had told her this happened every day at this time, Maxine shouted to herself, 'Crazy woman! This I don't believe!'

She went through a moment of acute indecision. The index finger of her right hand moved towards the horn button. She'd meant to give the crazy broad such a blast that she'd jump sky-high. Then she decided to swerve round into the opposite lane and carry on and forget the bizarre sight she'd just seen.

But the road was narrow and there were vehicles approaching from the opposite direction, so she had to pause and in that pause, she saw at close hand the poverty of the tent and the small wooden cross and the homemade blue and white flag with a hand-painted overfed looking dove on it which said, QUAKERS FOR PEACE.

In a mixture of pity, exasperation and curiosity, she killed the engine and got out of the car.

The kneeling woman was not disconcerted. 'Won't you join me?' she asked Maxine in a clipped, refined, English voice.

'You mean . . . ?' Maxine was alarmed, and indignant at herself for having stopped. Indignant at this middle-aged mousy little woman for doing anything so ridiculous, so blasphemous really, as to pray in public, and most indignant of all at her invitation for Maxine to join in.

'Yes,' the Quaker woman went on cheerfully. 'Won't you join me in prayer? I pray every day at this time. Very often passers-by join me. We pray in silence.'

Maxine asked suspiciously, 'What for?'

'They pray for whatever they want to pray. I pray for peace.'

'Is that all?' Maxine was unconvinced.

'And grace,' the woman added.

It seemed harmless. They were not praying for the Base to be spirited away or anything subversive like that. And though Maxine obviously could not, as the Commander's wife, be funnyfooted into doing anything so crazy or disloyal as to get down on her knees, she did stand with her head bowed, and the woman, who didn't seem to expect such a smart American woman to kneel down, gave her a sweet and grateful smile and closed her eyes. She must have stayed with them closed for two or three minutes. In that time, a milkman stopped his float and stood beside her, head bowed and moving his lips in vigorous prayer. Maxine said a harmless one for Sharon and Cas and that they might be a family one day. That surely couldn't hurt anybody.

Luckily there wasn't much traffic. Maxine would have been devastated if anyone had seen her there. The more she thought of it, the more crazy it was to have stopped, like getting out of your car on a safari or in a nature reserve.

Then, thankfully, the woman opened her eyes, got to her feet, shook Maxine's hand and the milkman's, whom she addressed as George, told Maxine her name was Anne, paused for Maxine to reveal hers, and when she didn't, wished them both Godspeed.

God or something certainly sped Maxine on the rest of her journey into Haddington village. Of course Caspar had had this crazy Quaker lady thoroughly investigated, and she was not sufficiently subversive yet to cause worry. So far she hadn't done anything worse than pray in the wrong places and sometimes take place in a candlelight vigil, but Maxine had been a fool not to avoid such an encounter.

Worse still, for all the lunacy of the situation, for all the pitifulness and hopelessness of the woman's efforts, Maxine had momentarily felt a flicker of sympathy and admiration. As if, instead of the woman being a lunatic in the midst of sanity, she had glimpsed a tiny flame of sanity in the huge self-destructive lunacy of the real world.

The flicker of sympathy quickly went out. But Maxine's feelings were still in a state of some turmoil by the time she turned the car through the impressive stone entrance pillars of Haddington Hall.

The wrought iron gates were open. Maxine swept up the drive and brought the car to a halt outside the porticoed entrance.

She sat for a moment lost in admiration. Here was another England, and one she warmed to. The façade of the great house was early eighteenth-century, of mellowed stone with brick quoins. The sun was catching the bluey glass of the long Georgian windows, and the air smelled of late roses, chrysanthemums and cut grass and some flowering shrubs in ancient stone urns.

The door was opened by a butler who was not nearly as impressive as Jarman, which made Maxine feel immediately more confident – but the drawing room could have been designed to cut Yanks down to size. It was a long room, ending in French doors to the terrace. It was not lavishly furnished, sparsely in fact – but

Maxine could recognise fine furniture. Hepplewhite sofa-tables, Chippendale chairs, faded Aubusson rugs, a large Gainsborough portrait over the Adam fireplace, Meissen bowls and Sèvres ornaments, and a lovely *épergne*, holding pink roses.

The figure that rose stiffly from a high-backed chair by the open French doors might herself have stepped out of a Gainsborough frame. Tall and thin and straight as a die, narrow shouldered, flat-chested, her silk dress hanging loosely on her bony frame, she was nevertheless possessed of a certain aloof and aristocratic beauty. Behind *pince-nez* on her aquiline nose, her eyes were violet and oddly youthful, her smile welcoming and gracious.

'Mrs Craddock . . . how nice to meet you.' A skeletal hand pressed Maxine's vigorously. 'Or may I call you Maxine? I may? How nice! Christian names always make me feel younger. Do sit down! I'll ring for coffee.'

She lifted an authentic, old-fashioned bell pull that took Maxine back to her childhood. She said so. Lady Haddington was enchanted. She asked Maxine about her childhood in Georgia and whether her parents still lived there, which made Maxine feel younger.

So all in all, they got on well.

The coffee came, served by the man who wasn't half as good as Jarman, and whose coffee wasn't either. But it was a *tête-a-tête*, just Maxine and Lady Haddington, enjoyable because they liked each other. They skirted dangerous subjects like aircraft noise, nuclear weapons and village protest, and concentrated on social interchanges, what Lady Haddington called 'accenting the positive'.

They had just decided on a date for the dance, when in through the French doors came as good-looking an Englishman as Maxine had ever seen. The quintessential Englishman. About Caspar's age and height, but slimmer. Dark-haired and dressed in jodhpurs and hacking jacket, his features declared him at once Lady Haddington's son. As did her look of exasperated tenderness.

'I'm sorry, Mother. I do hope I'm not interrupting . . . ?'

'You know perfectly well you're interrupting! I do hope Mrs Craddock will excuse you. Maxine . . . may I present my son, Charles? He and my grandson are staying with me at present.'

She didn't say why, nor if there was another Lady Haddington. And even at that first handshake, a treacherous little voice inside Maxine hoped there wasn't.

'I'm delighted to meet you.' He had his mother's charm and her strange violet coloured eyes but a fleshier, fuller, passionate mouth. He held Maxine's hand a moment longer than politeness demanded under the pretext of a heartfelt apology. 'And I'm really most sorry to interrupt but . . .'

'He isn't sorry at all,' Lady Haddington said roundly. 'He always interrupts when I'm entertaining attractive ladies.'

'With respect, that is just not true, mother. You rarely, if ever, entertain attractive ladies.'

Lady Haddington swept his protest aside. 'So why did you interrupt? What is your excuse this time?'

'My excuse is, Mother,' he gave Maxine a conspiratorial smile, 'that you have never entertained anyone as attractive as Mrs Craddock. So I was determined to meet her. It was as simple as that.'

It was all very simple, in fact. Maxine guessed it was all part of the ingrowing British aristocrats at play. Lord Haddington rang for more coffee. He eyed Maxine over the rim of his cup, as if the sight of her gave him the most intense pleasure.

He asked her how she liked England, and when she replied that she was reserving judgment, he laughed heartily as if she'd made a most witty remark. He told her with a strange mixture of reticence and openness which the British seemed to have, that he hoped to devote more time to the Anglo-American Committee and to his estate and his horses, because he was now 'between wives'.

'I thought it was business affairs that kept you occupied, not poor Cynthia.' Lady Haddington looked severely at her watch.

'Both, Mother dear. But without poor Cynthia, I do have time for other things.'

'So we'll see more of you, shall we, Charles?'

'Indeed yes, Mother. Much more—' and in the same breath, 'do you ride, Mrs Craddock?'

'I do. But not since I came to England.'

'We must remedy that, mustn't we, Mother?'

Lady Haddington said nothing.

When Maxine rose to leave, Lord Haddington jumped up.

'I'll see you to your car, Mrs Craddock.' And at the car, bowing over her hand, he asked, 'If I found you a suitable mount, would you trust yourself to come riding with me?'

'Thank you. I'd like that.'

It was all very flattering. And though Caspar had told her that

Lord Haddington, owner of vast properties and director of many companies, stood to gain from the American presence, his flattery warmed her. It wiped away the memory of last night's dinner with Vosper, it shrank to its appropriate ridiculous size the incident with the Quaker lady.

And it started Maxine on a different way of looking at life here in England.

Eight

'Jonathan . . . I'd like your opinion.' Helen Mansell came up to Scott as he stood alone at the Open Mess bar counter. It was four nights after the bombing display for General Vosper, since when there had been no flying. For three of those days the four black-painted F-115s had been in the TABVS – the Theater Air Base Vulnerability Shelters – under the care of the Equipment Maintenance Squadron, having 'modifications' done and being brought up to MCA (Mission Capable Aircraft). On the fourth day, unaccountably, the squadron had been given a twenty-four-hour stand-down.

Glenn had hightailed it off somewhere, and at the far end of the bar, Grunter Gruber was buying a case of Bourbon for Buzz Barlow to take to his future father-in-law. In the centre of the room, a noisy bunch of horny jocks were gathered round a girl Stratotanker pilot like yellow-jackets round a fig tree.

Scott turned to eye Helen with a mixture of welcome and wariness. She avoided his glance by studying the half-empty glass in her hand.

'Always ready to oblige.' He gave her his slow, slightly condescending smile, and still smarting from her attitude the other night, asked, 'Some facts you want to wise up on?'

'You could say that.'

'Then you've come to the right guy, Major.'

He picked up his drink, put his hand under her elbow and guided her to a corner by the window, tucked away behind a wooden stand that held periodicals. Gruber and Barlow exchanged meaning looks, but the rest of the jocks weren't interested. They were too busy preening themselves in front of the girl, like a flock of peacocks.

'Well?' Scott settled himself back in his chair. 'On what subject, Helen?'

'On whom,' she corrected him, and listening to her own words, heard how cool and pedantic they sounded.

Under the sandy lashes, Scott's grey eyes narrowed. He had somehow grown in maturity, she thought irrelevantly. Always good-looking, his face now was getting carved in lines of self-confidence and resolution.

'Strictly between ourselves,' she added.

'Uh-uh!' Scott frowned warningly. 'Not doing your psychological ferreting, I hope?'

'Only sort of.'

'Which means yes.' Scott took a gulp of his whisky. 'Who?'

'Rod Ryan.' She looked up suddenly, studying his now forbidding face.

'What about him?'

'Nothing precisely. Just what d'you think of him?'

'He's a bloody good pilot.'

'You pilots all stick together.'

'We gotta.'

'Even when you reckon . . .'

'Reckon what?'

'That he cut in on you.'

'Jeezus, I was just flipping my lid! Letting off! Releasing tension, like you psychiatrists would say. I dunno. Maybe he did. Maybe he didn't. Maybe we were all hyped up. It's all in a split second. One second, he's there. One second, he's not.' He frowned. 'You were always too literal, Helen.'

'Was I?'

'Yeah. Too black and white. Too precise.'

'But isn't flying precise?'

'Yeah . . . to a point. But people aren't. Life isn't either.'

'Thanks for the sermon.'

'You're welcome.'

They sat eyeing each other coldly. Why, she wondered, were they always at pains to make it clear they didn't find each other attractive. When the silence went on uncomfortably, with no real hope of ever finding enlightenment, she asked, 'Is he a good AC?'

'Are we still on Ryan? Is he a good AC?' He repeated her question with mild derision. 'Yeah, I guess so. He brings them back in one piece. He waxes the target.'

'Good husband?'

'Now how the hell would I know that?'

'You know Samantha.'

'Jesus!' Scott threw back his head and laughed. 'You are a little ferreter, aren't you! You've been listening to the poop. Sure, I know Samantha. So why don't you ask her?'

'Because she isn't over here, as well you know.'

She had heard a tangy wheeze through the grapevine that Samantha had a big thing for Scott and had married Ryan as second best. But that was another story – probably untrue.

What she had set herself to find out was whether or not Colonel Craddock's only half expressed misgivings about Ryan were justified. But she was up against the stone wall of pilot solidarity. 'Do you know why she hasn't come over yet?'

'How would I know that either?' Scott shrugged. 'Maybe she's busy buying her fancy new gear. You're the woman, Helen, you should know.'

'D'you reckon it would help Ryan if she came over?'

'Jesus, Helen! You ask the most goddamned questions! How about me asking you one.'

'Go ahead.'

'Why the hell does Ryan need help?'

'I'm not sure.' She got to her feet, scooped up the empty glasses and walked over to the bar counter. She returned and set the drinks in front of them. 'D'you reckon he's a stable personality?'

'You're the shrink, Helen. You're supposed to answer those sort of questions. And anyway, what's stable?' He eyed her over the rim of his glass. 'Are you stable, Helen? Am I? Is Glenn? Is Craddock? Is Dief? We're all liable to wobble off the wire.'

He studied her thoughtful earnest face with a mixture of exasperation and tenderness. 'You can delve too deep, Dr Mansell. There are certain things you just can't dig up and study and put back the way they were. And if it's any consolation, I'll tell you one thing. Ryan's a survivor. He does best under pressure. Give it us For Real, and he's your man!'

The subject of their conversation was at that moment roaring out of the main gate of the Cage in compensation for being on stand-down, which he wanted like he wanted a hole in the head. In times of frustration and disaster, relief usually came from a piss-up, singing sexy songs, the degree of dirt dependent on the depth of the depression. But there were certain times when the only compensation on the ground had to be a woman.

He was still hyped up from last Sunday night's bombing. That had been close to For Real. The difficult targets, the precision bombing, the General up there like God in his chopper, and better than all that, the tension, the whiff, the promise of Action To Come. And on top of it all, General Vosper's praise and his blessing.

As he opened up the Suzuki and raced down the main road, he relived that night. Not just the triumph of waxing the target, but it all. The power thrusting through his body, the delicate feel of the pickle button nipple under his thumb, the massive excitement of release.

He'd been eight years in the Air Force and never fired a shot in anger. But never had he gone on a low-level sortie when he didn't see a bloody Vietcong village down there, or done a practice interception when he wasn't in a furball with the Russkies. Hell, they were taught that, brought up on it! He loved the Red Flag exercises when they fought their own Aggressor squadron. The F-15 fighters were in Russian camouflage with Red Stars on their wings and you hated the guys inside like they were Commie bastards.

But the day after such an exercise he always felt cold and flat, like he'd shot off without a woman. It was like having Samantha and knowing you didn't have her. But right now he didn't feel like that. He still felt high, rarin' to go, because last Sunday's exercise was a beginning, not an end. Even the letter he'd had that morning from Samantha, reckoning it was time she came over to join him, didn't alter his mood.

Came to join Scott, more like. He was pretty sure he'd only gotten her because she couldn't have Scott. He had not yet figured how he would reply. Just as he hadn't decided on how far he would go with Harriet, always supposing she'd let him in. He'd expected she would have sent him a bill for the damage to the old jalopy, and had been irritated and intrigued when she hadn't.

She lived, so she had said, in the flat above the Health Centre, half way down Haddington High Street. Ryan burned up the road from the Base to Haddington in a couple of minutes.

The door to the flat had a little round spyhole in it. He put his thumb on the bell, and pressed it as decisively as a pickle button.

Wondering if she was studying him through the peephole, he smiled engagingly. Maybe he should have phoned her, but that would have given her the chance to make excuses. He pressed the pickle button again.

This time the door opened.

'Why, Captain! Captain Ryan!'

He looked her over slowly and appreciatively. She was wearing a sleeveless silk dress, her arms were very touchable, lightly tanned and smooth-skinned. The dress was low-cut, showing the cleft in her bosom. She was prettier than he remembered. He decided two could, *should*, play Samantha's game. Explaining swiftly, but penitently that he had come to settle about her car, he asked if she was going to invite him inside.

She stepped back and waved him in.

The flat was small and cosily British. A chintzy sofa and two deep armchairs faced a fireplace with a gas fire. Matching curtains blew at an open window, a big bowl of flowers on a polished table scented the room.

'I'm going out in a moment.' She looked at her watch. 'But can I offer you a drink? Oh, and there's nothing to settle about the car. My insurance took care of that. So you needn't have worried.'

He had a feeling she almost said . . . so you needn't have come.

'I wanted to see you again.'

Maybe she didn't hear. 'Scotch? Beer? Gin? I've no bourbon, I'm afraid.'

'I said I wanted to see you again.'

'I know.' She returned his stare, her eyes deliberately impersonal and shielded, but he saw the slight flush that crept up her throat, and smiled.

'Scotch, please. Straight. And do you *have* to go out?'

She poured the drink – a discouragingly small one – and handed it to him. Then she perched herself on the arm of the chair opposite, as if at any moment she would take flight. She didn't answer his question, so he asked another. 'Aren't you drinking?'

She shook her head.

'Where I come from, Harriet, that's inhospitable.'

'I'm sorry.' She smiled as if she meant it. 'I don't mean to be inhospitable. But I am in a hurry.'

He smiled engagingly. 'Like last time.'

She laughed. 'No. This is social.'

'Someone special?'

'No. I'm dining at the doctor's house.'

'Uh-uh.'

‘With the doctor and his wife.’

Ryan sat back in his chair and sighed reminiscently. ‘That sure was an experience. Last time. Guess I’ll never forget it.’ Then he added, ‘Or you.’

‘I suppose you’ve heard they’re going to be married? Jennie and the baby’s father. Lieutenant Barlow.’

‘Sure have. They’re tying the knot in our Base chapel. And we’re putting on a wing-ding afterwards. An Anglo-American marriage, all that crap. I know Buzz Barlow. One of the best. She’s a lucky girl.’

‘I hope so.’

Harriet looked tremulous-lipped and moist-eyed the way women did about marriage and babies. Judging this a good moment, he leaned forward and asked pleadingly, ‘D’you really have to go out?’

‘Yes, I do.’

‘I could show you a good time.’

‘I’m sure.’

‘We could go along to that place by the river.’

She shook her head.

Dejectedly, he stared into his whisky. His disappointment must have got through to her, for she suggested, ‘Some other time, perhaps.’

It was a compensation, though a very small and distant one. He needed her right now, but he swallowed his feelings. ‘When?’ He took a swig of his drink. ‘You say a date and then I’ll go.’

She wanted rid of him, so she suggested the twenty-first of October, a Saturday. To meet at the Riverside Inn at seven-thirty.

With a flourish, he polished off the drink and put down the glass noisily. She jumped to her feet with relief. As she opened the door, he put his hands on her shoulders and kissed her lightly on the lips.

‘I find you very attractive.’

He had on occasion, a rich warm caressing voice and he could use it effectively for that sort of remark. Then suddenly he pulled her close so that she could feel through that thin dress just how goddamned attractive he found her, and kissed her again.

She drew away quickly as if she’d been stung. He half expected she’d cancel the date, but she didn’t. As she closed the door behind him she looked uncertain and unhappy. Maybe she was regretting she hadn’t let him show her a good time.

Outside in the cool evening, he didn't feel exactly on Cloud Nine himself. He stumped across the sidewalk to his motorbike, kicking a stone with the toe of his boot and cursing women.

He had no clear idea of what he was going to do. He kicked the bike like it was a lazy mare, and off he belted. At the end of the High Street, he almost ran down a black cat which leapt over a high wall and a stout woman in a man's hat – typical British eccentric – waved her umbrella furiously at him.

Over his shoulder, he shouted an obscenity at her, but he doubted the old broad heard him.

It was getting dark now. He could see the powerful glow of the Base in the distance, but though that glow always excited him, gave him a sense of his power, American power, he didn't want to go back right then.

He was drawn by other lights. Jazzy little lanterns and fairy lights outlining the name of the nearest British pub to the Base – the Haddington Arms – stone built and quaint and favoured by sergeants and other ranks. A few officers went there, but not many, so there wasn't much chance of getting into conversation with anyone he didn't want to. But there were usually plenty of local broads waiting to be picked up, especially by an officer.

Ryan turned his motorbike in. The car park was already half full. Against the wall of the pub itself, next to the entrance porch, coyly rested two shiny new bicycles of the kind to be bought at the Base Store – one male, one female, almost indecently embracing each other.

The bikes had bugged Ryan even before he knew to whom they belonged. Then he pushed open the swing doors in the Saloon bar, and saw their owners.

No matter what company he was in, Glenn Robinson stood head and shoulders above the rest. There he was, standing by the bar counter, one hand holding a glass of his goddamned Coke and the other resting on the shoulder of a pretty young girl, who was sexily perched on a high stool beside him and looking up at him like he was God.

Ryan had no doubt in deciding who she was. He'd heard Barlow joshing Glenn about the enlisted sentry he'd met. He had even less doubt in deciding what Glenn and the girl were up to.

He felt himself break out into a sweat of indignation. As he thrust his way through to confront them, Glenn suddenly switched his glance and saw him.

His face broke into a smile of idiotic welcome. 'Hi, Rod! C'mon in.' He beckoned Ryan over. 'Let me buy you a drink.'

Obligingly, the Brits in the bar and a group of airmen from the Base made way for him.

'What'll you have, Rod?'

'Captain Ryan.'

That gave the son-of-a-bitch a clue. But the goddamned Bible-banger just went on steadily, 'OK, Captain Ryan, sir, what'll it be?' and winked at the girl who had begun to look scared.

'I'm not drinking.' And then he let Glenn Robinson have it. His pent-up frustration supplied his tongue without the words having to go through his head. He wasn't sure what he did say, but everyone in the bar sure sat up and listened. He knew how he finished. 'You know damned well, Lieutenant, officers are not allowed to date enlisted personnel.'

'Aw, c'mon, Rod – Captain Ryan! You know that's never really enforced. Never! You an' me know lots of guys've dated enlisted girls. You have yourself. What's got into you, Rod . . . Captain Ryan?'

He looked so concerned, and somehow more than concerned, as if he could see something worrying deep down inside Ryan, that Ryan really flipped his lid.

'I'm not arguing, Lieutenant!' he said, or maybe shouted. 'Rules are rules. Orders are orders! Discipline is discipline! We're a front-line station! And right now, Airman – ' he rounded on the shrinking girl – 'you can get out!'

A titter of ribald laughter went round the Brits. A thin reedy voice said, 'We've heard the Yanks don't know their arses from their elbows, but blimey, they don't seem to know their women from their men! That's a girl, Captain! Look at her skirt!'

'Airman!' Ryan had gone white with rage. 'Hear this! I'm ordering you out of here!'

'Just a minute, just a minute! Hang on!'

A hoarse voice sounded from behind the bar counter. Unhurriedly and with stagy deliberation, the counter flap was raised. Out came a large, fat, florid man with balding sandy hair, bulbous bloodshot eyes, a big red beery nose. His shirt sleeves were rolled up over large bruiser's arms, but he made a gesture of rolling them up further as if preparing for action.

'I'm the landlord here, Yank!' He thrust his face into Ryan's, fanning him with a beery breath. 'Did I hear you have the bloody cheek to order a customer out of my bar?'

'Yes.' Ryan stood his ground. 'She's an enlisted airman.'

Again, that goddamned titter of laughter went round the bar. The landlord joined in. Suddenly Ryan felt as if he'd been caught up in a nightmare, like some comic opera of hatred and derision.

Abruptly the landlord stopped laughing. He grabbed a handful of Ryan's jacket. His face came close again. Bloody eyeball to eyeball. 'I'll do the ordering round here, Yank! This is my bar! And this is still our own bloody country. If there's anyone leaving, it'll be you!'

'C'mon,' Robinson said. 'Have a drink, Captain. Lighten up. Della and I were jest leaving anyway.' He put his arm round her and kissed the top of her head. 'A large bourbon for the Captain, landlord.'

The landlord grudgingly set the whisky on the counter and Glenn counted out the money.

The laughter died away. The Brits lost interest. Ryan stood for a moment, staring at Glenn's bloody sincere black face, at the landlord still scowling, at the Brits now laughing and talking to one another.

He hated the lot of them! The whole motherfucking lot! He took a step forward and picked up the drink. He saw a relieved smile break over Glenn's face.

Then he raised the glass, tipped the contents over the other side of the counter into where they washed the glasses, and marched out.

Nine

Milton Ames stood at the counter of the Officers' Open Mess bar, like something left on a deserted beach when the tide had gone out.

So he was. He felt washed out, drained, empty, yet too stilted up to go to bed. He felt as if an unseen hand had tossed him up in the air and the force of gravity hadn't pulled him back to earth again. He stared at the jazzy array of liquor bottles on the wall, at the big-faced clock that audibly creaked as every second passed, and above it the silent globes of the readiness lamps, with only the white lamp lit.

Ames knew he wouldn't sleep yet awhile. The squadron guys who'd dragged him into the bar for a drink had gone off to a dance at the Amenities Centre, and Ames was alone. They were proud of him, they had said. Real proud of his performance in front of the General last Sunday. It reflected well on all of them.

They were a good bunch, Ames told himself. Maybe it was this sudden popularity that made him feel as if his blood was full of air bubbles, maybe it was recovery from fear.

For he had been afraid. Shit-scared. He'd seen how Ryan had almost shaved Scott's wingtip. He'd been in the righthand seat, for chrissake! He'd looked right into the Reaper's face, as the guys would say. His heart had all but choked him. But he kept his mind steady and then it was all over. They'd pressed their pickle buttons and were heroes.

But would they get away with it next time, and the time after that, and the time after that?

Ames ordered another bourbon from the bar corporal.

'Have one yourself, Jim.'

'Thanks, sir.'

The corporal opened a can of Budweiser and raised it. 'Guess we're all proud of you and Captain Ryan! Station's in line for best in NATO.'

'Could be.'

Ames watched the corporal draining the can and begin stoppering up the bottles. Above that array, the clock creaked its way to a quarter before midnight. Only fifteen minutes of stand-down left.

Ames was about to finish his drink when Ryan came in. He could tell right away that his AC was in a real mean mood. He had a way of walking when he was mad – head down, shoulders hunched, as if ready to throw a punch. And close to, his mouth was tight-lipped and his eyes looked black, the blue irises all but swallowed up by the pupils. They made you feel queer, like you were looking down gun barrels.

But he seemed real glad to see his wizzo, raised his hand and said, 'Hi, Milt!' Then he turned to vent his anger on the corporal. 'Don't try to close up the bar, corporal! You're open as long as we want you to open.'

'Yes, sir.' The corporal pulled out the stoppers, unhooked glasses at the double.

'Well, Milt, what're you drinking?'

Suddenly Ames wanted desperately to go to bed. The force of gravity had worked. He'd come back to earth with a socking great thump. He felt if he had another bourbon, he'd throw up.

'Thanks. I'll have a Coke.'

'Christ, Ames, I'm not gonna buy you a Coke! That's for Bible-banging sons-of-bitches, not for men!' He shoved Ames's glass over the counter and told the corporal, 'Same as before. And make it a big one.'

'Glenn's OK,' Ames said with daring. 'One of the best.'

'Sure! Sure! In the air.'

Ryan was going to say more, but he saw Ames's face close up against him, and right then he needed someone to spill the load on. He was fucking full of frustration. He'd had his bellyful of Samantha and Scott and Harriet and Glenn and the whole bloody nation of ungrateful, ignorant Brits. But when he did spill his load, it didn't come out against any of them.

It was against Craddock, the chickenshit of a Colonel that was jealous of his own men. Always had been. Always would be.

'I'll tell you somethin', Milt, that chickenshit was jealous of my father. Yeah, in Vietnam. Because my father did what he was too shit-scared to do. An' now he's jealous of me.' Ryan drained his glass and called for the corporal, who had retreated tactfully behind the screen of bottles, to refill it with the same. 'I jest wish you'd been at the Craddocks' dinner last Sunday. You should've bin by rights. Craddock should have asked you. You'd have seen then. I took a lot of flak. He was needling me. All the goddamned time! He told me, right there in front of the General, that he reckoned I'd cut in on Scott. Can you get meaner than that?'

Ames marshalled his courage to say, 'So you did!'

But he never got the last word out. Suddenly it was as if he and Ryan were turned to stone. For abruptly the white readiness light went out. And in its place lit up, not the next state of readiness, half yellow, but the full yellow of active involvement.

It took time for the pair of them to react. Ames felt as if his bowels had turned to water. But Ryan let out a great glad whoop like an Indian war cry, and threw his arms exultantly round Ames and hugged him like a brother.

A minute later, Diefenbaker came in. His expression was that of a man who knows a lot, but isn't going to say.

'Sure, we're on full yellow,' he said when Ryan pointed triumphantly at the globe. 'But take it easy, Rod. Along with that, stand-down's been extended for twenty-four hours.'

'Why?' Ryan demanded.

'Orders,' Diefenbaker replied. 'All four special assignment crews to get maximum rest. You guys go hit the sack. And that's an order too.'

Ames lay awake for a long time, thinking. A full yellow alert, and all of them to be rested. It didn't need a brilliant mathematical brain like his to figure out what it added up to – Something For Real.

Ten

At first light the following morning, Mr Lawrence Priestley, the warden of the bird sanctuary, wakened to a strange sound. He rushed out into his patch of garden on the edge of Haddington Fen, and stared up at the shimmering oyster sky. As he told Harriet Harper three hours later, his ears had not deceived him.

There, against the dark grey, was a skein of Brent geese descending like a black arrow to the tarnished surface of the water.

'I couldn't believe it, Harriet!' he said, as she gave him his monthly arthritis injection. 'I thought the Yankee aircraft had scared off the geese for good. They'd gone up river, you know. I'd seen them. A whole flock up beyond Thwaite Lock. I was sure they'd deserted us. A few nights' peace and they're trying us out again. Nature,' he sighed, 'is truly marvellous. And forgiving!'

Harriet snapped her medical bag shut and smiled. 'Let's hope so! Nature's got a lot to forgive. But it was lovely to have another peaceful night, wasn't it? I've just been to the old people's home to check on their flu injections. There seems to be no flying this morning either, so they could all hear themselves speak.'

'This morning,' Mr Priestley said as he showed her to his cottage door, 'I can actually hear the birds twittering in the eaves.' He pointed up to where the sparrows were taking over the nests left behind by the migrating house martins. 'And there's a robin been singing all morning on that hazel.'

'I think we should be grateful to Steven Naylor,' Harriet reminded him. 'He must have done his stuff with the Colonel . . . at last! And with the Anglophile General, if he exists!'

The two of them parted in a mixture of mutual congratulation and gratitude.

Throughout her calls in the village and its environs, Sister Harper found the same mood. The British point of view had got through to the Yanks. As Steven Naylor had promised, they were curtailing night flying. And apparently day flying too. For by noon, not a single aircraft had taken off.

Peace was being restored to the countryside. The sun shone. The air was full of small simple sounds – the hum of tractors and muck spreaders, the rattle of root crop sorters, the lowing of Muggeridge's now contented cattle. Muggeridge's cockerel could now crow from one end of the village to the other. Dogs barked in the seeming knowledge that today they would be heard. Horses trotted along the lanes beneath gulls and rooks wheeling in a clear blue unruptured sky.

The air was sweeter too, without the tons of burned fuel that normally descended on top of them. It smelled of moist, newly tilled earth, crushed grass, autumn leaves, chrysanthemums and fresh baked bread, as the village of Haddington gratefully returned to its time warp again.

Everywhere, Harriet found, the gratitude which she most heartily endorsed was for Steven Naylor.

Nowhere, of course, more than at the dismal looking thatched cottage by the fen at the end of the bumpy lane, where Captain Ryan had had to drive her that memorable afternoon. It was Harriet's last call. One she had left deliberately to the end, partly so that she could supervise the young mother bathing her baby and giving him his early evening feed, partly because she wanted to savour that rare occurrence, an unwanted pregnancy that had ended happily ever after.

Already, there were signs that fortune had begun to smile on Fenside Cottage. Mr Dann was pulling into the shelter of the porch a shiny new perambulator, the infant equivalent of the cars – Yank Tanks the villagers called them – that some of the young men drove.

'Afternoon, Sister.' A thatcher by day and a poacher by night, Mr Dann had a dour weatherbeaten countenance rarely lit by even the semblance of a smile.

But not so today. 'And a fine afternoon it's bin, too,' he said, waving Harriet inside. 'Jennie's in the bathroom with young Edward.' A fond indulgent smile creased his face. 'Mum's in there, too.'

The bathroom of the cottage was a breeze-block lean-to built up against the back wall. Mr Dann led the way through the kitchen. The dresser was piled with boxes of Yankee food and bottles of liquor. A stiff gift-wrapped flower arrangement sat in the centre of the table.

Lieutenant Barlow had also endowed the bathroom with infant scales and a plastic bath, and rows of powders and creams and rainbows of cotton wool and wipers. Jennie sat on a wooden chair by the bath, holding her baby, her expression dazed, as if she couldn't believe her luck.

After she'd checked his weight and watched him being nervously bathed, Harriet sat at the kitchen table while Jennie unbuttoned her blouse and suckled him.

Mr Dann went out to the back to prepare his little rowing boat for the night's iniquities, and Mrs Dann bustled upstairs to make sure that the cot, delivered only that morning, was aired and the room warm enough for her grandson. Her relief that Jennie was to have not only a willing bridegroom, but a white one, still kept her walking on the nearest her solid frame could get to air.

'I should have told Buzz before,' Jennie sighed, smiling down first at the baby then at the flower arrangement, then at her mother's back disappearing upstairs.

'Why didn't you?'

'Oh, I dunno! I just couldn't! Not when it came to it!'

She wasn't mentioning names, she told Harriet, but she had a friend who found herself in the family way. Her boyfriend was a Yank. And when she told him about the bun in her oven, he gave her the money to get rid of it, and told her to get lost.

She knew Buzz wasn't like that. But . . . she couldn't bear to see his face if he did want her to get lost. Breaking it to her parents had been bad enough. All the same, she'd screwed up her courage to tell Buzz that last time they met. But she'd been so scared and so unhappy and so uptight that the words wouldn't come out the way she'd prepared. She went all sulky on him, and he got cross and she got crosser, and they had a terrible row. She told him she hated him and that was that.

Harriet stroked the baby's downy head with her finger tip. 'And now it's all wedding preparations?'

Jennie nodded. 'More arguing there, mind you,' she smiled happily. 'Mum doesn't want me to get married in white. But why not?'

'Why not indeed.'

'I'm having a long veil, too. And lilies. The Base chapel has an organ, so we'll have the 'Wedding March' and hymns. The lot.

We're having the reception at the Assembly Hall afterwards. And we're having two clergymen. The Base chaplain and the Rector.'

'Who's the best man?'

'His aircraft commander, of course. Captain Gruber. And Dad's hiring a suit to give me away.'

At that moment, a knock sounded on the back door. 'Are you decent, girl?'

'Yes, Dad.' Jennie hastily buttoned up her blouse.

Mr Dann put his head round the door. 'I'll be off then. Tell your mum. Back about midnight.'

'Righto, Dad.'

'Goodnight, Sister. Hope you brought your mac. By the look of them clouds, it's going to rain.'

'I have, thanks. Goodnight, Mr Dann.'

'Trout should rise, Dad.'

But Mr Dann didn't deign to reply. In a moment, they heard the creak of the rowlocks and the splash of the oars, and exchanged smiles.

By twelve-thirty that night, the stars were overcast and it had begun to rain. Jarman put on his black oilskin jacket, snapped the bicycle clips on his trousers, and closed the back door of the Craddock house quietly behind him. On Mrs Craddock's instructions he had kept dinner for the Colonel until eleven. But there had been neither sight nor sound of him all day and while Mrs Craddock waited for her husband, Lord Haddington had phoned.

Jarman had not been a duke's butler without recognising the voice of a predatory gentleman, nor had he lived in Haddington without hearing of his lordship's reputation. He recognised a potentially dangerous situation. A beautiful, neglected wife, a suave aristocrat eager to make her feel desired.

The telephone conversation had been short, but Jarman saw trouble looming on that horizon.

Jarman wanted his employers to be happy, and Mrs Craddock manifestly was not. Worse still, he doubted if the Colonel recognised her unhappiness, or how he neglected her. So it was with relief that he saw, as he wheeled his bike down the path, two big cones of headlights fanning through the mizzling rain as the Commander's Chevrolet squealed to a halt outside the gate. Out leapt Colonel Craddock.

About to offer to return and serve the Colonel's dinner, Jarman was waved impatiently into silence.

'Jarman,' the Colonel put a hand on Jarman's shoulder, turning him around. 'I want you here.' Walking him back up the path, Craddock bent his head to talk in his ear. 'No, I don't want dinner. But I want you to stay at the house tonight.'

Jarman looked at the Colonel, head tilted, not questioning his orders, but respectfully waiting to be told why.

'The Base is still on full yellow readiness,' the Colonel said quietly, opening the front door. The light from the hall fell full on his face. His voice was sober, but Jarman thought he had never seen the Colonel look so invigorated and so young.

Basically they were all alike, these military men. Even Jarman himself felt a frisson of mingled excitement and apprehension.

As he made coffee and sandwiches, he examined the possibility that the yellow alert meant the Base was about to be attacked, a repeat of the horrendous bombing of the American civil plane at Reingarten. He could hear a low desultory murmur from the sitting room, but nothing his ears could interpret, and when he carried the tray through there was a sudden silence like a radio snapped off.

Proffering their refreshments, Jarman saw that Mrs Craddock, like so many artistic and highly strung ladies, was taking whatever the Colonel had told her with determined bravery. But the Colonel didn't seem to notice how she was taking it. It was as if he was in a space capsule, rocketing off into some macho man's world.

Mrs Craddock stood up. 'Let's get some sleep while we can, Cas.'

'Go ahead! I've some calls to make.' He yawned. 'But I'll follow you up soon.'

As she passed her husband, she touched his arm. 'You won't be in any danger, will you, Cas?'

'Why should I be?'

'I don't know, Cas. Will you be?'

'No.'

'You won't be taking part in . . . anything?'

He hesitated for a moment before saying, 'No.' Regretfully, Jarman thought. But that reply seemed to satisfy her.

'Don't be long then, Cas.'

'I won't be.'

The Colonel turned to Jarman. 'And don't you wait up now.'

The Colonel was still in his study when Jarman retired, but he heard him come upstairs soon afterwards.

The house settled down to absolute quiet. But Jarman couldn't sleep. The sounds of the Base – louder than usual, lorries trundling, the hiss of tyres, jet engines running up, the hum of generators – kept him awake. When he did doze off, he slept with one ear open like a cat.

It was past two on the luminous dial of the bedside clock when he heard steps quickly descending the stairs then, just audible above a low-flying aircraft, the sound of the front door opening and clicking shut.

Within seconds, a huge crescendo of clattering sound shook the house. Jarman leapt out of bed and parted the curtains.

Immediately above their roof, its landing lights blazing, hovered a helicopter. Its rotor blades chopped up the light and the rain into whirling rainbows, its engine noise was deafening. For one horrified moment, Jarman wondered if it belonged to terrorists about to lob a bomb down the chimney. Then, more calmly, if a visiting chopper had missed the landing strip in the fog and rain.

But as he watched, it dropped to the ground on to the playing field just across the road. And running towards it, head down, to be gathered up with startling immediacy, was Colonel Craddock.

Jarman dozed and pondered uneasily till six-thirty when he rose, dressed, and went downstairs to clean the house and prepare madam's breakfast.

Despite the earliness of the hour, the paperboy had already delivered the morning paper.

Jarman saw it spreadeagled on the mat, its bold headline uppermost: 'ANOTHER BOMB OUTRAGE AGAINST USAF IN ITALY. THE PRESIDENT PROMISES ACTION.' Jarman picked up the paper and carried it through into the kitchen. In smaller type below, he read: 'General Akhbar, dictator of Hammadaz, has continued his anti-American campaign by a further bombing of a USAF base in Italy. There have been six casualties.' There was a map to show how close to the toe of Italy was the oil-rich, once pro-Western republic of Hammadaz, with lines like advancing septicæmia linking its capital to the sites of previous anti-American atrocities.

Thoughtfully, Jarman folded the paper as neat as a napkin and stowed it in the linen drawer. He was not at all sure what he was protecting Mrs Craddock from, simply that he wanted to protect her.

Earlier than usual, he prepared her tray of tea. He was not sure he should wake her, but he doubted she was asleep.

He knocked gently. A wide-awake voice bade him enter.

He put the tray down on the bedside table. 'Good morning, madam.'

'Good morning, Jarman.'

'I trust you slept well, madam?'

She eyed him derisively, as if the question was too damned silly to answer. She looked at the tray. 'Where's the morning paper, Jarman?'

He hedged. 'That wretched paperboy . . .'

'Jarman, don't give me that! Go and fetch it! No. Don't bother. I can guess. I'll see it soon enough when I come down.'

She sank back on the pillows, her mouth tremulous. In a shaky, little girl voice she asked, 'Jarman, do you ever wish time away? Twenty-four hours? One whole day? One whole night?'

'No, madam. At my age, madam, never.'

She smiled thinly and closed her eyes.

'Shall I draw the curtains, madam?'

She nodded without opening her eyes.

With a swishing sound, the curtains opened. Revealed was a veil of mist covering an airfield deceptively still. But even as he watched, the stillness began breaking. Almost invisible as it broke cloud, a strange aircraft was descending down to the east-west runway – pencil thin, with long narrow wings and black as night.

Human memory is notoriously short. But not Jarman's. In the course of thirty years' successful buttling for the gentry, his memory had become a computer of useful facts.

Immediately Jarman saw the aircraft, he was back in time, seeing all those photographs in the newspapers of a US plane being displayed in Red Square after Gary Powers had been shot down over Russia.

This was the first Stealth Aircraft, supposedly almost impervious to radar, that flew at eighty thousand feet above the reach of flak and fighters – minutely photographing all details of the terrain below.

Its name was the U2 – the USAF's spy in the sky. Where had it come from, Jarman wondered, as he fussily straightened the hang of the curtains.

And why was it here?

Eleven

'Say nothing of what I told you, Dief.'

Craddock got up from his desk and walked over to the window, staring out at the weak October sun that had finally struggled through the overcast. 'At least the weather's improved.' He turned back to the Squadron Commander, still sitting behind him. 'Get the Strike and EW crews on readiness.'

'So this is it, sir? We're going for the score?'

'Still not definite. We're waiting for the President to decide. Might be called off.'

'I sure hope not, sir.' Diefenbaker got up and saluted. 'Time we showed the bastard!'

The office door closed softly. Quick steps echoed down the corridor. He's locked on to the mission, Craddock thought, reaching for the half-filled cup of coffee that had been his only nourishment for the past ten hours. Like they were at the American Embassy last night. Maybe like he was. If the Strike was aborted now, they'd all flip their lids.

He hadn't had this sort of feeling since Vietnam. 'We've been alerted to a further atrocity,' General Vosper had told the assembled diplomats, politicians, scientists, and senior Air Force officers in the War room at the American Embassy. 'And now the time's come. Uncle Sam's taking no more. Akhbar has gotta be neutralised.'

You could have heard a pin drop as Vosper outlined his carefully prepared plan.

For most of the time, Akhbar kept himself safe from reprisals in his specially fortified eyrie in the Ghat Mountains. But they had secret information that for the next two days, he would be in his Hammadaz palace for a special high-powered meeting with his allies. This was where and when they must strike.

To preserve maximum security, one base only would be used – and Haddington under Colonel Craddock had been specially selected. As this was no act of war, but a surgical operation, only four of the finest USAF bombing crews would be dispatched.

As the heads of all those present had turned round and the eyes fixed on him, and the voices murmured appreciatively, Craddock had felt this must surely be the justification of his whole Air Force career. And yet he had experienced a strange unease. The fly in the ointment was Rod Ryan. On the surface, Ryan was the man for this sort of job, a real balls-to-the-wall jock. Yet underneath, how like his father was he?

But Jesus, how could you really forecast what any man would do? Or any woman, come to that. He picked up his coffee cup and drained it, pulling a wry face at the cold dregs.

He looked at the clock. Past ten already. At this very moment, signals were flashing across the world, diplomats were conferring, the French President, the Spanish and British Prime Ministers were being consulted. Senior operations officers of Strategic Air Command were organising support aircraft, were working out times, heights, bomb loads, routes, refuelling positions. All the way down the line the logistics of the mission were being finalised. And he had been sucked into the exhilarating vortex of all these preparations. Get the bastard! That was the one thought that obsessed him now. His only regret was that he wouldn't be leading the attack.

Suddenly the telephone rang. His secretary told him, 'General Vosper on the scrambler, sir.'

Quickly, he lifted the red receiver, fearful only that the mission would be cancelled.

'Craddock.'

'Cas.' General Vosper's voice, unusually quiet, unusually subdued. 'The President has agreed and the Brits are with us. But the bloody Frogs and the goddamned Dagoes won't let us fly over their territories. Means a helluva long way round. Route weather's godawful. But the mission's on! First take off 23.00!'

That Sunday morning, the solitary silent arrival of the U2 and the brief descent from the skies of the helicopter returning Colonel Craddock to his Base had gone unnoticed by the Haddington villagers.

The F-115s still remained on the ground. Not a hint of their all too familiar ear-splitting scream.

Peace on earth – a text indeed for Anglo-American unity which the Rector was quick to pick up in his sermon, bringing in at the same time the forthcoming wedding of Jennie Dann, spinster of this parish to Lieutenant Edward Barlow of the USAF.

He pointed out not only the bonds of cousinship, but also the fact that the Americans had finally carried out their promise to curtail night flying and once more quiet sleep had returned to Haddington.

As the congregation, led by Lady Haddington, spilled out of the south door and walked down the damp brick path between the ancient gravestones, it did seem that a new era of Anglo-American friendship had begun.

'Good sermon, Rector,' Mr Whittaker, the used-car merchant, shook the clergyman by the hand. 'That's the stuff! I've always said the Yanks are a good bunch! Treat 'em right, and they'll treat you—'

His voice was drowned by a sudden whistling, shrill as a hundred flutes.

The knots of worshippers stood where they were amongst the gravestones, shading their eyes. Looking up, Lady Haddington was suddenly spun back forty-five years to the Liberator bombers of the Eighth American Air Force that used to roar out of Haddington then. She had always said a prayer then for those that flew in them, and for those that cowered beneath them.

'What do you suppose they are, Lady Haddington?' Mrs Brunswick, the doctor's wife asked.

'707s,' the much travelled primary head teacher, Miss Tarrant, answered.

'But what are they coming here for?' the doctor's wife persisted.

'Certainly not picking up tourists for the Costa Brava,' Lady Haddington retorted drily.

One after the other, the four aircraft landed. Miss Tarrant's aircraft recognition was almost, but not quite, right. The aircraft were indeed 707s, but redesigned into Stratotankers for flight refuelling.

On the Base, everyone knew now that something was on, but some still regarded it as simply another practice like the 'terrorist attack' four weeks ago. Officers and airmen would soon be hustling at the double, the aircrew would go to their aircraft. Then with the whole Base keyed up, someone would blow a whistle and say, 'OK, you guys. Just a practice.' And everyone would feel let down.

But as Sunday wore on, the realisation began to catch on to

everyone that this was no practice. Too much was being thrown in. An hour after the Stratotankers had landed, the acrobatic black corporal on the gate was looking up at what looked like four F-115s in formation above them.

Only these aircraft had long thin ant-eater noses and were camouflaged a silvery white. Unlike Miss Tarrant, he identified them accurately. These were EF-115s of the Twelfth Electronic Warfare Squadron, equipped with every known radar and radio jamming device.

Half an hour later, the strangest bird of all arrived with what appeared to be a mighty mushroom growing on top of its fuselage.

Ames and Ryan had had a long lie-in and a late lunch. Now sitting together by the window in the Open Mess lounge, they saw the stranger coming lower and lower, wheels and flaps down.

Both of them knew exactly what it was and what that skunk-striped rotodrome stuck above the fuselage meant. An AWACS 135 – an Airborne Warning and Control Systems Aircraft, containing a fully equipped high-power radar and radio Station and Operations Room combined.

'Jeez, Milt!' The exultant excitement had come back into Ryan's eyes. 'Looks like we're goin' to Rock an' Roll!'

The whole of Haddington Airbase was now like a little hygienic cell, shut off from all contamination from the universe. All gates closed. All roads to the Base blocked. All personnel wearing helmets and carrying revolvers or sub-machine guns. Guards and military police everywhere. A tiptoeing silence in the deserted Officers' Mess, now packed with all the newly arrived airmen – with the exception of the pilot of the U2, which had departed as silently as it had arrived.

From everywhere else on the Base, sounds of feverish activity. A crescendo of orchestrated engines being run up and tested on hard standings and in Hush House. The squeak of long lines of trolleys carrying iron bombs and 'smart bombs', the new laser-guided Paveway 3 stand-off bombs and Sidewinder anti-aircraft missiles, the chug of pumps as aircraft were refuelled. Jeeps and lorries sped round the perimeter, carrying mechanics, radar technicians, armament and avionics officers.

Meals were forgotten, daily routine forgotten, office work forgotten.

Everywhere, the excitement was catching. Cooks preparing

flying rations, nurses in the Hospital, barmen in the empty bars, assistants in the shops, kids in the schools had become electrified by the knowledge that something was cooking.

Even the rain that poured down on the Base late that afternoon could not dampen it. The hardened hangars, the Messes, the Avionics section, Operations rooms formed a continuous muzzy blaze of light. At 19.00 hours, officers and sergeants were checking the carefully selected ordnance under the wings of the four Strike F-115s, and half an hour later their crews arrived at the locker room after a huge steak meal in the Mess.

'This'll zap you up for your wedding, Buzz!' Gruber had called across to his wizzo.

The ceremony was to take place in the Base chapel the following Saturday. The British registrar from Cambridge had been laid on to attend, and the USAF chaplain, assisted by the rector, was going to tie the knot. Gruber was to be his wizzo's best man and half the Sixth TFS and dozens of villagers would be attending the reception in the Assembly Hall.

Ryan had eaten little, Ames noticed, impatient to get on. In the locker room, he was first to be dressed in his G-suit, flying suit, gloves and boots, and carrying his helmet and oxygen mask, he led the way into the Briefing Room. 'C'mon, Milt. Front row of the stalls for us!'

Within minutes, Operations was filled with crews from the tankers, the EW and Strike aircraft. On the dais, directly facing them, was a blackboard on which was balanced a big map covered in a sheet. Beside it, as straight as the black pointer he held in his hand, was Lieutenant Colonel Burke, the Chief Intelligence Officer. Beside him, stood Colonel Craddock.

For a full minute there was a breath-held quiet, broken only by the shuffling of feet, the rustling of flying suits and the creak of chairs.

Then a tiny clunk as the minute hand of the electric clock on the wall jumped to 20.00 hours. Like a marionette jerked into action, Colonel Burke raised the pointer and flicked the black cloth back from the map.

'Jee – zus!'

A sighing whistle ran round the room.

'There it is,' Burke said in that stilted voice that matched his straight back. 'Operation Grand Chasm.'

Nobody said anything. All eyes were still on the long red tapes that stretched from Haddington, south-west across England, down the Bay of Biscay to parallel the coasts of Spain and Portugal, then turning east through the Straits of Gibraltar to the bite out of the North African coast that was the Bay of Hammadaz, then inland due south to the capital.

The pointer came down on a big green star.

'Hammadaz,' Burke went on. 'I don't have to name the guy who lives there. The deadliest terrorist dictator in the world. The man responsible for two hijacks, the murder of an American diplomat, six bombing attacks, including three on American bases that caused numerous casualties to our men, women and children. For the last four months, the US government has sought a concerted effort of reprisals against this crazy guy amongst its allies. Result, zero. After this last outrage in Italy, the President has decided to go it alone.'

Burke paused. Then he said, 'That's why you're here!'

A different sort of silence now. No longer suspenseful and apprehensive. A grim silence, purposeful and determined.

'Operation Grand Chasm is no act of war. It is not against the Hammadaz people. That is why the minimum number of Strike aircraft are being despatched. Operation Grand Chasm has one objective. And one objective only. The precision neutralisation of General Ahmed Akhbar.'

A blown up photograph of a huge ornate building was flashed on the screen to the right of the map.

'Akhbar's palace,' Burke continued. 'We have information that for the next forty-eight hours . . . and only forty-eight hours . . . he will be resident here before returning to his impregnable eyrie in the Ghat Mountains. This is our one and only chance to get him.' Again Burke paused. 'No easy gig.'

Another blown up photograph replaced the first one on the screen, clearly showing gun-posts and missile sites ringing the palace and its approaches.

'Now here we have a photograph from the U2. Look carefully. Like you see, the whole target area is heavily guarded. All the latest radar-warning and jamming devices, radar-controlled twin 40 millimetre cannon, Crotak surface-to-air missiles and long-range radar-controlled rockets. And right here—' the pointer moved to encircle the palace —'a ring of 4.5 AAA.'

A series of photographs followed, showing two airfields on which were based three squadrons of MIG Supersonic night fighters, the roads leading from the coast to the city, even shots of soldiers drilling.

'The Strike will attack the palace. And this is the schedule. The AWACS will be in position off the Hammadaz coast, just out of radar range, at 03.00 hours. The Stratotankers,' the pointer returned to the map, 'will be stationed off the Spanish coast at this point. And here, just east of Gibraltar. They will refuel F-115s outbound, and will be replaced by the second wave of Stratotankers to refuel homebound. The four EW aircraft on "the Shell" will take off at 23.00 hours followed twenty minutes later by the four strike F-115s. At 03.00 hours, all F-115s will group up at the AWACS position. Then under AWACS Control, in go the EW aircraft to jam the radars, followed closely by the bomb carriers.'

More photographs on the screen now, diagrams and maps.

'They will follow the main coast road the sixty miles south to the city, turning port at this main intersection to proceed to the palace. Lieutenant Colonel Diefenbaker will go in first with Strike anti-radiation missiles, scatter-bombs and five hundred pounders for defence suppression. After the explosions, in go Captain Scott, Captain Gruber and Captain Ryan in that order, using Target Acquisition through the new radar, dropping both stand-off and iron bombs with delayed action fuses. And after that—' for the first time, Burke permitted himself a frugal smile —'max after-burners, bat-turn port on to due north . . . and speed-o-heat . . . back to the barn!'

After Burke's briefing, the weatherman's contribution came as almost comic relief. A deep Low over the north tip of Spain, giving thunderstorms and heavy rain over the whole route to Gibraltar and the western Mediterranean.

In contrast to Burke, the forecaster was a little man with big owlish spectacles. As though in compensation for the appalling route conditions, he promised them, 'No cloud and fifty mile visibility over the target.'

At least that raised a laugh. But the only genuine one came from Ryan, who had been sitting on the edge of his seat, absorbing every word, his pleasure increasing with every hair-raising detail of that incredible briefing, just like a kid at Disneyland, enjoying every bang and cliff-hanging thrill.

When the main briefing was over, just behind them, Lynch muttered, 'Where's Superman?'

Ryan didn't exactly say, 'Here.' But he did turn round and tell

Diefenbaker's wizzo, 'This'll sort the Tigers from the Candy asses!' Ames and the other wizzos got up to go to their special radio and electronic briefing, on frequencies, radar, armament and computer details, at the same time being reminded that radio silence was to be maintained at all times, even on refuelling – no 'porky pigging' – the rule to be broken only after the operation had been completed, when they were to give the signal 'Feet Wet!' meaning they were homebound over the sea.

The pilots studied the routes intently, the heights to fly, memorised the refuelling order, the position of the tankers, the tactics and timing of each one's approach to the IP – the Initial Point for the bomb run to commence.

Watching it all from the dais, for a moment Craddock was back in that tin-roofed shanty that served for an Operation Room in Vietnam. He felt the same elevated excitement he had felt then, but now the emotion was laced with foreboding.

War statistics showed that most aircrew were killed on their first few combat missions. Once they had completed ten, however, statistically they were far more likely to survive. The Top Brass had therefore decreed Mission Ready airmen should have completed ten missions simulating (as near as possible) actual war conditions, thinking thereby they would become battle-hardened.

Craddock had doubts. Certainly pilots became obsessed with 'the game', some of them practically hypnotised into believing this was For Real. But like all airmen who had been through fire or actual war, he believed that such Flag exercises were no more than good practice in operational techniques.

To his experienced eyes, these boys were still green. None of them had heard a shot fired in anger, only in such simulation. On the whole Base, he was the only one who had seen war in all its horror and bloodiness. Yet tonight, these guys would be required to carry out a far more precise and difficult operation than he had ever done. As a dedicated serving officer, he could not concern himself with the morality of the mission. But there was bound to be world reaction against it. And what if they failed? Then his own countrymen would join the chorus, and the Yanks would be shown up as incompetent aggressors.

And even if they succeeded, would they all survive? Or would they be flying the Missing Man Formation? And then American families would demand the reason for the sacrifice of their sons.

Just before they filed out to walk through to the Personal

Equipment Room, where each crew-member had his own stall in which he kept his gear – helmet, oxygen mask, gloves, survival vest, G-suit, pooping suit and piddle-packs – Craddock said a few words, wished them good luck, added from his heart, 'Just wish I was going with you.'

They appreciated his sincerity, sympathised with him for missing the party. Jonny Scott called back at him, 'They're saving you for the Big One, Colonel.'

All that is, except one. As together they went out into the wet darkness, Ryan said to Ames, 'Same old chickenshit!'

Twelve

Strapped in, engines lit, Ryan and Ames sat silently side by side in the *Probe*, watching the four EW aircraft take off down the muzzy flarepath, waiting with the three other Strike F-115s for the Controller's green Aldis to flash permission to taxi.

Haddington Base now resembled a gigantic illuminated tank filled with dirty water, through which swam phosphorescent fish of many colours. Everywhere lights – red, white, green, yellow. Everywhere aircraft moving, tractors moving, weapon dollies moving. Steady lights, flashing lights, revolving lights. The sounds of multiple engines – aircraft, fire-trucks, ambulances – mingled with the continuous drumming of rain on the concrete.

Ames glanced across the throttle box at his aircraft commander.

Still on a high. Still balls-to-the-wall. Triple A, missiles, MIG fighters – all the threatened bogies that had made Ames feel sick at the briefing, had just hyped up Ryan like he felt he was Superman. Ames had been scared of his split-ass flying, but now that knife-edge skill was what was going to keep them safe. When it came to dodging cannon fire, escaping radar, outmanoeuvring MIGs in a furball, and out-turning Sam 7s, there wasn't a goddamned jock could touch him – now it was For Real.

A blur of wet green blossomed on the darkness.

Immediately Ryan took off the brakes, and pushed the throttles forward. Squeaking and shivering, the *Probe* wheeled right round to take up rear position behind Gruber's *Thunderbird* in the little line of F-115s nosing their way round the perimeter track.

At the quick-check area lay-by, Ryan pulled in. While the ground crew removed the safety pins from the bombs and made a final check of aileron and elevator movement, Ames finished off the last items on the before take-off check.

'Jet pipe temperature normal,' Ames called.

'Magnetic indicators checked – hydraulic pressure three thousand pounds.'

Ahead of them, Diefenbaker's *Lightning Lady* turned on to the runway. The ground shook. The wet sky reverberated. The afterburners gushed orange flames. As the *Probe* was waved out of the quick-check area, Ames saw Ryan's face profiled against the glow. Purposeful, deadly, the face of a killer.

Now it was Scott's *Pacemaker* burning up the night.

Now Gruber in *Thunderbird.*

Now, for chrissake, them. This was It.

As Ryan lined up on the centreline and advanced the throttles to max afterburner, Ames stole another glance at his face.

For the first time, he was glad to be beside him. For the first time, he almost liked the bastard.

Climbing at three hundred and fifty knots, all four aircraft broke cloud at flight level 250. Levelling off, at cruising revs they flew south-west over England in loose formation.

In *Pacemaker*, Glenn Robinson was watching the big round face of the new Attack Radar in Short Range Map Mode, giving Scott a running commentary on the marvellous magnification of detail being portrayed on its green screen.

'. . . girl on a bicycle . . .'

'Jesus! This time of night?'

'Sure.'

Scott leaned right for a look. 'That's a glitch!'

'Maybe you're right.' Robinson turned down the brilliance knob and the fault disappeared.

'Trouble with you, Glenn . . . you see cute little girls everywhere.'

'Della's not just a girl. She's an airman!'

Thirty yards away on the port side, Grunter was joshing Buzz Barlow, as his wizzo checked the F-115's defences against attack – the Chaff chutes down which aluminium strips would be sent to confuse enemy radar, the hot flares that would be dropped for the heat-seeking missiles to home on instead of the engines, the radar and radio jammers, air-to-air rockets and the aerial mines.

Surrounded with all that, and their Stores list of delivery ordnance, the only safe subject to talk about was girls.

'This'll be your last night out with the boys, Buzz.'

'So what?'

'You'll be home with the baby while she goes out!'

'Couldn't ask for better company. Eddie's a great kid.'

'Is he coming to the wedding?'

'Sure is.'

'He's wearing the white dress, huh?'

They bickered amicably as turning over Cornwall, the aircraft flew southwards into the Bay of Biscay.

To starboard in *Lightning Lady*, there was no talk of girls. Diefenbaker and Lynch were both married men with wives on the Base. The Squadron Commander recognised that this was a one in a hundred career opportunity and he wasn't going to pass it up. Right then, as he squinted at the high castles of cumulonimbus ahead, he was getting edgy about the wind. He pointed to the arrow on the INS indicator.

'Wind's getting up. And dead on our nose.'

Ryan realised they were dropping behind schedule, and by going up to Mach 1.2 had taken up position at the tanker first, just as the last of the EW aircraft broke away to follow his three companions into the night.

Looking upwards, Ames saw the long stick of the boom with a light on its nozzle descend from the KC 135's tail. There it hung, like Excalibur's sword, while the boomer 'flew' it towards the *Probe*'s receptacle.

Silent connection was made. Joined together, Stratotanker and F-115 bucked vigorously up and down in uneasy embrace on that damp ballooning bed.

Watching Ryan turn the *Probe*, jittering in the upcurrents, into a steady platform, once again Ames took comfort from his skill. People often talked of a pilot's 'marriage' to his aircraft. He'd once heard Dief's wife say she'd sue *Lightning Lady* as her husband's co-respondent.

But with Ryan it was different. With Ryan, man and machine were one. Its every movement anticipated before the computers. Its changing moods immediately understood.

Ryan *was* the *Probe*.

Within five minutes, they had taken on board five thousand gallons of gas. Only a faint smell of kerosene as they broke off for Ryan to begin circling the tanker, waiting in uncharacteristic silence for the others to complete their sucks.

Then in loose formation, keeping station on their radar, their navigation lights appearing and disappearing in the tops of the cloud, the four Strike aircraft shot south at five hundred and thirty knots.

The wind began dropping. By the time they had turned ninety degrees port and headed for Gibraltar, the weather had improved. The second refuelling in the Western Mediterranean was completed dead on schedule in bright starlight with a sliver of moon rising above the eastern horizon.

Off went their navigation lights. Down to the water they dived.

Like four black angels of death, stealthily they advanced towards their target. Nobody saw them. On no radar did they appear. Only the calm surface of the sea mirrored the orange glows from their engines amongst the shimmering stars and the phosphorescent tongues of tiny waves.

In *Lightning Lady*, Lynch turned to Diefenbaker and put up his thumb. 'Got the AWACS!'

'How far?'

'Twenty miles. We'll be five minutes early.'

The Squadron Commander nodded in satisfaction. As in all the other four Strike cockpits, he and his wizzo had exchanged fewer and fewer words as the moment for action approached. Older than the others, he took his responsibilities harder. As Craddock had told him in a private word before take-off, he was in effect, the leader of an orchestra. He had brilliant players, all with different personalities, but there was only one tune. No heroic solos, the Colonel had warned him. No prima donna stuff, by which presumably, he meant Ryan. Everyone to do exactly what was briefed. Sure, each jock and wizzo had their contract with each other, but all that recognised and worked out understanding had to be within the frame of the Operation.

And – Craddock's final words – 'Bring 'em all back to the barn, Dief!'

They were just the same words his wife had used. And whatever the odds, as far as he was able, he'd make goddamned sure he did that duty.

Ames actually saw the AWACS five hundred feet above them, silhouetted against a crescent moon. One after the other, he caught sight of the four long-nosed EWs – circling, waiting. One after the other, he watched the other Strike aircraft join them till all eight were going round and round the AWACS, anti-clockwise, like black moths round a lightless candle.

Four minutes to go. It was eerie – this waiting. Ryan sitting beside him, tense as a coiled spring. Up above them, under the strange mushroom of the AWACS, would be eight men and two women sitting at long tables staring at screens and listening to sounds.

The slightest indication that any foreign country knew they were there, and warnings would be flashed to them.

Nothing. Two minutes to go.

Eighty miles south lay Hammadaz. Street lights on. Houses shut up and dark. Little traffic on the roads. Sleepy guards exchanging monosyllables.

One minute. The guys in the EWs would be going through their final drills. How agonisingly slowly, Ames thought, as he watched the clock on the instrument panel, a second hand sometimes moves!

03.00 exactly. A green light from the AWACS.

Immediately the EWs formed up in line astern and disappeared south into the night.

Five more minutes to go for the Strike aircraft. Three minutes. Two minutes – and still no warnings of anyone being alerted.

It was all like a game of Grandmother's Footsteps, Ames was thinking, creeping up stealthily, unseen, unheard, when suddenly Ryan broke his silence.

'Goin' to catch those sons-of-bitches with their pants down!'

'Hope so.'

'Jesus, hope not!' his AC snapped. 'Or there'll be shit-all for us to knock down!'

A double green at last.

Like a snake uncurling, first *Lightning Lady*, then *Pacemaker*, then *Thunderbird*, finally the *Probe* left the circle formation and one behind the other and at max afterburners tore towards the target at eleven hundred knots.

No radios on. No radars. Nothing to give away electronically their position.

Staring ahead, nose pressed against the windscreen, in the lead aircraft, Lynch saw the long string of yellow lights linking ahead.

'Coast, Dief!'

'Roger.'

Behind the lights now, a cascade of red and white stars.

'Shooting at the EWs!'

The Squadron Commander raised his eyes momentarily from the instruments. 'Warm welcome, huh? Radars and jammers on! Drop Chaff! And look out for Bogeys!'

The coast was coming hurtling towards them. A searchlight rose and began waving up and down, followed by another.

A bead curtain of white cannon fire ahead of them now.

'Got the road south, Lynch?'

'Dead on track.'

A jangle of interference patterned the attack radar.

'They're jamming. Can you follow the street lamps?'

'Sure can!'

The surface rocketing beneath them turned from black water to grey-yellow sand.

'Sam battery!' Lynch yelled. 'They're shooting! Four, five . . . see 'em?'

'Yep. Drop the hot flares!'

'Have done! One of the bastards trying to lock on to us! Get ready to turn!'

But it was *Thunderbird* that the missile made its target. Barlow could see its fiery tail twisting out of the darkness towards him.

'Sam at two o'clock! Turn starboard! Starboard!'

Port wing already vertical, Gruber's eyes were being burned out of his head. A searchlight had got them and was hanging on more grimly than any heat-seeking missile.

'Bogeys on the radar!' Barlow yelled. 'Two . . . three coming right at us!'

A dark shape of a MIG 28 flashed above them.

'At six! At six! Hostile . . . coming right up our ass!'

'Fire sidewinders!'

'Sidewinders gone . . . Bogey catching up! Firing! Missiles locked on us! Turn!' Barlow yelled. 'Starboard! Starboard!'

Still in the searchlight, *Thunderbird* went into a screaming right turn.

But the missile turned just as steeply. Seconds later, a colossal bang. The whole aircraft shivered. Alarm bells went. On the screen in red flashing letters, TURBINE FAILURE ON PORT ENGINE.

'Did he get us?' Barlow shouted to Gruber.

'Yep. Port engine.' The F-115 was vibrating badly. Gruber began adjusting the power on the starboard engine. The speed built up again. The juddering stopped. 'But we're OK. The *Bird*'s flying. We're turning on target.' Ahead was like a goddamned wall-of-fire circus. Just for a second, Barlow was bloody glad he'd made a will.

Ahead in *Pacemaker*, they were so low and so fast that the

telephone poles were merging together on the radar. From every side, strings of white light AA. In the side glow from the searchlights, Glenn Robinson could see square boxes of houses. All the street lights had gone out, but it was still possible to follow the road visually.

'Coming up time to turn on target, Jonny!'

'OK, Glenn.'

As they turned, the wizzo saw *Thunderbird* still floundering in the searchlight beam.

'Grunter's having a bad time.'

'He'll beat the bastards!' Scott began pulling the throttles back. 'Slowing for target!'

Ahead of them now, the sky suddenly erupted like a red and yellow volcano.

'Dief's waxed the target!' Glenn said. 'Our turn now!'

'Auto-pilot?'

'In.'

'Master Armament Safety Switch?'

'Off!'

'Bombing switches?'

'Auto.'

The bombing computers now had control of the steering, and when to release the stand-off Paveway Threes and the iron thousand pounders.

'How's the radar?'

'Clutter.'

'See the palace?'

'Just.'

Wobbling as though under water, what looked like a parade ground. Barracks behind – the terrorist training school. To the right, a vast building topped by a high dome.

'Coming up to the IP point.'

Glenn was keeping the electronic cross-hairs exactly on the target.

'All Readiness Lights check. Bombs ready to go.'

The F-115 rocked under the blast from heavy AA. 'Two miles to drop.'

Speed now was right down to three hundred knots. From all sides, a stream of red and white anti-aircraft fire.

Through the windscreen, Glenn could see the left side of the palace had crumbled under Diefenbaker's bombs.

Now on the bombing run, the dial on the computer was already counting down to drop . . . four, three, two—

'Bombs gone!'

Immediately Scott went up to max afterburners. As he made a vertical turn to port, behind and to the left, Glenn saw *Thunderbird* twist out of the searchlight.

'Grunter's got away!' he reported exultantly.

'Told you he would,' Scott said, screaming through the sound-barrier north.

Last of all, way behind the others, in the most dangerous position, thundered the *Probe*. Twice caught by searchlights, three times by Sam 7s, by his own inimitable manoeuvres – slowing, pulling up vertical, corkscrewing – Ryan had evaded all of them. But his violent jinking had inevitably slowed them up. Now some of the ice-cool calculating man was beginning to dissolve into impatience.

As they came up to the suburbs of the city, Ames saw ahead of them a solid wall of searchlights and AA. Two lost missiles came out of the inferno and started chasing each other's tails like illuminated snakes. At ten o'clock, suddenly a huge cascade of fire – the third.

'Gruber's dropped his load.' Ryan banged his fists hard on the control column. 'Shit-all of the palace left for us!'

'Coming up to time to turn!'

'Say when.'

'Will do.'

But Ames never did. On the scope, suddenly he saw a procession of cars and trucks moving away from the palace.

'Hang on, Rod!'

'For chrissake – what gives?'

'Look! Something's up!' Ryan leaned over. 'Jee – zus!'

Ames switched to the two-mile Mode. In the scope could clearly be seen a big car, surrounded by gun-trucks and lorries.

'Wow! If this is what I reckon it is – ' Ryan snapped the auto-pilot out and flew towards the procession. 'Drop flares!'

The *Probe* was right over the convoy now. Strings of cannon fire streamed up from the trucks. Deadly brown mushrooms of heavy AA tilted the wings.

As the flares swung high above them, the line of vehicles was doused in an eerie yellow light.

'It is! Jesus, it is!' Ryan pulled against his straps to point through the windscreen. 'Akhbar's armoured Rolls-Royce! The chicken-shit's punching out!'

He swung the F115 to starboard. 'Set-up for pilot release, Milt! We're gonna hose the bastard!'

Two miles north, Ryan climbed to two hundred feet, slowed down to three hundred knots and did a hundred and eighty degree turn back to the convoy, through a criss-cross of gunfire.

Coming up to it, he pulled hard back and then pressed the pickle button.

It was like aiming darts at a dartboard – only these were a lethal mixture of deadly ordnance. The stand-off bombs streaked forward, landing exactly on target as neatly as a player throwing a double sixteen.

Now climbing vertically, Ryan wheeled round to watch.

Seconds later, the flash momentarily blinded Ames's eyes. Even high above the explosion, the metal sides of the bomber vibrated.

Flames and smoke billowed upwards.

It was like nothing Ames had ever seen or could have imagined. He felt exhilarated, horrified, triumphant. It was like hovering over an erupting volcano of your own making. A volcano tossing up not melted rock, but fragments of lorries, guns, cars, people. None of it seemed real. Just the power. It was like having fused inside his body both God and the Devil.

But his most urgent thought right then was to get the hell out.

'Got him! Got him! Got the bastard!' Ryan was exultant, banging his clenched fists together and laughing. Then he turned to punch Ames on the arm. 'Milt! You're the greatest! The Ace of Gauges, no kiddin'.'

'It was your shooting.'

'And hear this! We still got another two in the Storehouse!'

To Ames's dismay, Ryan turned to port and dived to the road again – so low that now he had to hedge-hop over the roofs of smouldering vehicles. Then he released two delayed-action thousand pound bombs before pulling up.

The flames this time almost reached the *Probe* as it circled overhead. Smoke filled the cockpit and both of them started coughing.

'Akhbar's funeral pyre!' Tears from the smoke were running down Ryan's cheeks. Coughing and laughing, high above the roaring of the engines, came the whoosh of the afterburners as he went into max.

Then above that smouldering ruin, Ryan did his second Grand Salute – an even more spectacular version of the one he had done for Colonel Craddock. Without warning, Ames found himself upside down, held by his straps. The thought flashed through his mind, 'We've been hit! We're going in!' Then just as suddenly, he was right side up again.

Above that massed rubble of men and metal, Hotrod Ryan had done a victory roll.

'*Lightning Lady* . . . Feet Wet!'

Diefenbaker reported over the coastline, and going up to Mach 2, left three following MIGs behind him and shot over the Mediterranean towards the first tanker.

The MIGs turned to fall like wolves on *Pacemaker*, now coming up from the south.

'We got company,' Glenn told Scott. 'Three bogeys at ten o'clock.'

'Jesus.' Just as he thought it was over – now this. He glanced at Glenn. He didn't know if his wizzo was praying, but *he* sure was. 'Release Sidewinders.'

There came a hail of AA, followed by the sound of whining thuds as cannon pierced the fuselage. Now the whole of Hammadaz seemed to be aroused to what had been done to them, and was erupting in fury. The sky was alight with a false dawn of red and white tracer and the flashes of heavy AAA.

'Port, Jonny! Port!'

Scott went into a corkscrewing left turn. As he did so, he saw a huge fireball light up the sky. One of the blips melted off the radar.

'A hit! A kill!' Scott leaned over and punched Glenn's arm in triumph. 'We got him, Glenn! We got the bastard!'

Just slightly, Glenn seemed to shrink away from him.

'You OK, Glenn?'

'Sure.'

'Have we still got the other two?'

'Negative. They're headed for the barn.'

'Wise guys. We'll do the same.'

Five minutes later, *Pacemaker* also reported, 'Feet Wet,' followed by Gruber calling, 'Feet Wet. On one engine.'

Dief's voice came immediately back. 'How's she flying, Gruber?'

'OK.'

'Make for Crotoni then.'

'Roger. Will do.'

Finally, ten minutes behind the rest came the *Probe*'s, 'Feet Wet.'

Mindful of his promise, with relief, Diefenbaker turned to his wizzo. 'All four in one piece, Ben! And three heading home.'

Dawn was breaking as the three F-115s came up for the first refuelling east of Gibraltar. As beside him, the wizzo tried to reach for the checklist, a shaft of sunlight illuminated *Pacemaker*'s cockpit.

In its sudden golden light, Scott saw the jagged bullet holes through the wizzo's side window, and the spreading stain of blood on Glenn's flying suit.

'Glenn! Glenn, for chrissake!'

With painful slowness, Glenn turned his head. His great dark eyes met Scott's and filled with an almost apologetic regret.

Thirteen

Glenn died just after they made landfall over England. Some time between 08.30 and 08.45, he'd seemed to drift away. Scott had kept his hand on Glenn's, and from time to time the wizzo had returned the pressure of his fingers. But about then, his hand had gone limp and fallen away.

They'd both known he was going to die, but with afterburners ablaze, Scott had gunned the F-115 for all it had – desperately coaxing, belting, squeezing every ounce of speed out of the engines, muttering about help, doctors, patching him up in no time.

Speed saved – the pilot's credo. Speed would save now.

Glenn had kept up his AC's illusion. Since the second shot of morphine from the Survival Pack behind Scott's head, he was in no pain. He was also manifestly unafraid.

When they lowered into Haddington circuit, the first to return, Scott was flashing all his lights on and off to signal emergency as if the ambulances and fire-engines wouldn't be there anyway, and as if Glenn's hand wasn't stiff and cold, and there was still hope.

But when the canopies were lifted, and he climbed out of his seat, his own flight suit was soaked in Glenn's blood, and the paramedics took one look at Glenn and shook their heads.

Scott waited beside the aircraft till they had taken him off. Then he walked alongside the stretcher to the ambulance and stood still while the metal doors clanged shut.

As the ambulance accelerated away, he waited – not just out of respect to Glenn – but to get his composure. He watched till the blipping light became a pinprick and was lost among the myriad moving lights of a base at war.

Then he climbed into the waiting jeep. There was only the sergeant driver beside himself, and the sergeant had the sense to keep his mouth shut just for the short trip to debriefing. Scott felt an almost physical sense of amputation at Glenn's loss. He surprised himself at how fond he'd gotten of the Bible-banging bastard. Now his only hope was that the bloody raid had been worth it.

It was certainly assumed to have been. When Scott arrived at Hard Operations, he was congratulated by General Vosper, even though the General then had no precise details of the raid. Colonel Craddock, on the other hand, looking like he hadn't slept for weeks, said very little.

'Tough about Robinson,' said the General.

Scott nodded, not trusting himself to speak.

'Great guy,' said the General, though he had only shaken Glenn by the hand.

Again, Scott silently nodded. He was half way through his own debriefing, reporting hits on Akhbar's HQ and the training barracks and hosing the bloody MIG, when Diefenbaker came in.

He was much more forthcoming. 'The whole zoo on fire, sir! Akhbar, staff, terrorists . . . hosed!'

That was what the General wanted to hear, and his spirits reached a new high.

Then in came Ryan with his story of the fleeing convoy, and the Colonel's forehead clouded. Beset by Vietnam memories, Craddock said sharply, 'You didn't attack your briefed target, huh?'

Sassily, Ryan retorted, 'Akhbar was the target.'

'The target was his palace.'

'He wasn't there.'

'How come you're so sure?'

'His car.'

'How d'you know he was in it?'

'Just did.'

'You disobeyed your orders. Four bomb loads were necessary to ensure the palace's destruction. That's what Intelligence said. And you—'

The euphoria was evaporating. Quickly, Vosper came to the aid of the blue-eyed boy. 'Cas . . . reckon young Ryan'll be right!'

'It could have been an ordinary military convoy.'

Ryan reddened. The Colonel was trying to steal his thunder. 'That was no goddamned ordinary car! It was Akhbar's Rolls-Royce.'

'So? He might not have been in it.'

'But he was!'

'You have no way of knowing.'

There was an icy silence. Everyone, even Vosper, was considering the awful possibility of failure. The recriminations, the complaints at the United Nations, the pious condemnations by the eastern block and General Ahmed Akhbar himself addressing the Assembly with his arm in a sling, accusing the USA of attempted assassination.

The news that there had been no further contact with Gruber dampened the proceedings further. Radio conditions in the area were bad. The lights of Gruber's *Thunderbird* had been seen a hundred miles south of Crotoni, but no further information had been transmitted.

'What time's the 71A due back?' Vosper asked. This high speed reconnaissance aircraft had been scheduled to make its survey two hours after the attack when the smoke had cleared.

'We'll know the way the cookie's crumbled then.'

The debriefing continued in a subdued atmosphere of suspenseful waiting. Even Ryan during those electric ninety minutes appeared knocked off his high horse. To Ames's surprise, he did not elaborate on the reason for deviating from his orders, and said very little about his attack on the convoy through intense AAAs, and said nothing at all of his victory roll.

Just before twelve o'clock, the crew of the SR71A came into Hard Operations to report on their Post-Strike survey.

You could have heard a pin drop.

Then everyone saw the smiles on their faces.

'Total devastation!' the aircraft commander told them. 'Palace, training school, the convoy. The lot! Jesus, but did you guys wax the target! Not a goddamned chance of anyone left alive!'

Question after question was answered the way the General wanted – sure, it was Akhbar's Rolls-Royce all right. But not any more . . . Everything reduced to ash and twisted iron.

'You bet, General! That's what the photos and videos will show.'

When the videos and photographs from the Strike aircraft and the SR71 arrived, and showed, if anything, that the reconnaissance crew had underestimated the devastation, the cheering and the shouting almost blew the roof off Hard Operations.

But when it came through CIA intelligence that a month of mourning had been proclaimed in Hammadaz for their leader, Ryan became the man of the moment.

Further reports that Akhbar's Foreign Minister was on his way to the United Nations just served to broaden the smile on the General's face.

'Sure they'll bellyache! But Akhbar's gone! Without him, the whole goddamned country's a chicken without a head. We did it! We won! And everything's fine – if you win.'

He put his arm round Ryan and hugged him like a son. Ryan's very quietness beforehand on his exploits highlighted them more brilliantly.

'Told you, Cas! Told you, this youngster's got it!'

Then he came across to Craddock for what he called a quiet word.

'An immediate Medal of Honour for him, Cas! Same as his father! The PR boys are going to love it!'

'What about the others, General?'

'Something of course, Cas. But something less.'

'I reckon they should all have the Medal of Honour. Or none. Besides, Ryan disobeyed orders.'

'I call it quick thinking under changed circumstances. I call it initiative. I call it skill. I call it guts.'

The General walked away, intent now on overseeing that the photographs, videos, briefing reports, 71A survey, and his recommendations were sent post-haste in the waiting 135C to the President in Washington.

As the excitement began subsiding, Ryan the hero detached himself from his admirers and walked over to where Scott was sitting alone, drinking a cup of coffee.

Now a different sort of Ryan emerged. Scott felt a bastard at ever having nurtured a distrust of him. For Ryan at his best was powerfully persuasive. He was no longer smiling, but choking down his own exultation, showing what looked like genuine grief.

'Gee, I'm sorry about Glenn, Jonny!' He put his arm round Scott's shoulders. 'Christ, I guess we all loved that guy! One of the greatest! I'm proud to have served with him.' Ryan stared for a few seconds at the floor. Then he added, 'But it's the way he'd want to go!'

'Mebbe,' Scott grunted. He was not sure he didn't prefer Ryan the son-of-a-bitch, to Ryan the sympathiser.

'In action,' Ryan continued. 'Not some damnfool accident. But in action. The way he'd have wanted.'

'But later rather than sooner.'

'Sure,' Ryan shrugged. 'Guess that goes for us all.'

It was afternoon when Scott left debriefing and headed for the Mess. He was hungry, but he knew he couldn't eat. He was dog tired, but he knew he couldn't sleep. He showered and changed, then left the Mess again. He wanted to keep on walking till things sifted down inside himself and found their allotted place. Only now as he turned left at the foot of the steps, someone had fallen in beside him.

Helen must have been waiting round the Mess for him. She didn't say anything. Her presence wasn't disturbing. Quite the reverse.

They tramped round the whole complex of that bustling American township till they ended up at one of the less popular coffee bars used mainly by airmen. They sat in a corner, watching the sun go down, drinking coffee, talking about nothing in particular, till in the end, she must have judged it right to mention Glenn.

She took both his hands and said her sympathy – not like Ryan, but as if she felt it, and with real love. For Glenn. And, amazingly, for him. By then, he was getting things into place. He could look at that sunset and not see it as red flames exploding behind his aircraft, that whole wild holocaust they'd left of fire and billowing smoke.

That was what he was trained for. He was a professional pilot and a professional killer. He'd seen his first action. For the first time fired in anger. Seen his best buddy die. And he had survived. It was as simple as that.

He could talk about Glenn quite steadily to her now. How much the rest of the squadron would miss him. Ames, for instance. Glenn had been like a big brother to him. Really taken him under his wing. It'd be like a death in the family to Ames.

At that point, she deftly and daringly turned the conversation on to who would succeed Glenn as Scott's wizzo.

'That'll be up to Dief,' Scott stirred his coffee slowly, unwilling to discuss.

'Won't you get a say?'

'Oh, sure. If I want to. When I want to.'

She drained her cup and looked at her watch. 'Guess Ames isn't that happy with Captain Ryan. And vice versa.'

It wasn't news to Scott. Just news that this too had reached Helen's ears.

She stood up. 'You and Ames might be better suited.'

He got to his feet and stared down at her derisively. 'You being the expert!'

She stuck out her chin. 'In the matter of personalities, maybe I am. Anyway, it's worth thinking about.'

But he didn't want to think about a replacement for Glenn. He didn't want to see someone like Ames sitting in Glenn's seat. Part of him resented Helen's cool pragmatic approach, part of him found it as therapeutic as a dressing on a burn – and loved her for it.

But though he was most comforted by the tender, carefully shielded warmth of her concern, he was not yet ready to admit it, even to himself.

'Still the little preppie!' he said, putting her in her place.

Then they walked back in silence to the Mess.

There he went straight up to his Single Officer Quarter – and slept like a baby.

When he woke sixteen hours later, all hell had broken loose.

The man who stood in the centre of that hell was Squadron Leader Naylor. This was where the buck stopped at the man who was titular head of the Base, as everyone liked to pretend. It was obvious that Naylor had been selected by a not usually over-perceptive Air Ministry because of his amazing capacity to be all things to all people. He was liked by most people from Colonel Craddock to the lowliest airman, and from Lady Haddington to that crazy Quaker lady, with her way-out notions of loving one's neighbour. Squadron Leader Naylor liked and disliked the Americans in almost equal proportions and he was able to bounce off most situations and give comfort to both sides at once.

But not today. With the Hammadaz raid, the Yanks had gone too far. The British were incensed. The reasons for their anger were convoluted and no doubt very psychological. Deep down the country that had fought the Battle of Britain and the Battle of the Atlantic resented the Yanks taking over their defence. They resented the Yanks themselves, and most of all the British resented their airfield being used for a big guy to hit a little one, however repulsive.

The radio, breakfast television and the later editions of the morning papers were full of protest, though the government kept its end up with gung-ho support. The whole of East Anglia had tried to crowd into his office that morning. The road to the airfield was choked with cars, whose owners were hell bent on putting in their two pennyworth. And the two hundred police whom Squadron Leader Naylor had under his command didn't enjoy their strong arm role against their own kind, even though they knew that was what they were there for.

To make matters worse, because the Americans had suffered casualties – one aircraft and crew missing and Glenn Robinson killed – they were more than usually sensitive to criticism of any kind.

God, what a situation, Squadron Leader Naylor thought, as he stood at the salute, while Lieutenant Robinson's body, draped in the Stars and Stripes, was loaded on to the waiting Hercules, for burial in the States.

It was a terrible and moving moment.

The mist was rolling in from the sea, the sun was going down on one of life's most unpleasant days, and the Americans, God bless them, were making the most of their emotions. They couldn't help it, and he liked them for it, but Brits in general didn't. And the send-off for Robinson was all very American.

Colonel Craddock stood in the centre of the small, hastily erected podium, flag-draped like the coffin. He was flanked on one side by Lieutenant-Colonel Diefenbaker, and on the other by Lieutenant Colonel Evan Walton, the Vice-Commander, who'd had return-of-the-body arrangements to make.

In crisp ranks in front of them were all the squadron not on duty, and a vast number of HQ staff as well. Naylor hoped that none of Akhbar's reputed hit squads paid them a visit, for they'd all be sitting targets. A number of the female airmen were in tears, especially one little shrimp, so small she could have only just made the physical grade. She had got herself standing near to Scott and was weeping like a child as Colonel Craddock spoke his words of respect and thanks, of tribute and farewell.

Scott must have known the girl for when the Colonel had finished and had stepped over to place Glenn's cap and wings on the coffin, Scott put his arm around her shoulders, and kept it there, hugging her tight, while the bugler played the 'Last Post'.

There wasn't a woman and hardly a man with dry eyes then. But the emotion, naked or otherwise, was not what got to Squadron Leader Naylor. It was the terrible setting to it. For the huge Hercules loading bay was near the perimeter track. And beyond that was the perimeter fence, ten feet tall, of thick wire mesh, surmounted by barbed wire. And that fence was lined, *thronged* with the British, five or six deep, pressed against the fence, black shadows against the pink sunset, like bees pressed on a honeycomb. Except these were weirdly silent.

They were still silent as the loading bay closed. But when the band party struck up with the 'Star Spangled Banner' and every man and woman, including Scott and the shrimp, came rigidly to attention, it was like a pre-arranged signal to the watching British. One by one, each watching Briton lit a candle till the whole Base was ringed by small white petals of light.

Squadron Leader Naylor could see by the set of Craddock's shoulders that he was furious. But when he came over to talk to him, the Colonel's expression was calm and inscrutable.

'Come round this evening, Steve,' he said, issuing an order, not an invitation. 'Round about nine. Bring your wife. I've invited those locals who,' he paused, and smiled thinly, 'who ought to be invited. The opinion-makers. We need to get together. Mend fences. We've got a good case. We need to put the best spin on it. Right is firmly on our side. It's time they heard about it.' He touched his cap in an easy salute. 'But we'll probably need you to referee.'

Fourteen

The meeting at the Base Commander's house lived up to Colonel Craddock's worst expectations. It was a small gathering, select, intense and sticky.

When Steven and Elspeth Naylor arrived punctually at nine, the guests were standing with their backs to the imitation fire. Their faces were disapproving and they uneasily held brimming glasses, as if they might contain hemlock.

Maxine Craddock dressed in slender black with a double choker of pearls, glided forward in a cloud of expensive perfume to lightly kiss them on the cheek. 'Steve and Elspeth! Am I glad to see you!' she whispered conspiratorially and led them forward.

Colonel Craddock turned. 'Come on in you two! Get yourselves warm by the fire!'

Steven pushed forward, rubbing his hands and holding them out to the electric glow. 'Good evening, Rector! Councillor! Mrs Muggeridge! It's what we call over here "parky", Colonel.'

Parky inside *and* out. The Rector gave a wan smile, and the Muggeridges shuffled their feet.

'Ah, that looks good!'

Steven took two rich ruby glasses of punch from Jarman's tray and handed one to Elspeth.

Elspeth who was everything a regular RAF wife should be – charming, chatty, ambitious, and good-natured into the bargain – immediately set about thawing the Muggeridges. Steven had met Elspeth when he was a boy entrant at RAF Halton and she had worked at the local Ministry of Agriculture. She knew a little about subsidies and a lot about farmers, and she soon had that lumbering turnip-head eating out of her hand.

The Rector buttonholed both the Craddocks about what would happen to the Barlow marriage and the baby and Jennie if . . . the Rector coughed delicately at that point . . . if the father failed to return.

Embarrassment made the Rector phrase his question badly. It sounded to Steven Naylor as if he were implying some default on Barlow's part, and was relieved that the Colonel took the enquiry with understanding and compassion.

'The way I look at it, Rector, we all go on hoping. No news is good news. But you have my promise. Come what may, that child will be taken care of.'

'Sure it will,' Maxine said, 'you have to believe that,' then hearing the sound of the front door bell, followed Jarman to welcome the Haddingtons and the real business of the evening began.

Dear loyal Elspeth detached herself from the Muggeridges to work her magic on the Haddingtons. But Lord Haddington had eyes for no one but Maxine Craddock. He was friendly enough with Elspeth in a glassy-eyed dismissive way.

'Yes, we've met, Mrs Naylor. Of course we have! I remember now. How nice to see you again! How are you?'

He didn't want to hear her bubbly enthusiastic response. He put his hand under Maxine's elbow and walked her over by the window.

'You've had a ghastly day, Maxine?'

'Do I look it?'

He held his head on one side. 'No. You look simply marvellous. As always. But I've some imagination. It's besieged, isn't it? The Base? Reporters ringing up. It must have been awful!'

'Not only reporters,' she said, and hid her face in her drink. 'My beloved daughter!'

'Approving?'

'Jeezus, no!'

'It was a silly question. When do the young approve? My son doesn't approve of me.'

She laughed. 'Crazy guy!'

'Exactly my sentiments.'

He smiled at her warmly. Too warmly maybe.

'I must talk to the others.' She turned round guiltily. Lady Haddington was in earnest conversation with Cas and the Rector and Elspeth Naylor. The Muggeridges were getting redder of face and louder of voice with their third glass of Jarman's punch.

'You do much better for Anglo-American relations by talking to *me*.'

She smiled. 'I guess you're telling me *you're* the most important person hereabouts.'

'I am indeed!' He took another glass from Jarman's tray and lifted it to her. 'And I have a proposal to make. A very honourable one. You told me you ride and the first meet of the Hunt is a week on Thursday. Will you come? Then you'll meet some of the other important people.'

She shook her head. 'I haven't a horse.'

'That's no problem. I'll provide your mount. Hand-picked.'

'I haven't the gear.'

'You can hire it in Haddington. Stop making excuses!'

He stood sipping his drink, watching her over the rim of his glass.

Maxine flushed. 'Thank you, then. I'd like to. If Cas doesn't mind.'

'Take my word for it, Cas will be absolutely delighted.'

'How do you figure that?'

'I know the military mind.'

He looked over at Cas and smiled. 'My mother is in full flood. She wouldn't want you to interrupt.'

But Lady Haddington was being interrupted. And by a more authoritative figure than Maxine. Jarman had pussyfooted over to tell the Colonel he was wanted on the telephone.

Obviously the call was urgent. Cas went out hastily.

Elspeth Naylor was left with Lady Haddington and the Rector, who, now that the baby's interests had apparently been safeguarded, had fallen into an embarrassed silence.

'How are your chrysanthemums faring in this dry weather?' Elspeth began, for Lady Haddington was a keen gardener and an expert on chrysanthemums.

'Not well,' Lady Haddington waved a withered dismissive hand. 'More to the point how is your husband coping with *this* dreadfully difficult situation?'

'Oh, *very* well,' Elspeth assured her loyally. 'Very well indeed!'

They both turned to where Naylor was gamely defending the Yanks from the Muggeridges and having a hard time. Jarman's punch had made the Muggeridges more, not less, aggressive. Naylor's forehead was pink and sweaty, the hefty farmer, no longer the turnip-head charmed by Elspeth, bending over him, his big red hands clasped.

'Yes! Yes, indeed! Mr Muggeridge is absolutely right! The

village *is* incensed.' Lady Haddington held her head on one side, the better to listen to Muggeridge's diatribe. Now she snatched up a phrase and trumpeted it to Elspeth and the Rector. 'They're furious! *You* know that, Rector!'

The rector nodded but spread his hands disclaimingly in Christian regret.

'*Of course*, they see it as a violation of British sovereignty! You're *so* right, Councillor Muggeridge!'

She moved arthritically but nevertheless determinedly closer to the Muggeridges and Steven, and the Rector and Elspeth had to move with her.

They joined up like spawning amoeba to become an uncomfortable sixsome in the middle of the room. Jarman topped up every glass he could decently reach, and tried to close the gap or make the gap less obvious between that vociferous group and the laughing twosome by the window.

The Naylors were doing their best. The Rector from time to time inserted healing phrases, but Elspeth wished to heaven that Maxine and Lord Haddington would break up their *tête-à-tête* and that Colonel Craddock would return to take charge.

'When we arrived here tonight,' Lady Haddington told them in her penetrating voice, 'the roads were absolutely lined with cars belonging to protesters. It must have been the same when *you* arrived, Rector?'

The Rector nodded and spread his hands.

'Cars, bicycles, vans,' Lady Haddington went on. 'And masses of people on foot!'

Lady Haddington waved her hand expansively to encompass the whole world.

'Oh, CND.' Naylor shrugged them off. 'We get used to *them*!'

'No! Not CND! Not any initials of *anything*! Just *people*! British people, Squadron Leader. *Village* people! Who didn't like what happened.'

'But Lady Haddington,' Naylor said with a sweetly reasonable smile, 'the British welcome the Americans here to defend them . . .'

She interrupted smartly. '*Do* they? Welcome them? We try to, certainly. But to *defend* us? We have our own Air Force. Whose uniform you wear. I always thought we welcomed the Americans as equal partners. And that as Allies, we were to preserve the peace.'

It was a well known fact that two of Lady Haddington's sons

had been killed in the Battle of Britain. The two good ones, the locals said. The flower of the flock. So she was a tricky person to argue with. Sometimes pro-Yank, sometimes not.

'You saw the six o'clock news, I suppose?' Muggeridge put in challengingly.

Naylor shook his head. 'I was much too busy.'

'Well, sir. You didn't ought to have been too busy! You ought to know what you're sticking up for, by God!'

'Civilian casualties,' Lady Haddington chimed in sorrowfully. 'Children. Blown apart. Limbs everywhere. Dreadful! Quite dreadful!'

'Very regrettable.' Naylor sighed and shook his head sagely. 'Very, very regrettable. No one would be more sorry than the men and women here. But in war . . .'

'We're not *at war*, sir,' Muggeridge unclasped his hands to wave a fist. 'Not so far as we know! And we don't want to be! We don't want another Vietnam! Yanks use other people's backyards to fight in. An' they never know when to stop. Bloodthirsty buggers! I've fought with them. Which is more than *you've* done, Squadron Leader Naylor.'

'My husband wasn't born till forty-seven,' Elspeth piped up protestingly. 'The war was over.'

'My dear,' Lady Haddington put a hand on Elspeth's arm. 'Don't get upset! If you saw the village tonight, I think you would understand that what we're saying is only the tip of the iceberg.'

And then just as Elspeth was beginning to feel she could take no more stick, the door opened and Colonel Craddock came back in.

'I apologise for my absence, ladies and gentlemen,' he began gravely.

And then he paused. And not just for effect.

He was dog tired. He had not slept for thirty-six hours. And in those thirty-six hours, while outwardly calm, outwardly unmoved, he had run the whole long gamut of emotions and opinions. He was proud that Haddington had been selected. It had to be a feather in his cap. It augured well for the Base and for himself personally. The raid in its daring had amazed him. If there were reservations about the moral aspect of the raid, speculation on that was a luxury for the Brits and for those long-haired liberal academics back home who taught kids like his step-daughter, Sharon. He was a front-line wing commander. He had been given his orders. He had supervised the final planning and execution.

The American crews had carried it out brilliantly. In Ryan's case, beyond brilliance, beyond orders, on that perilous knife-edge between disobedience and daring. Between military sense and madness.

Ryan. Craddock's particular ghost at the feast. Best not thought of until another day.

For the moment it was the British and their bellyaching. And this for him was a whole different ball-game. He had expected protest. But not like this. This was protest of every shade of the spectrum from the professional protesters, through the religious, to the authoritative vehemence of the dowager Lady Haddington. Worst of all, the protest touched a tiny buried chord in him, which made him feel that much more angry, that much more alienated. As if he were in enemy territory. A little Vietnam.

Vosper on the blower with a personal congratulation from Downing Street didn't take the bitter taste away. Add to that Glenn Robinson killed, and now the news that he'd just received that wreckage of *Thunderbird* had been found on a mountain in Italy – both Gruber and Barlow dead.

Ordinarily, when he returned to the lounge, he'd have said nothing beyond the apology. He'd have done the British stiff-upper-lip act. But that evening he felt not just a savage need to make the Brits squirm, but the knowledge that he had the power to make them.

'I have just received an important telephone message,' he announced weightily, looking around at the flushed group in the centre of the room, and then at Maxine and Lord Haddington, obviously flirting with each other by the window.

'I'm afraid it was bad news. Our losses last night were heavier than we reckoned. The missing aircraft crashed. Both crew members were killed.'

He had the grim pleasure of seeing the British squirm all right. Muggeridge ran a clumsy hand through his scrubby hair, and shuffled his feet. 'Sorry to hear that, Colonel, very sorry. Deepest sympathy to all concerned.'

'Both dead? Gruber *and* Barlow?' the Rector asked questioningly as if he'd misheard.

'Yes, Rector. *Both* of them.'

'We're dreadfully sorry,' Lady Haddington murmured. 'Such fine young men! Such a loss!'

'Thank God for such fine young men!' Lord Haddington came

down firmly on the side of the Yankee angels. He would have done anyway. But this was the opportunity to do so without offending his dear but wayward mother. 'We should *all* be very thankful to them.'

Jarman was meanwhile padding around discreetly and generously filling up the glasses. There was no more argument. A murmur in Craddock's ear from the Rector. Should he tell Jennie the sad news, and could he relay the Colonel's promise? Then drinks were hastily swallowed. Farewells were said. Caps and coats smoothly handed out by Jarman.

'You can rely on me, Colonel, to minimise any damage,' Lord Haddington assured Craddock. 'There are many, many people who think as I do.'

Craddock gave his guests one parting shot, as they began to step out into the moonlit night. 'After all,' he said loudly and with apparent good humour, 'your Prime Minister gave permission. Your Prime Minister has sent congratulations.'

'So who are *we* to question?' Lord Haddington kissed Maxine's cheek, and took his mother's arm. The Muggeridges said a discomfited goodnight. The Naylors chugged off home like twin tugs relieved of a heavy duty.

Maxine stood for a moment in the lighted doorway. She could see a little segment of the perimeter fence, and the tiny candles still burning. They gave her a funny shivering feeling as if those were hostile fires beyond some wild west palisade. She wanted Cas to return quickly from seeing the Haddingtons to their car. Even with Lord Haddington, or maybe especially with him, and despite his heavily laden admiration, she'd been aware all evening of a gap of nationalities. She wanted Cas to come and put his arms around her.

'Thanks, Jarman,' she said, turning and going inside. 'You were great. But it's been a long day. You go now.'

She poured herself and Cas another drink and waited.

In times past, they would now have discussed the evening, 'shot the breeze' as Cas would have said. Unwound together. But it was a long time past since they'd done that.

When Cas returned, he raised one eyebrow at her recharged glass, and then as she handed him his, reluctantly, 'Oh, well, mebbe.' He gulped down half. 'It'll help me sleep.'

'You need a good sleep.'

'Sure do.' He glanced at the clock as if he were about to go right upstairs and claim his rest.

'I'm sorry,' she said softly, 'about Gruber and Barlow.'

'Hell, yes.' He stuck out his lower lip. 'And Robinson. They were three good guys. The best.'

'Then tonight on top.'

'Uh-huh, that's what Uncle Sam pays me for.' He gave her an abstracted smile. In the kindly tone he might have used to Jarman. 'You were great with Lord Haddington.'

'He's a good friend to us all. Not just to me.'

'More to you, I guess. You got him round your finger.'

Maxine glanced sharply at her husband's face, in search, hopefully maybe, of jealousy. But there was none there. The Wing Commander was pleased at her efforts. The husband was compliant. She felt a strange anger, faint enough to pretend it wasn't there.

She went over and kissed her husband lightly on the forehead. 'You go up first, Cas. I've got some shopping lists to make out for Jarman.'

By the time she went to bed, he was asleep.

Fifteen

The candlelit watchers didn't sleep that night. Nor did Ryan. He saw those bloody lighted candles, but somehow they didn't get to him. He was stilted up, high on action and success. It was like nothing he'd ever known.

When he was a kid, the fat old priest at his downtown school had described what he called 'touching the hem of God's garment'. He must have cribbed that from some book of sermons, for Jeezus, the only garments that fat man had known about touching were positively not God's. Even at seven, Ryan had recognised that. Touching God's garment, the old sinner had said, was like nothing in heaven or on earth. It was ecstasy. It left you wanting nothing else but to touch it again. Well, God's garment, Ryan didn't have time to speculate on. But real action, war, sure left you hungering and thirsting for nothing but it.

It.

The best feeling he'd had in his life, including fucking. The taste of it, the euphoria of it lasted through night after night. It made Ryan impregnable against such minor irritations as the pathetic ring of candles. Boy, could he huff and puff and blow those piggies' candles out! One blast from his after-burners and . . . pffff!

Now he knew what his father must have felt like. Now it was as if he'd really known him, shared an experience with him. Above all, placated his father's ghost. Proved himself.

Ryan was still in a good mood at breakfast time. In the Mess, he helped himself to a man-size platter of ham and eggs and hashed brown potatoes. He was early, the place was three-quarters empty. He sat himself down at a table by the window.

He saw Scott come in and waved a friendly hand at him. No one was doubting who was Ace of the Base now. Ryan felt magnanimous. The man of the moment. He could afford to be off guard.

Which just went to prove to himself that he was too trusting a guy, and you could never be off guard.

As soon as he'd collected his tray, Scott came over. 'Mind if I join you?'

'Be my guest.'

'Thanks. You're just the guy I want to see.'

Then Scott came straight to the point. He needed a new wizzo, which of course everyone knew. Would Ryan object if he asked Diefenbaker to give him Ames.

Would he object? Ryan threw back his head and laughed out loud at the bloody hard nose of the man. The request didn't diminish his good humour. Boosted it, if anything. But it sure made him suspicious.

If Scott had asked him a week ago, he might have said, 'You're welcome.' But now, when he'd stopped laughing, he said, 'This is one hell of a surprise.'

'I don't see why – you've bitched enough about Ames.'

'Aw hell! Maybe. In the past. But I've brought him on. Gotten him into my ways. He's all right. He understands me.'

'That's not what I heard.'

'Then you heard wrong. Have you asked him?'

'No. I guessed I should ask you first.'

'You guessed right.' Ryan carved up a piece of ham, a smile playing round his lips. 'And I'll tell you something else, Scott. Don't! Don't ask him! Him and me are sticking! We're a winning team! Hear that? That's why you want him.' He stuffed the ham into his mouth and chewed it before stabbing the fork in Scott's direction and adding, 'You've gotten into the habit of wanting what I've got.'

'Which is supposed to mean?' Scott asked evenly, staring coldly into Ryan's eyes.

'Oh, you jest try to figure it out.' Ryan mopped up the last of the egg with a piece of bread, swallowed it and got to his feet.

He toyed with the idea of mentioning Samantha, and then thought better of it. Instead, he went in search of Ames on his Suzuki.

He found him, as he knew he would, in Soft Ops, studying.

In his present munificent mood towards Ames, Ryan came up behind him and clapped him on the shoulder, and said, 'C'mon, c'mon, buddy! Give yourself a break! The war's over! For the moment! Time you had some fun.'

Ames screwed his head round nervously. He mistrusted Ryan in his expansive mood. The Greeks and their presents were as nothing compared to Ryan and his fun.

'Let's get out of this bloody cage, Milt. You an' me. C'mon! I've got my bike outside. We'll go down to the pub. Have a wing-ding!'

'It's early.' He looked at his watch. 'It's not ten yet.'

'So? They'll soon be open. C'mon.' He smiled kindly at Ames. Not just because he'd done a good job, but because he couldn't help valuing him that much more for Scott wanting him. 'We need to get out of this place.'

He led the way out to his bike. Reluctantly, Ames followed and took the back seat. Ryan started up and roared round the perimeter.

'I just hope those cars aren't still there,' Ames muttered, as Ryan decelerated before the guard-house.

'Sure they're not,' Ryan called over his shoulder. 'Bet you they're not. The Brits don't have staying power. The dumb bastards have had their little bellyache. Made their protest. Then they'll go off home to their tellies. Safe in Uncle Sam's bosom.'

He thrust his ID plastic at the black corporal guard, who quivered his arm into the most respectful salute the human arm was capable of. 'Thank you, Captain Ryan, sir,' he said. 'Can I just say how proud we all are of you, sir.'

The corporal seemed for a moment so like a pocket-sized version of Glenn that Ames's eyes filled with tears. If the British cars and the British protesters were there, then hell, he'd look them in the eye and ride right past.

But they weren't. At least only a few. A bunch of homely looking women with a CND placard, a couple of cars with stickers which read, 'We want Glasnost'.

'What did I tell you?' Ryan yelled over his shoulder, gunning the engine exultantly for all it was worth.

Ames caught his mood, laughing out loud as the hedges whipped by. It was a beautifully sunny morning, slightly hazed. The harvest was long in and the sun gleamed on the golden stubble fields.

Then as the road passed the northernmost tip of the perimeter fence, over Ryan's shoulder, he glimpsed what looked like a small brown sack in the middle of the road. He heard Ryan shout out something. Then he saw it wasn't a sack, but the kneeling figure of the little Quaker woman.

He braced himself for Ryan slamming on the brake and swerving. But he didn't. He accelerated. He screamed, and yelled, profanities streaming behind him in a wild incoherent jumble, and aimed the bike like a missile, in a fangs-out attack, dead at the kneeling woman.

Time telescoped. It was forever and at the same time only a few seconds that they hurtled towards her. Ryan's hands were locked on to the handlebars, his shoulders rigid.

It was a moment Ames would remember forever. He knew he ought to do something, but he daren't. And even if he dared, he didn't know what.

But something, instinct perhaps, made him scream out a warning, rise up crazily, lean over Ryan's shoulders, seize the handlebars and wrench them sideways.

They missed her by a whisker. The bloody woman hadn't moved. Whether it was part of her campaign or whether she'd been frozen in fear as he'd almost been, Ames didn't know.

Whatever it was, though she'd stuck where she was, they missed her. They went scraping along the grassy verge for half a mile throwing up great clods of earth. On and crazily on. Then Ryan seemed to come out of whatever it was he was in, his hands unclenched. He steered the bike back on the road. He didn't stop though till they got to the local pub another mile down the road.

Then he dismounted, threw back his goggles, and hissed in a small deadly voice, 'Never do that to me again, you hear, Ames?'

'Do what?' Ames croaked. His mouth was dry. His shirt wet with sweat.

'*Panic*! That's what *you* did! *Panic*!'

'You might have killed her!'

'Panic.' Ryan repeated. 'Don't you ever panic.'

A minute later, he was punching Ames's shoulder and laughing, 'C'mon, let me buy you a beer!'

Sixteen

Ames had nightmares that night. He woke in a cold sweat, screaming. He dreamed that he and Ryan were back on Operation Grand Chasm again. Only they'd run out of bombs and Ryan was doing a kamikaze right at the target.

He reached for his cigarettes, muttering, 'Crazy bastard!' His hands trembled as he lit up, for somehow the dream was like as if it had happened, and from that moment he began to think, Ryan really was crazy. He wasn't just kidding. He *was*.

When they met up in Ops later that day, he eyed his AC carefully. His blue eyes had those pinpoint pupils, though maybe that could be explained by his high. His movements were jerky and he jumped from one subject to another like a tick.

Ryan was still full of love for the human race, except for protesters and Commies and Ruskies and Craddock.

Craddock, he reckoned, had been bloody tight-assed in his praise for him personally. The old green-eye of the little yellow god. Craddock had been jealous of his father and now of *him*. Because he himself was yellow. Hadn't the balls to stand up to Commie bastards.

But he had a date that evening with a pretty little nurse, and so long as she didn't turn out to be a protester or a Commie or a Ruskie, he was, he told Ames, going to lay her. A plush dinner first at the Riverside Inn. He'd booked their best table by the window. Then afterwards, her place. He'd bought her a corsage from the Utility store. Ames should take note of how you went about getting a woman.

Ames watched him roar away from the Mess on his bike. He wandered back into the bar and bought himself a beer. It was deserted except for Scott and his new wizzo, Gorringe, chatting up Dr Mansell.

If they'd had Glenn with them, it would have been OK for him to drift over and join them. But only Gorringe was facing him and he was obviously trying to make an impression on his new AC, and didn't even raise a smile.

The evening stretched before him. The cinema perhaps, the bowling alley, the dance at the Galaxy club with the bussed-in broads. He was not in the mood for any of them.

He thought of Glenn again, pounding his way round the perimeter, and his oft repeated homilies on exercise.

Maybe, at the back of his mind, Ames nourished the hope that like Glenn, he might run into some nice girl. There were after all a few left in the world, and though his physique didn't match up to Glenn's, he looked all right stripped down.

So having changed into shorts and singlet, looking as purposeful as he could, he set off, pounding the perimeter.

It was a fine evening. The fall in Britain hadn't the glory of North America, and East Anglia had only small sparse woodlands, but in quieter golds and browns and oranges, the British fall had its own modest splendour.

The sun had gone down, and there was a pink afterglow over the flat fields and the tarnished inland waterways. The air smelled sweet. A long skein of geese was flying toward the marshes so low that he could hear the squeaking of their wings. Then high above, the big black bulk of the weekly Hercules shuttle from the States, red and green wingtip lights carving a jazzy track over the first faint pricking of stars.

It had landed by the time he completed his first circuit of the perimeter. He watched it turn off the runway and taxi round to Dispersal. He loved aircraft and he always liked watching them. Maybe flying wasn't in his blood like it was in Ryan's, but he thrilled to that black monster tamed by a single pair of hands.

When the Hercules came to a halt, under the arc lights of the Passenger Reception Apron, he hung around. He watched the steps run into place, and the doors being opened. A smiling flight attendant was bidding her passengers farewell.

Ames's jaw fell wide open.

The first to emerge was a very pretty, very expensively dressed little blonde, who looked around expectantly as if for the guard of honour to strike up.

Samantha Ryan.

With studied, sexy grace, she began to descend the steps, her eyes travelling around the handful of people on the tarmac. At the bottom, her gaze alighted on Ames, still rooted to the spot. She screwed up her eyes as if not quite believing what she saw. 'Milton? Milt Ames? Christ, is that *you*? What the hell are you doing in that get-up?'

'Running.'

'Who from? What's her name?' She went into a fit of the giggles at her own humour. 'Jeezus!' She ran her eyes speculatively over him. Their expression changed a little. 'Say, you don't look bad though!' And in the same breath, 'Where's Rod?'

'Does he know you're coming?'

'Hell no! It's a surprise. Rod's quite a celebrity now, eh? Where is he?'

Though in the long run it might have been the best turn he could have done his aircraft commander, it naturally never entered Ames's head to tell her. At times he might reckon Ryan was crazy, at times he just about hated him, but he would never have let him down.

Ames shrugged, looked vacant and said nothing.

'C'mon! C'mon, Milt! You gotta know! Or,' she giggled teasingly, 'is he with some other woman?'

'Hell, no! You know Rod!'

'Hell, yes!' Her expression momentarily darkened. 'I sure do!'

'You're the only woman for him. Gee, he's got it real bad!'

'I guess so.' She preened herself. 'So where is he?'

'I reckon he's in Ops.' He caught her arm as she turned as if to make off for wherever Ops might be. 'You can't go in Ops, Samantha! Go through that door over there. Personnel Relations Reception. Then grab yourself some coffee. I'll run right over to Ops and tell him the good news!'

Ryan had arrived early at the Riverside Inn. There were a few cars in the parking lot to the right of it, but no sign of Harriet's ancient jalopy. He retrieved the corsage from the carrier box, straightened his tie, ran a comb through his hair, then went inside.

It was a nice quaint place. The sort the Brits did well. Rather low in the ceilings with big dusty black beams. There were logs burning in the brick fireplace, though it wasn't cold outside, with all sorts of shining brass utensils on the walls.

A waiter with oily black hair and a funny French accent confirmed that his table was waiting. And just as he was asking if sir would like to be shown there, in came Harriet.

She was a sight worth waiting for. She got prettier, sexier, more desirable every time Ryan saw her. Or maybe it was just that he had been away from Samantha too long.

Harriet was wearing a dress of some soft material that clung to her figure like the proverbial second skin. It parted company with her first skin just below the knees and flounced out in a way that attracted the eye, at least Ryan's eye, and showed off her pretty legs and neat high-heeled feet. The dress was green. The old green light to airmen. *Come in to land, boy*!

He didn't comment on it then. He played it cool. 'Harriet! Hi! You look . . .' he waved his hand as if words failed him. 'I would say a million dollars. But you look better'n that.'

He presented the corsage to her with his well-known smile. And then he realised he was barking up the wrong tree, playing the wrong record, over the wrong bloody approach beacon. A closer look at her face showed she had not come in the mood for corsages and pretty compliments and an intimate dinner and certainly not *afterwards at her place*.

She said in her neat precise English accent, 'Thank you, Captain Ryan. But . . .'

'Rod! And no *but*, for chrissake . . .'

'Thank you, Rod,' she went on steadily and coldly. 'But if you knew how I felt, how I *still feel*, I'm not sure that you would have wanted me to come.'

Her eyes looking up at him were earnest and he liked that. She was trying to pick her way through a minefield of words. But all the time she was doing her picking and choosing, he had his hand lightly under her elbow. And on the other side of her, the oily rag of an imitation Frog had his hand, not touching her, but wafting her in with a folded napkin over his miserable little arm and a menu in his hand the size of an F-115 checklist.

So by the time she'd finished, they were beside the table, her chair pulled out, the giant menu thrust into her hand and the oily rag cutting off her retreat.

She sat down with a flustered smile at the waiter, then leaned across the table. 'Before we go any further . . . before we order or *anything*,' she whispered urgently, 'there's something I feel I ought to tell you.'

He deliberately misunderstood her. 'My, my,' he said in a mock-avuncular manner. 'What have you been up to? Whatever it is, I forgive you, my child.'

'It's not what *I've* been up to. It's what *you've* been up to.'

She handed the menu back to the waiter and gave him one of her quelling glances that sent him back to his position by the cold buffet. Then she took charge of herself and the situation.

'I tried to phone you,' she said. 'But I couldn't get hold of you. I wanted to tell you before we met tonight, just how I feel.'

'About *me*?'

'No.' She frowned. 'Not about you.'

'What then?'

'About the raid.'

'Jeezus,' he said, pressing his fingers against his temples. 'Not that.'

'Yes, that!'

He gritted his teeth. 'OK . . . get it off your chest.'

'I thought,' she began slowly, tracing a pattern on the damask tablecloth with her fork, 'that it was wrong. Most of us thought the raid was wrong—'

'Then, Jesus, *you* were wrong!'

'—and we didn't like our country being used for it.'

'Oh, for chrissake!'

'And I took part in the vigil.'

'All those goddamned candles?'

'All those candles, yes.'

He made a noise with his lips as if he were blowing them all out. He was surprised that he didn't feel angry. At least not with his head. With different parts of him, maybe. Whatever he felt made it that much more urgent for him to lay her.

Harriet saw a multitude of expressions cross his face. Like the rest of the villagers, she had reacted to the raid with disbelief and bewilderment. The loss of Barlow had added a terrible personal poignancy. Professional though she was, Jennie's suffering had deeply distressed her. Jennie's resigned words, 'I always knew it was too good to be true.' In an afternoon spent comforting the poor girl, she had stifled her condemnation of the raid and fallen back on that self-perpetuating myth of all victims of wars that the misery was worthwhile.

But it wasn't. And she hated herself for her spurious comfort.

'You know we lost two other guys besides Barlow,' Ryan said thickly, as if he'd been following her thoughts. 'Barlow, Gruber, Robinson, three of the very best,' he added with theatrical emotion and covered his eyes.

'Yes, the Rector told us. I'm sorry. Dreadfully sorry. We all are. But it doesn't make it any better. It makes it *worse.*'

'Don't let's talk about it, honey! It chokes me! I knew Glenn Robinson, for instance, real well. He came over with us. That day I met you, honey, we'd just flown in. The four of us were like brothers.'

At that point, she stretched out her hand across the table and touched his, and he knew it would be cruising altitude from here on.

'OK, you've had your say,' he said briskly. 'And I've taken it right here.' He patted his outthrust jaw. '*I* don't see why the Brits object. Hell, I don't! They weren't their men. And that raid made the world a safer place. But like we say, life's gotta go on. And you and me . . .' he smiled winningly, and squeezed her finger tips. 'Guess it doesn't bring those guys back for us to fall out.'

Harriet hesitated. 'I suppose it isn't individuals,' she said, still making patterns with her fork on the tablecloth.

'Sure it isn't,' Ryan agreed.

'Well, let's not think about it tonight,' she smiled.

Tonight! Her words gave him abundant hope.

'I've been wondering all day what I'd say to you.'

'Least you were *thinking* of me.'

She laughed. And then immediately reproved herself. 'I shouldn't laugh. It wasn't funny.'

'Jeezus-Christ-on-a-crutch, I'll say it wasn't!'

She laughed and then put the brakes on again. 'I was only laughing at your expression. I'm sorry. It was thoughtless of me. It must have been hell.'

'Hell!'

'Were you frightened?'

'Shit-scared!'

She nodded. 'You must be very brave.'

'Hell, no!' he said unconvincingly.

'I hear a rumour,' she went on reluctantly, 'that the Colonel's put you up for a medal.'

'Not the Colonel. The General.' And on that note he banned the subject. 'Let's talk about something else.' He jerked his head for the waiter. 'Food, for instance. I'm starving.

Despite the bad start, or maybe because of it, the evening progressed with a slightly hysterical merriment. Ryan ordered with extravagance. The waiter responded with constant attention. Harriet never said no to her glass being refilled. Guilt made her drink more, say more, be more kindly to the brash airman opposite her. They talked about the village and the Base and about how they first met. The baby. Jesus, that had been another time he was shit-scared. 'Now I come to think of it, more shit-scared than on the goddamned raid.'

She smiled. 'Oh, surely not!'

'Sure was!'

'You were very good about it. You stayed. I thought you might have dropped me off and left me.'

'Nope. I always bring 'em back. That's what I tell my wizzo. "You'll always make it in my bird".' Ryan paused. 'Kinda weird that it was Barlow's brat.'

'Tragic.'

'Shows that if you're aircrew, you gotta live for the day.' He paused. 'Or the night.'

By the third course, his language had become more suggestive, his glance more challenging, his knees under the table more frequently brushing her own. Ryan was sure that the evening was going to end with mutual satisfaction.

And then just as he was choosing a fantastic-looking sweet from the trolley, a figure gesticulating urgently in the doorway caught his eye.

'Christ-on-a-crutch!'

He didn't know the exclamation had escaped him. But it must have done, for Harriet turned her head.

'Looks as if someone wants you, Rod. Friend of yours?'

'No! Stupid son-of-a-bitch!'

He stabbed his finger at a yellow and white confection. 'A piece of that, waiter.'

He raised his head to glower at Ames.

'Shouldn't you see what he wants?'

Then Ryan made a big mistake.

'No.' He shook his head. 'He'll be wanting a lift back to Base. Stupid dummy! Wet behind the bloody ears.'

'Who is he?'

'My wizzo. For my bloody sins! I've treated that guy like a son. Taught him all he knows. Time he stood on his own two feet.'

'He looks worried.'

'Let him!'

He lifted a fork preparatory to digging into the yellow and white confection, when suddenly he saw Ames lurch forward into the dining room and come right over to their table.

Without any preamble, without dressing it up or whispering it down and with the goggling look of any bearer of bad news, he said in Ryan's ear, 'Samantha's landed.'

Christ, he made it sound like bloody Martians! And Christ, he was right!

'Why don't you sit down?' Harriet nodded towards an empty chair opposite and smiled at the discomfited man hovering in front of her.

The minor furore in the dining room had died down. Ryan had thrown down a handful of ten dollar bills on the table, and with simply an aghast look at Harriet, and another at the astonished waiter, had rushed wordlessly out. The other diners had gone back to their food. The waiter now looked merely undecided as to when he could decently pick up all those ten dollar bills.

'You might as well eat his pudding,' Harriet suggested as Ames slid into Ryan's empty chair. 'He didn't get time to start it.'

'Sorry to interrupt, ma'am.'

'Don't be. It wasn't your fault.' And after a pause, resignedly, 'Samantha's his wife?'

'Yes, ma'am.'

In self-justification, rather than in anger, she said, 'I didn't know he was married.'

'I guess he hadn't been married very long.'

Her eyes crinkled up. 'You mean it slipped his mind?'

He laughed nervously and relaxed his shoulders a little. 'Not exactly. Maybe he hasn't gotten used to being married.'

'I'm sure he hasn't.' She picked up her spoon and fork and ate daintily of a mound of chocolate ice-cream. Ames attacked the yellow and white confection with relish.

They exchanged names. Harriet ordered coffee and brandy. They exchanged ages. Milton Ames was six months younger than her, but he seemed much younger than that. He had the aura of someone who emotionally has been kept too long in artificial light. A clever lad, studying and working his way up, naïvely supposing that was the way of the world.

'Where d'you come from, Milt?'

'New York.'

He told her about his father. The best read man he ever knew. What a great man he'd have been if he'd had Milton's chances. 'I'm with you up there, son.' That's what his father said. 'All the way. Every trip.'

'He'd have liked to fly, would he?'

'Sure.'

'Even on the Hammadaz mission?'

He looked across at her steadily, his face composed. He looked older than her now. Much older. 'I guess I couldn't answer that.' He stirred his coffee. 'I reckon most people back home support us.'

'That's because they are *back home*.'

'They reckon you've gotta put down terrorism.'

'Not by governments behaving like terrorists.'

A spasm of surprised pain creased his youthful face and smoothed out again. 'Ma'am,' he said, 'we're here to defend,' he waved his hand to encompass the dining room and its greedily absorbed eaters, 'you all. To hold back Communism!'

'No.' She shook her head vehemently and leaned across the table. 'You're here because America is a militaristic nation. A *colonial* nation. You expect sooner or later to fight Communism, in spite of *Perestroika*. And you want to make sure the Third World War's in Europe again.'

'That isn't so.' Ames shook his head vigorously and drained his brandy glass.

'And,' she went on, 'who gave Uncle Sam the divine right to topple any government he doesn't like? As for defending us, you're more likely to *annihilate* us. You're too immature to play with such lethal toys.'

Suddenly she bit off her words. The sight of his face, his nice, vulnerable, startled face, so genuinely surprised, offended and even distressed by her apostasy, melted her.

'I'm sorry,' she said and stretched her hand across the table. He took it self-consciously. 'Don't let's talk about it any more. What right have I to preach, you might ask.'

'No, ma'am. I reckon it's an interesting viewpoint. I shall think about what you said.'

Odd, she thought, he was the first Yank she'd spoken to who seemed capable of examining another point of view. Who didn't reckon you were a Commie or KGB sympathiser. And now she had made that tiny dent in America's self-esteem, she wished whole-heartedly that she hadn't. She tried to make amends.

'And after all that,' she smiled apologetically, 'would you like me to drive you back to the Base? Or would you like some more coffee, and we'll talk about something else?'

'Coffee, please. And another brandy.'

She lifted one of the ten dollar bills, and eyed him humorously. 'Your captain left enough for a bottle. I'll just have coffee, though. I've got to drive.'

It was close on midnight before they left the restaurant. He held her hand as they walked to the car. Ames walked on air.

Despite her opinions, in those few hours they had really gotten to know each other. And liked each other. They'd talked about everything under the sun and laughed like kids. And for the first time in his life, he had felt really comfortable with a girl.

It was a funny old car she had, and it chugged along at about ten miles an hour. Good for sightseeing, she said, pointing out the church, the market cross, the smithy and a row of olde worlde houses, all bathed in unclouded moonlight.

She let him out just before the guard-house. And even with the myriad patterned lights of the Base, and the black crouching mounds of the bomb-dumps and the hard hangars summoning him back to the real world, he felt sufficiently confident of her to make a joke about the unjokeable.

'If *I* promise not to start the Third World War,' he put his head through her open driver's window, 'will you promise to see me again?'

She cupped his face in her hands and lightly kissed his lips. 'Sounds fair.'

'Where can I call you?'

'It's easy to remember. Local exchange, then four-three-two-one.'

It sounded like a countdown, and for a moment, ominous. But it was a countdown to happiness, he told himself, still walking on brandy-assisted air. To having a girl of his own, a girl Ryan had been hot for.

To beating Captain Ryan at his own game.

Seventeen

Ryan had gunned the bike through Haddington village like a bat out of hell. There was a smell of burning rubber and a squeal of tyres as he pulled up sharp at the guard-house. The guard smiled his approval, gave his rubber-limbed salute and waved him through, watching as his hero accelerated and roared round towards Dispersal.

Something hot and throbbing between your legs – that's what they reckoned a bike is to you. Well, he had that without the bike. He was as mad as hell with Samantha. Mad that she had come at all. Mad that she hadn't warned him she was coming. Mad that she had picked just the right time to flip it for him with Harriet. But mad as he was, or maybe because he was as mad as he was, he wanted her.

If he couldn't have Harriet, then Samantha.

He parked his bike under the bright arc lights in front of Relations Reception, and strode inside. He threw open the double glass doors. He had gotten used this last day or so to the admiring glances, but the pretty sergeant behind the enquiry desk gave him the best to date. She stood up, smiled, and almost genuflected.

Yes, Mrs Ryan was waiting in the lounge, she told him as she lifted the flap, preparing to conduct him in person. Lucky Mrs Ryan to be married to *him*, her glance said.

The lounge was a big comfortable open area, two carpeted steps down from the Reception Hall. As they descended them, he heard her tinkly laughter and immediately saw just how bloody well they had looked after her.

Samantha was the only remaining unclaimed passenger-relative from the Hercules. There she queened it centre stage, having the time of her life, her little face flushed, her golden head thrown back in laughter, holding a tall glass in one hand, playfully wagging the finger of the other at her companion.

Her companion was, of course, he might have figured that, none other than Scott. Scott who liked to pretend that he didn't fancy Samantha. Now caught off guard, leaning forward, talking earnestly, intimately, saying what?

Bastard! Ryan glanced quickly at the smiling sergeant to see if he had spoken aloud. But no, she was still smiling, looking fondly at the two of them like God looking on his handiwork and finding it good. 'We got Captain Scott over to look after your wife. She said he's a family friend.'

'Sure is!' Ryan said through his teeth. 'A very *intimate* friend.'

She did look sideways then as if not quite sure, but his wide grin reassured her. Samantha had got the shortest skirt on that could reach below the hem of a knicker, and she had her legs crossed so that Scott could have the benefit of all that thigh.

Scott saw Ryan first and got to his feet. Following his eyes, Samantha put down her glass, clapped her hands and let out a little shriek half of pleasure, half of reproach. She was always one to get her reproach in first.

She jumped up and flung herself at him, fastening her arms round his neck. He lifted her off her feet, swung her round, squealing, pressing her to him so that she was in no doubt as to what was going to happen when he got her home.

'*You* took a long time coming,' she pouted when he put her down. 'Didn't he?' she turned round to Scott. 'Poor Jonathan.'

Scott looked uncomfortable, as well he might. 'It was a pleasure.'

'I'm sure it was,' Ryan agreed.

'So what took you so long?' Samantha asked, head on one side, winking at Scott.

'That dumb clown Ames! Couldn't find me. I guess I'll have to do something about that son-of-a-bitch.'

'You had your chance,' Scott put in.

'Hear him, Sammy!' Ryan put his arm round her. 'He wants everything I've got, including . . .'

He kissed her on the mouth lingeringly.

While they kissed, the sergeant, with an abstracted smile, disappeared back to her counter. Scott picked up his cap.

Samantha struggled free of her husband's kiss, and asked with wide-eyed innocence, 'Including *what*, Rod? Jonny wants everything you've got including *what*?'

'*Whom*, honey. I guess even Vassar couldn't drum an education into you!'

'Oh, for chrissake,' Scott said, 'I'm going to hit the sack.'

'Us too.' Ryan laughed loudly and suggestively. And turning to Samantha, 'You're lucky they assigned me a Married Quarter.'

Scott grunted a curt goodnight, and nodded at Samantha. 'Nice seeing you again, Samantha.'

When he was half way across the lounge, Samantha said shrilly to Ryan, 'You didn't thank him for looking after me.'

'*He* should've thanked *me*. Come on, wife.' He playfully pulled a handful of her hair. Then gave it a little hard tug, just to show her the way it was going to be.

Samantha liked it the way it was going to be. So did he. He zoomed her off to his Married Quarter, and even if it was a disappointment to Mrs Rich Girl, she couldn't wait to get upstairs.

Then it was like something else that fat old sinful priest of his childhood had told him. Something about the best-laid schemes of mice and men and how they went up shit creek.

Ryan didn't suppose what happened to him ever happened to mice – or Jeezus there wouldn't be so many of them.

Whatever it was, it happened to him. And it wasn't the first time with Samantha. Coming right up to the target, his engines failed. And he couldn't help feeling it was all something to do with Craddock, and Scott fancying her and her fancying Scott.

The following day, Colonel Craddock took a calculated decision. It was nothing to do with Operations, but everything to do with the Base. On the surface frivolous, it was highly important. Beside up-to-date information from higher authority, he had monitored every news report, studied the local papers, been in frequent conference with Naylor and sought advice from Jarman who was probably the best interpreter of local feeling.

On the strength of all that, the seemingly frivolous decision was that the dance should go ahead, despite the Brit's anti-American sentiments.

'Aren't you tempting providence?' Maxine asked him when he sought her aid over dinner that night.

'If by providence you mean his Lordship,' Craddock gave a faint smile to show that what wasn't a joke was one. His Lordship had phoned Maxine twice since the meeting about arrangements for the Hunt, a fact he found himself simultaneously deploring and applauding. He was using his wife for the sake of the Base. He felt less of a man for it.

'I didn't,' she said tersely.

'But if you didn't, reckon maybe I *did*! He's the first one we've got to get here. Then his mother. Then as many of the Brits as we can. The Brits are snobs. They follow where his Lordship leads.'

'What I meant was it's too soon. The whole goddamned lot might decide to boycott it.'

'There are always those that won't.'

'I guess you're right.' She waited till Jarman had cleared away the pudding plates. 'So I'm to nobble the Haddingtons.'

'You're to use your good offices.'

She gave a derisive curl of her lips. He could never be quite sure with Maxine. Over the last week, she had suffered almost as much as he had. Sharon had been a pain in the ass with her pious phone calls about how the campus pundits had reacted to the Hammadaz raid. There'd been a whole lot of grief on the Base, and she and Helen Mansell and the Padre had the job of giving what comfort they could. Maxine was good at that. She was a warm human person underneath. But instead of the shared grief bringing them together, it seemed to have turned Maxine away from him. Made her resentful of him and the Air Force.

'I'll try,' she said shortly. 'Charles will come. His mother won't. Who else?'

They went through the list over coffee, Jarman flitting between them, eyeing them closely, keeping silent till spoken to, then replying with carefully thought-out decisiveness. The Chairman of the Council, Muggeridge, wouldn't come, but his deputy would, the local newspaper editor would. On balance the Member of Parliament wouldn't dare. On the other hand, he wouldn't dare to refuse. So Parliamentary business would keep him in Westminster. The Rector would come, the pub keeper, the tradesmen, led by Mr Whittaker . . .

The furore was dying down. The public soon forgot. Self-interest largely dictated their opinions. But they must cast their net wide.

The net was not only cast wide, but the budget was made even wider. No expense was to be spared. But despite its lavishness, it wasn't to be a victory dance or a celebration dance, that certainly would get up British noses. And to avoid being either of those it was in the end called, at Squadron Leader Naylor's suggestion, by a good Anglo-Saxon title that they all could identify with: a Harvest Home Ball. The date was set for the first Saturday in the month.

'A Harvest Home Ball,' Lady Haddington said, studying her

invitation through a magnifying glass. 'I hope they don't reap a bitter harvest.'

'Oh, Mother! For heaven's sake, we've had enough doom and gloom. They only did what they had to do. And there haven't been any terrorist reprisals.'

'*So far.*'

'All right, Mother, *so far.*'

'Nevertheless, *I* shan't go.'

He clicked his tongue with exaggerated despair, but he didn't try to persuade her. Frankly, he preferred to go on his own. Despite her failing eyesight, she was altogether too observant, and despite her failing memory, she remembered too many of his unhappy loves.

'I expect you will be missed, but I've no doubt there will be plenty of others only too willing to accept.'

In fact, he was for once right. A variety of motives sucked the British into the Base that night. Rumour had spread that it was to be a fabulous party. Though flowers were regularly flown in from the States, a huge order had been given to the local florist. Though pastrycooks in the Officers' Mess were first class, the local baker was asked to produce batches of *vol-au-vents* and rolls and cheese straws, the butcher several haunches of beef and a dozen legs of pork for the cold buffet. So the patronage and the money were really spread around, and with all those orders went invitations to attend.

For mixed reasons, Harriet accepted Ames's invitation. She liked him. She could talk to him. She felt he needed friendship. She felt sorry for him. She felt underneath the highly trained brain-programmed youngster was a man of integrity. And, more frivolously, she was curious to see inside this great wen on the British landscape, and more curious still to see how the Yanks went about their expensive PR exercise.

That was undoubtedly an exercise the Yanks did well. A security pass was issued with her formal invitation. It was examined at the gate by the immaculate white-gloved corporal guard, who waved her through with a salute and a, 'Have a good evening, ma'am.'

Ames was waiting for her outside the Mess, lined up with other officers waiting to claim their women. In blue and silver Mess dress, his face flushed, his eyes expectant, he looked like the lead in an old-fashioned romantic musical. Behind him the fairy lamps outlined the squat structure of the Mess, pink light and the throb of syrupy syncopated dance music flooded out through the uncurtained window.

And behind all that, the dark curves of the hardened aircraft shelters, housing their black monsters, and the hillocks like ancient tumuli of the bomb dumps, housing God knew what, all stark silhouettes, now cardboard theatrical cut-outs against the fading evening sky.

The contrast made her shiver. She shouldn't have come. Or if she came, she shouldn't think like that. They should have a notice over the gate, a paraphrase of the one over the Styx, ABANDON THOUGHT ALL YE WHO ENTER HERE.

She almost turned and ran back to her car. Then the lead in the million dollar musical, who had the voice of Milton Ames, stepped forward.

'You look so beautiful,' he said and with abashed sincerity took her arm, leading her inside and on-stage.

She abandoned herself to the lavish production. Perhaps at midnight she would wake up, lose her glass slipper, return to rags and rational thought, but meantime everyone from the Colonel and his lovely lady downwards, smiled. Everybody welcomed. The music was lovely, the flowers everywhere were lovely, Ames was rather lovely, *she* felt lovely.

But the magic of the dance began to fade before the clock chimed twelve.

Ryan and Samantha arrived late. Samantha couldn't make up her mind which dress she should wear. At nine o'clock they'd got as far as their front door with her wearing a white satin outfit with a skirt like a half inflated parachute, when she'd changed her mind, gone back upstairs and changed into red silk with a great big bow on her backside that made her look like one of those dolls you shoot for on the Coney Island rifle ranges. She took as long to change from the white to the red as it would take the fitters to do a bloody engine change.

When he told her so, they had a row. About the fifteenth to date since she'd come over. Only this was a real mean one. And she'd ended it up by saying if he didn't think her well worth waiting for, Jonny would. He *loved* her in red.

Scott was not however the first son-of-a-bitch that Ryan saw when they arrived. The first they had to greet, of course, was Craddock.

It was clear to Ryan that the Colonel wasn't averse to Samantha either. He held her hand to the count of twenty-five.

'And how are you settling in over here, Mrs Ryan?'

'Oh, all right, I guess.' She looked up at Craddock all big eyes and baby face and talking in that little voice she used to reserve for him, of a girl intimidated by so much masculine vitality. 'A bit homesick, maybe.'

Maxine chimed in to urge her to join the officers' wives' club (some hope of that) and murmured *she* had a daughter of Samantha's age at College in the States. She knew how homesick she must feel. Then Craddock released Samantha's hand. Ryan gave him a stiff bow, and he and Samantha submerged themselves in the multicoloured sea of dancers.

That way, he almost collided with the son-of-a-bitch, Ames. Christ! He'd been right to be mighty wary of Ames. There he was, dancing with Ryan's cast-off girl. And not just that. He was hugging her pretty close, and she was looking all right. Put side by side in a beauty contest with Samantha, the little nurse might just have had the edge. Her bare shoulders were smooth and touchable. Her dress had that certain something Samantha's lacked.

At the end of that dance, Samantha said she wanted to renew her friendship with the squadron boys. Which of course meant Scott. He was talking to the medico, the tight-assed one with the frosty blue eyes and the buttoned-up lips. Scott would get no joy there, and he was most likely just killing time with her till he could home in on Samantha.

Or she on him. Samantha gave a little squeak of pleasure when she saw Scott, rustled over and put her hand through his arm.

'Hi.'

He turned. 'Hi, Samantha.'

'Aren't you going to introduce your friend, Jonny?' She smiled winningly at Helen Mansell. 'Yes, I guessed that's who you were,' she went on, when introductions had been effected. 'I've heard so much about you, Helen. I may call you Helen, mayn't I? Say, we're not intruding or anything are we? But well . . .' she then said something that made Ryan's blood turn first to ice, then to a boiling real red rage '. . . I guess some time I'd like to come to your wives' sessions. Your *counselling* sessions.'

She gave Dr Mansell a soulful little girl lost look which somehow managed to include Scott.

'Do that,' Helen Mansell smiled encouragingly. 'I'd be delighted.'

They would *all* be delighted, Ryan thought. It didn't take much imagination to hear Samantha spilling it all out. Their marital difficulties. *His* difficulties. Christ! It'd be all round the Base. The Ace of the Base who couldn't.

He had a good mind to whisk her off home before her venomous little tongue did any more damage, and was grabbing her arm preparatory to making their exit, when over came Craddock, to make a bad situation worse.

He wasn't, as Ryan and also Samantha first supposed, making for Samantha. Ryan's scowl was wasted, so was the demure lowering of Samantha's eyes, and her greedy expectant little smile.

'Excuse me, Mrs Ryan . . . gentlemen . . .' The Colonel stretched out a hand towards the frosty-eyed medico, and lo and behold, a miracle. The frosty eyes melted, the mouth unbuttoned. A-ha!

'May I have this dance, Helen?'

'I'd like that.' Even her voice had melted. She slid into his arms like a hand into a glove. And thereby, most likely, hung a tale. Hand in glove the two of them. Any psychological information Dr Mansell picked up, no doubt went direct to Craddock, the cunning chickenshit! Anything Samantha spread around, likewise!

Then Scott really did the dirty on him. While Ryan was watching the Colonel and Dr Mansell pirouetting around, Scott had gotten Samantha's hand and led her on to the floor.

After that, the screw tightened. When the dance finished Scott, the bastard, didn't bring Samantha back. Though Ryan stood on tiptoe he couldn't see them anywhere in the goddamned ballroom. Instead, the Colonel escorted Dr Mansell over to him as if they were in the same party. He bowed and left her with him.

Ryan considered just bolting off and leaving her. But as if she was a bloody mind-reader, she put a hand on his arm and asked if he would fetch her a drink.

'A drink?' He repeated her request mindlessly. 'A drink?'

'Anything. Fruit cup if they have it. Otherwise anything.'

And when he returned, almost in the same breath as she thanked him, she asked him about Samantha.

'Samantha?' Again he repeated her question foolishly.

'How is she settling?' After that, did he think she needed counselling? Was she homesick? She was very young, wasn't she?

He just couldn't take any more of it. He mumbled something

about finding Samantha. Then he pushed his way through the dancers, searching for her. In and out of the red and green and blue spotlights, his anger and embarrassment growing. At one point, Dief's wife peered over Dief's shoulder and asked him, 'Is everything OK, Rod?'

Ames's guilty face swam into a green spotlight. He was still hugging the nurse close, as if she was a bloody prize he'd won. No, he hadn't seen Samantha. Which wasn't surprising since he was dancing with his eyes half closed. Squadron Leader Naylor hadn't seen her either, but Mrs Naylor who was nobody's fool said she thought she'd seen Samantha going outside to cool off.

Jesus Christ! Cool off! Come on hot, more like!

He found the pair of them right outside the circle of the Mess lights. He homed on them by her bloody red-for-danger dress.

She had her arms locked round Scott's neck, and if his weren't round her, it was a technicality. They must just have been.

To Scott, Ryan's appearance was the last and final straw. He had listened reluctantly to Samantha's gripes about her husband, reckoning it would do her good to get it off her chest. He had no way of knowing if what she said was true or false. He didn't trust Samantha any more than he trusted Ryan. But Jeezus, it had him worried. If what she told him was true, Ryan was more than half way to the funny farm. A menace to fly with.

Then just as the silly kid put her arms round his neck, out comes Ryan breathing murder.

'You bastard!' Ryan rushed right up and before Samantha had time to drop her hands, he punched Scott on the jaw. Then he broke Samantha's hold with a savage sideways jerk of the elbow, which sent her whimpering backwards.

While Scott rubbed his bruised jaw, Ryan danced in front of him like a dervish, his face contorted.

Scott tried desperately to take a tight hold on himself and his temper. His hands itched to wring Ryan's neck. Talk about seeing red! He could see the angry blood pounding behind his eyes, feel the adrenalin surging through his body. He clenched his fists till the nails bit into the palms.

He was nearly a head taller than Ryan. Once he started, he would give Ryan the thrashing of his life. And then they'd both get a court martial. Right then, thrashing Ryan, better still, half killing him, looked worth the consequences. But it wasn't. He was a career officer. Like a drowning man he saw not the past, but his future prospects rushing away in front of his eyes.

Not given, like Glenn, to prayer, he yelled, 'Godalmighty! Christ!' He shoved his bruised face into Ryan's. 'Got a bloody good mind to thrash you and to hell with it!'

'Try! Just *try*, Jonny boy!'

Ryan danced a couple of backward paces. His right hand flicked inside his jacket to his belt and out again. He held it up like a conjurer. And there was the knife. The sacred knife! His father's knife, catching a murderous glitter from the Mess lights behind.

Christ almighty!

'Don't be so bloody crazy, Ryan.'

'Try! Just *try*! Thrash me, you said! C'mon! *C'mon*!' He gave a quick glance over his shoulder. 'Samantha's scarpered. There's no one to see. No witnesses. C'mon.' He beckoned with the finger of his free hand. 'Or are you yellow as well?'

A light wind rustled among the shrubs. Cars changed gear along the main camp road. From Hush House came the sound of an F-115 engine run up. The sickly sweet music throbbed from the Mess. But above all those sounds, Scott could hear Ryan's heavy breathing and the slugging hammer of his own heart.

Then a new sound. High heeled footsteps crossing the strip of tarmac in front of the Mess. Behind them Helen Mansell's voice, 'Are you there, Jonny?'

Like whipping off a mask, Ryan's expression instantly changed. The knife disappeared inside Ryan's jacket, so quickly Scott almost wondered if it had ever been there. Ryan folded his arms across his chest, regarding Scott blankly as if nothing had happened.

Scott succeeded in keeping his voice steady. But he could only manage the single syllable, 'Yep.'

'It's supper, Jonny.' She sounded mildly exasperated. 'You were going to take me in.'

Samantha, the bloody cause of it all, appeared from behind the shrubbery, and put her arm trustingly and admiringly through Ryan's arm. 'Come on, Rod. I'm hungry!'

Scott followed them over.

Christ, he was thinking, wondering how much, if any, he should tell Helen; one of us is going crazy. One of us has got combat fatigue or whatever. I sure hope it's Ryan!

Eighteen

'Combat fatigue, Cas?'

'Could be, sir.'

'You're crazy, Cas! You hear me? Plumb crazy. Young Ryan's at the top of the climb. The peak.' The General's voice burst loud and clear and incredulous over the NATO scrambler.

'I'm only suggesting rest, sir.'

'Rest! *Only rest*, he says! Rest is for old dogs like you and me, Cas!'

Vosper laughed heartily at his little threat disguised as a joke.

Caspar Craddock gritted his teeth. Jeezus, he more than half wished he hadn't brought up the subject. Maybe Ryan was his, Craddock's, Achilles heel. Maybe he couldn't think straight about him.

'Did Ryan *ask* for a rest, Cas?'

'No, sir.'

'Hell then, Cas! There's your goddamned answer. End of message!'

A pause. Craddock said nothing.

'But what made you sail that crazy kite, Cas? I'm curious. Ryan's goin' to get the Medal of Honour, same as his father. He's the USAF flavour of the month. So what the hell? Is he hitting the bottle?'

'No, sir.' Craddock spoke slowly, carefully, chasing the words like he chased that nebulous sixth sense of coming doom. 'But I reckon he's showing signs of tension.'

'Tension! Tension! Jeezus, man! He couldn't bloody well fly without *tension*! Christ almighty, Cas! You know that. Any pilot knows that! You fly with your balls.' A long loud laugh. Then as if enlightenment dawned. 'Say, Cas . . . that pretty young Major you gotten there?'

'Do you mean Major Mansell?'

'Yeah. *Her*! Her and her P-sychology.' He separated the P from the s to make a derisive syllable. 'She bin putting her oar in a bit too far?'

'I don't reckon so, sir. But she *is* concerned with aircrew stress.'

'Sure she is, Cas.'

'And we consult, naturally.'

'And I don't blame you, Cas! So would I in your shoes! Christ almighty, in our day they didn't have 'em like that, did they? Remember those son-of-a-bitch shrinks? Jeezus! It was get-up-there-and-fly-you-bastard! They didn't hold your hand and ask if you was tired!'

'Neither does Major Mansell.'

'Naw-naw, course she doesn't, Cas! Only kidding! Guess she's a goddamned fine doctor. The best. Wouldn't have made Major if she hadn't bin. Not in *my* Command.'

'Exactly, sir.'

'But she's a *woman*, Cas. And women are softer'n us.'

'I'm not sure you're right, sir.'

Craddock frowned at himself . . . it was never wise to contradict the General. But that had to be said. He wished Helen herself had been more explicit. She'd mentioned a row between Scott and Ryan at the dance. It hadn't come to blows as far as she knew. But Ryan was getting edgy – that much Craddock could see for himself. There were other factors. The arrival of Ryan's wife had not been an unmitigated blessing – and though his relationship with Ames had improved, it was an up and down one, lacking stability. Helen would talk to Samantha if Samantha presented herself as promised, and some time she'd like to run the psychological ruler over Ryan.

'It's more a gut feeling I have, sir,' Craddock went on.

And even that for chrissake he wasn't sure of. Not unless memory was stored in the gut. Memory and that ominous sense of history repeating itself. A prickling at the back of the neck. The sins of the father inherited by the son. After all, if Helen had told him her piece on Ryan about any other pilot on the squadron, would he have suggested rest? Wasn't his own judgment distorted? Pre-set against Ryan from the start? Hadn't the past bit too deep into him?

'Don't go much on gut feeling myself, Cas,' the General snorted dismissively. 'Too much like good old-fashioned bellyache. Us old warhorses just can't take these youngsters doing what we can't do, eh?'

'Possibly, sir.' He nearly reminded the General that he at least was still MR, but he managed to bite his tongue.

'In any case, we can't do without Ryan or any of 'em, this awhile. We got Operation Sabretooth coming up. NATO's gonna make this Navy and Air Force exercise a real cracker. A fitting follow-up to what your boys did to Hammadaz! As I said to my good friend, the Air Sec,' General Vosper's tone became sunnier and sweeter and more mendacious, 'I was real proud of the Sixth TFS. I told you he had a message from the President?'

'Yes, sir, you did.'

'He praised you on two counts, Cas. Two. The way that raid had gone. *And* the way you handled the Brits afterwards.'

'Thank you, sir.'

'Thank *him*, Cas! Mr President has his eye on you. Same as I have. He said Caspar Craddock sure can cut the mustard. The President's word, Cas! And on Sabretooth we're really gonna show how you cut it. We're gonna show the flag. The Stars and Stripes. The Cold War sure isn't over yet, Cas. An' we're gonna do a whole lot better'n our so-called NATO allies. We'll sink the attack ships. We'll shoot the Aggressor craft out of the skies. An' what skies! You'll be getting the Battle Orders through any day now. But I can tell you the zone. Glasnost to you, Ivan! Right up the Ruskies' icy backside!'

'The Arctic, sir?'

'Sure! Knew that would please you, Cas. Well, we'll be talking about it.' He laughed heartily. 'Jest about as often as you talk to that pretty shrink of yours about overworked pilots!'

'I'll look forward to it, sir.'

'And how's that pretty wife of yours? Mavis? Millicent . . .'

'Maxine.'

'Yeah, Maxine.'

'Maxine is fine, thank you, sir. Never better.'

Never better, and maybe never worse. With, he might have added, the look in her eye and spring in her step of a woman who knows another man wants her. But with something gone from her. A tenderness, a warmth, that now he came to think of it had probably been a long time gone.

Craddock wondered how many of his officers, how many of the Brits had noticed Haddington dancing with her, gazing down into her face with that flattering, cherishing look it must have taken him God knew how many affairs to perfect. Was Maxine dumb enough to fall for that? Apart from Mrs Naylor and the wife of the local newspaper owner, Lord Haddington had danced with no one else. And when he wasn't dancing with Maxine, he was watching her, with that small prideful smile, as if she were some valuable oil painting he was adding to the Haddington collection.

'Well,' Maxine had demanded when they got back home. 'How did I do?'

Her eyes were luminous with unshed tears he might have thought, except that their expression was challenging, almost hostile.

'How did you do on *what*?'

'On cementing Anglo-American relations.'

He gave her a long, keen, steady look. She met his look defiantly. It was as if, for all her poise and elegance, she was a naughty child, a child demanding that he do something, show her he minded, punish her even. But then, all women, they told him, were children. And though part of him wanted to show her just how much he minded and yes, punish her, he couldn't. The last thing he wanted right then was a scene, or any emotion, come to that. He had enough on his plate.

'I think the whole thing went very well.'

The luminous light had seemed to die in her eyes. 'Glad you were pleased, Colonel.' She had put her right hand to her head in a mock salute, and gone up to bed.

'Beautiful woman, your wife!' Vosper said warmly. 'Got class. You take care of her now! Good wives don't grow on trees!'

'Certainly don't, sir.'

'And keep that Major . . . Major . . .'

'Mansell, sir?'

'Yes, her! Make her keep her goddamned oar out! Women don't understand, Cas. Action's a man's thing. A man's prerogative, as the wise men say. Always has bin. A man's gotta do what a man's gotta do. Women . . .' he blew a rude derisive sound down the line which the scrambler made ruder still. 'They don't realise. With youngsters like Ryan . . . it's like the old saying, Cas, the more you fly 'em, the better they be!'

Nineteen

Caspar was flying them all right. And the more he flew those boys, the further did he go away from her and the less did he see. Four days after the Ball, Maxine woke to the sound of Caspar's five-thirty alarm.

'Go back to sleep,' he touched her shoulder, as he padded unseeingly past that dark shadow on the wardrobe door and through into the bathroom.

'There's nothing for you to do,' he said irritably, when he emerged, passing the shadow again. 'Jarman's left everything ready.'

Jarman sure had left everything ready. Clean shirt and underwear laid out, uniform pressed, shoes polished, a light breakfast set downstairs. But today he had left something else ready which Caspar had forgotten about, not seen or not chosen to see.

Her hunting gear.

Before she had gone to bed last night, Maxine had hooked the hanger over the beading on the wardrobe door. So there the dark shadow hung, the new black jacket, the white stock, the fine cord jodhpurs, a headless ghost. Like something hanging from that old gibbet at Haddington crossroads, telling Cas, what? Here hangs a neglected wife? A disappointed woman seeing a man who wasn't there? Or was it to tell him that one of these days *she* might be the one to go away? And why not? Leave him, like Sharon had said? Start again.

Then bending over to kiss her goodbye, Cas elected to remember. 'Enjoy the Hunt, darling.'

She caught his hand. 'You don't mind?' She studied his face. She willed him to mind.

He smiled thinly. 'Should I?'

'No.'

'There you are then.' He straightened and stared derisively for a moment at the jacket and jodhpurs.

'If that's what you reckon you'll enjoy.' He crossed to the door, opened it. 'Give my regards to the Haddingtons. And take care now.'

She heard his brisk step down the stairs, felt his eagerness to be off. Never the one to be overly ambitious, Cas was now scenting real success, reaching for the big one that Vosper was dangling before his eyes.

He would no doubt tell himself he was doing it all for her. Men always did. But how could it be for her, when it cut them apart?

She dozed a little after the front door closed behind him, and the noise of his car engine died away. But an hour later, the now regular dawn take-off of the F-115's began. One after another, shattering the sky and everything beneath it, as Cas and Vosper continued to fly the boys.

She had showered and dressed, all but the stock and boots, by the time Jarman brought up her tea tray.

'Madam,' he elected to be quite bowled over by her appearance, 'you look exactly to the manor born.'

'Well, I don't feel it, Jarman. Jeans and sneakers is more my sort of riding.'

He watched her struggling with the stock. 'If you'll allow me, madam.'

She studied his face, small lips pursed in concentration, as he flipped one end of the stock over the other. What went on behind that composed face, that faintly furrowed forehead, behind the blank eyes?

'I always tied the Duke's stock, madam. I was better than his valet, his Grace was kind enough to say.'

Jarman spoke affectionately of his employers, and of course of his mother. But had he ever loved anyone else beside her, Maxine wondered?

'Did you ever think of getting married, Jarman?'

The forehead furrows deepened, the small lips tightened. 'No, madam,' Jarman sounded outraged. 'It would have interfered with my work.'

And thereby hangs a tale for all mankind, Maxine thought, but didn't say aloud.

'I would suggest, madam,' Jarman said, a little irritated by her enquiry (even the nicest and best Americans had very little *savoir faire*), 'that you let me help you on with your boots downstairs. We'll allow plenty of time. The boots are new.'

They were not only new, but the leather felt like iron. But finally Maxine was shod and her bright hair scooped up into a net. She looked, the mirror and Jarman's eyes both told her, stunningly beautiful. The severity of black and white complemented her colouring, the well cut jacket and jodhpurs set off her figure. But more than that, they changed her, gave her a new exciting identity. Now it was Jarman's turn to look enquiringly into Maxine's face. 'Lord Haddington promised you a quiet mount?'

'Oh, sure, but it's kind of you to worry, Jarman.'

He essayed the airing of one more worry. 'In England, madam, riding is often reckoned to be conducive to . . .' but at that point his usual flow of *mots-justes* dried up. He couldn't think of the right word. Promiscuity was far too strong, flirtation was too weak.

It was a peculiar warm animal easement between the sexes, a gaminess, a randiness, well recognised by his previous employer, but hard to explain to this American lady with the lovely haggard face and yearning, innocent eyes. So he ended up saying '. . . good health. Conducive to good health.'

She smiled. 'Sure it is. Just so long as you don't fall off, I guess.'

He smiled with her. 'You won't do that, madam.' He might have added a warning against falling for Lord Haddington's advances. But he knew his place.

Maxine waved at him as he stood framed in the doorway, and then pressed her booted foot on the accelerator and headed for what suddenly seemed like freedom, pausing to show her plastic at the gate and then out and turning left down the straight unbroken stretch of road.

It was a frosty morning, which Charles Haddington had told her he was going to pray for. So the ground would be crisp underfoot and the scent would hang. He certainly did better with his prayers than the Quaker woman whom this time she had remembered to avoid. The twiggy hedges on either side were rimed in sparkling frost, the verge grass whitened, and icy puddles crunched under her tyres. The cold air through the open car window, the clear sky, the brilliant sunlight filled her lungs, compounded her feeling of escape, of something new beginning, of youth recaptured.

Like that, escaped from the Cage, she had the courage to examine the new worry, the new one that till now she hadn't dared to admit to herself. That it wasn't just Cas's dedication to his work that was separating them, that there was in fact, another woman.

And that woman had to be Helen Mansell. Anyone on the Base would likely say the same.

A month ago, a couple of weeks ago, Maxine would have maybe dismissed that idea. But not now. Lately she'd begun to realise just how much time they spent together. Just how much he relied on her. Just how much he liked her. Just how much they shared that concept of Air Force duty, above all else. In her own way, Helen Mansell was *right* for him.

An F-115 taking off right over the road shattered her thoughts. The noise set her teeth on edge. She watched the driver of an oncoming lorry laden with beets, shake his fist up at the reverberating sky. They exchanged sympathetic smiles as they passed. In a field on her right a flock of sheep were dashing around dementedly. And just here, where the cottages of Haddington village began, the posters were out, and streamers and bunting hung from upper windows only not with 'Merry Christmas', or 'Happy Thanksgiving' or, like in Greece, with 'Christ is Risen'.

Just 'Yanks Go Home'.

Maxine didn't know whether to laugh or cry or what. All she knew was to tread harder on the accelerator and get as fast as possible through the High Street to the civilisation of Haddington Hall.

On a sunlit frosty morning, it was enough to soothe the most jangled nerves. The Virginia creeper on the walls was as red as north American maples. The stone urns and the flower beds were full of chrysanthemums and winter flowering pansies.

But the colour of brickwork, of stone, and creeper and leaves and flowers, were stolen by the assembled company. Fifteen or twenty beautiful horses, bays and greys and chestnuts, their coats brushed to velvet, leather gleaming, attended by grooms in livery, two dozen pairs of hounds with the whippers-in, florid faced riders, several formidable women riding side saddle, two rosy-faced teenagers on short fat ponies, and men in hunting pink. The air was full of the snuffle and snort of horses, the ring of hooves, the jingle of bridles, the husky yapping of hounds, and voices and laughter. So much laughter. It seemed so long since Cas and she had laughed.

As she brought the car to a halt, she spotted Charles Haddington on his big black deep-chested gelding, and immediately he courteously detached himself from his companions and rode over. He jumped down lightly and opened the door for her.

He looked very splendid. The hunting gear became him as the Air Force uniform became Cas. And as MFH, he was as much in command here as Cas at the Base. In command, but aware of her and concerned for her. That was the difference.

'You look absolutely marvellous, Maxine.' He put his hands on her shoulders and playfully lifted her bowler hat by the rim, pushed it to the back of her head to kiss her cheek. 'Leave the car there. Come and meet Diana.' He put his hand under her elbow, and with the other, led the black gelding to where a groom was holding a grey mare. She was about fifteen hands, fine boned, with full eyes and a dished, almost pony head.

Maxine let her snuffle her fingers. 'She has a kind face.'

'Kind? Of course she's kind, my dear. Would I mount you on anything else?' Charles put his hand on her arm. 'And perfect manners. Fast. But sure-footed.'

He looked Maxine over as he listed the mare's attributes, making it sound as if they were hers. 'In fact, admirably suited to you, Maxine. Let me give you a leg up.'

He clasped his hands together for her foothold, gently patting her thigh as she swung her leg over. With relief she found her joints still supple, and though the saddle was different, it was good to feel a horse's warm body under her calves again.

'Caspar sent his regards to you and your mother,' Maxine said, catching Lady Haddington's eye and waving as the old lady stood in the doorway watching them all.

'How kind! What a splendid fellow he is!' Charles said condescendingly. 'Now come along and meet some of our friends.'

They all seemed to talk the same way. Gargly, effusive yet condescending. 'Delighted to meet you. The American Air Force Commander's wife, eh? Ah, now! He's the fellah that's giving us all this stick. No sleep for Haddington. Deafened *me*, for one. What was that you said? NATO. Their orders? NATO eh? Mmmm. I see.' They didn't see at all, of course. But they supported the government and the government supported NATO, so the subject of noise was dropped for the moment. They asked her how she liked England and murmured, 'So glad,' before she had time to answer.

But Charles was at her side. The stirrup cup was delicious. Hot and potent, heavily laced with brandy. She took another from the proffered silver tray. She felt her nervousness, her worries, her inhibitions, melting away.

Then Charles put the horn to his lips, the whippers-in gathered the hounds and he led the way down the drive, with Maxine at his side. It was like living in another time, another dimension, another world. She felt regal, respected, maybe even loved. At the lodge gates a group of villagers were waiting. Some of the men doffed their caps to his Lordship, but it was all spoiled by a group of youngsters of about Sharon's age who suddenly pushed their way to the front bearing a banner. At least it didn't say 'Yanks Go Home', but it did say 'Ban Hunting. Killing isn't sport'.

Charles behaved impeccably. Through clenched teeth, he said, 'Take no notice, Maxine. Ride on.' He put a hand on her horse's bridle ready to steady it, and kept his eyes fixed ahead as if the protesters didn't exist.

'Don't look round, Maxine!' Charles said. But her head was already turned. As the tide of riders swept past them, the kids looked curiously forlorn. One of them, a girl in an anorak with tousled hair, shouted at Maxine, 'Why? Why d'you do it?' She came running alongside them, as if sensing a weak link in the heavily armoured chain, holding up her puckered accusing face, scowling like Sharon. 'Why d'you want to kill something?'

'Trot!' Lord Haddington bade Maxine tersely, and pressed his horse's flanks.

Gently, Maxine pressed her heels in. The shouting girl was left far behind. The road narrowed to a winding lane. The question hung unanswered. Why? For so many things, why?

'That's what happens when you disobey orders,' Charles chided, smiling an indulgent strong-man-to-little-woman smile.

'At least they weren't shouting "Yanks go home",' Maxine said.

'No.' Lord Haddington's expression became exaggeratedly grave, 'And don't you ever do that.'

'Go home?'

'By that I mean, my dear, go back to America.'

'We'll go back one day.'

'Don't, Maxine! Just when I've discovered you. Don't!'

They were trotting now through an avenue of trees. A few dead leaves still clung to the almost bare branches, just enough to send a dappling of moving sunlight and quivering shadow over the frost bleached road. The horses' breath hung white in the cold air. Sounds carried with startling clarity. The chime of the horses' hooves, the baying of the forward hounds, the snort of horses, the song of birds. It was all beautiful, immediate, exciting, the stuff of dreams. A picture book picture gilded with romance.

'Caspar can't stay here indefinitely.'

'I didn't say anything about Caspar! God forbid!' He turned to her with deliberate meaning.

'Caspar and I . . .' she began to say but he didn't want to hear. He was standing in the saddle squinting forward. The hounds were well ahead of them now, leaping one after the other over a low wooden fence.

He nodded towards the fence. 'Does that daunt you?' Somehow he made it sound as if it wasn't the fence he was talking about, but Caspar and her and him.

'No. It's easy.'

'Good girl! I'll take it first then. Just follow me, and don't rush it.'

'I won't.' She watched him take the fence with throwaway ease, then move aside to see her safely over.

Neither of them need have worried, Maxine didn't have to do anything but keep her butt on the saddle. The mare had springs in her feet – she followed the big black gelding daintily and effortlessly.

He threw a glance at the rest of the field shouting, laughing, thundering behind them. 'Answer me something,' he whispered as Maxine and he cantered to the front again.

'What?'

'Why are all other women like sacks of potatoes?'

Then he was off after the hounds, jerking his head for her to follow. The pack now were yelping, noses to the shallow tussocky hillside, sterns erect and waving. The Hunt was in full cry. The horn sounded.

A View.

Excitement swept Maxine forward like nothing she had known in years. Over ditches, with mud clods flying from their hooves, over fences, thundering across fields after the streaking hounds, splashing through shallow streams, her heart racing, her backside smacking up and down against the saddle, her whole body throbbing with sheer animal excitement.

When the hounds found, and the hunting horn sounded, Maxine felt nothing but wild exultation. The culmination. The orgasm. She followed Charles over a five-bar gate that gave on to a long stretch of winter-browned moorland. Charles reined in to watch and motioned Maxine to do the same. The fox had been flushed out of a spinney, and, 'There!' She shouted the word aloud and as quickly clamped her mouth shut.

Up the slight slope of the moorland, low to the ground hardly taller than the scrubby sorrel and ragwort, ran a small red-brown desperate animal, less than two hundred yards ahead of the pack.

'It's so . . .' Maxine began but she wasn't sure what she wanted to say. So small, so pathetic, so frightened, so exhausted, so wanting to live. Was this the culmination, this the climax, of all that wild and wonderful and powerful chase? Did all of *them* hunt *this*? Suddenly the bright day went hideously wrong.

The whole field now was behind them, watching with reverence. Horses were lathered, riders mud-splashed. The rich smell of horse mingled with the scent of crushed grass. The horses' coats steamed as they crowded together.

The gap between the small fox and the large hounds narrowed. Maxine turned and clutched Charles's arm. 'Do something! For chrissake, do something!'

He glanced at her, bemused.

'Do . . .' she began to say again. But the gap had closed. There came the most godawful screams of an animal torn limb from limb, the yelps and screams of its assailants, and the inhuman grunts and shouts of the human watchers.

Maxine felt the blood drain from her head. Reality shimmered like landscape in a heat haze. She thought for the first time in her life she was going to faint. All the riders were in a circle now. The mare had moved forward without the touch of Maxine's hand or heels. Beside her, Charles was too absorbed, too part of the grisly scene to notice either her pallor or her silence.

As though it were someone else watching, she saw him jump down and walk triumphantly towards the hounds. A huntsman was retrieving what looked like a scrap of sodden red fabric. He handed it to Charles who held it aloft, to the cheers of the circle.

Then he walked towards the two youngsters mounted on those little fat ponies, and solemnly wiped the red rag over their foreheads. Anaesthetised by a sense of unreality, Maxine saw him coming back toward her, smiling an odd smile, like the bearer of gifts.

Solemnly, ritualistically, he bowed in front of her. Then he straightened, still smiling, his eyes ardent. His right hand came forward. Now she saw what the red rag was. A blood-sodden fox's brush.

'For you, Maxine,' he said ringingly, 'with the compliments of the Haddington Hunt.'

She recoiled with immediate and violent revulsion. The other riders had begun to clap as if she were being awarded an honour. In a moment of frozen horror, she saw their red distorted Alice-in-Wonderland faces. Then with a desperate heave she backed the mare, wrenched round the bridle, caught a last glimpse of the Alice-in-Wonderland faces now registering outrage, and went galloping away across the moorland, not guiding the poor animal, just begging it to get the hell out of here.

She was cantering through a little woodland path when Charles caught up with her. Maxine was keeping her head low under trailing branches. The mare was blowing and he rode for a while in silence beside her. Then he said quietly, 'Ease her up, Maxine! She's had a hard day. Time to rest!'

He pulled up, dismounted, and threw his reins to the gelding which immediately began to lip at the last shoots of grass among the curls of bracken. He held out his arm for Maxine to dismount and still full of revulsion for the Hunt, and for him, she fell into his arms, burst into tears, and let him clasp her tightly to him, as if that were the safest place on earth.

It was a catharsis, as violent and total as the orgasm of the Found, and it was for many things: for the fox, for the bestiality of the Hunt, for the cruel Alice-in-Wonderland faces, for the protesters, for the girl who scowled like Sharon and for Sharon herself. For Jennie and the baby, for the Hammadaz babies torn like the fox in the American raid, for Gruber and Barlow and Robinson, for the whole mixed up bloody world. But most of all, selfishly maybe, for Cas and her.

Beneath all that weight of misery, revulsion receded.

Aloud, she said, 'I'm sorry. I guess I spoiled the whole goddamned day for you.'

He pulled her down on to a fallen log, cupped her face in his hands. 'On the contrary, you made my day. And Haddington Hunt history.' He kissed her almost without her noticing. 'I can always rely on you, Maxine, to be different.'

'Were the rest of them sore at me?'

'The Field?' He shook his head. 'Not sore, no.'

'What then?'

He shrugged. The right word eluded him. 'It was perfectly all right,' he said. 'They understood. Nobody minded. The British like eccentrics.'

'Not *Hunt* eccentrics.'

'I promise you. *Nobody minded.* So why cry?'

Ah, why? She clasped her hands, twisted them together. Tears still streaming down her face, she sorted through all those profound and terrible reasons for crying. The mangled fox was in every one of them. Because you could see it, touch it, hear it, feel its blood-sodden stump of a tail, you could grieve with it, and see them all.

'It's Cas,' she said at last, 'I guess he doesn't love me . . . not now. Not any more.'

Even in her distress, she noticed the quick flash of triumph in Charles Haddington's eyes. His sudden intent, alert expression.

'I wondered,' he said softly. 'Last time I saw you together, I wondered.' He paused. 'I realised all wasn't well. But you'll survive, Maxine. You're still young and beautiful.'

She shook her head. 'No.'

'Of course you'll survive, Maxine. My wife no longer loved *me*. *I've* survived. I've very happily survived. And now I realise,' he put his fingers under her chin and kissed her lips, 'it was the best thing that ever happened to me.' His mouth went round to her ear. He nibbled it gently. His hand was busy at the buttons of her jacket. But it all seemed to be happening to somebody else, while her mind scurried round, weighed, measured, mourned the problem of her and Cas.

'Had your wife found someone else?'

'Oh, yes! Don't they *always*?' Now his fingers were unfastening her shirt.

'So you reckon Cas . . . ?'

'But *of course*. Don't be naïve. A virile man . . .' he edged closer to her.

'Did you still love your wife?' She pushed his hand away, and turned his face so that she could stare searchingly into his eyes.

He smiled at her earnestness. 'Certainly *not*.'

He tried to close her mouth with his lips. She wriggled her head away and stood up. 'It's different for me. I still love Cas. I don't want to lose him. I just want to find him again.'

The truth of it surprised her, and maybe the hopelessness too.

Charles Haddington pulled a wry face and got to his feet and squinted down at her in mingled exasperation and what could well be genuine tenderness. 'Listen to the voice of experience, Maxine! That's not much good if *he* doesn't love *you*. Face facts. Especially if he's found someone else.'

Suddenly she wanted to get back to the Base more than anything else in the world. 'I don't know that he has. Not yet.'

'Yes, you do.' He gave her a leg up on to the mare. 'Of course you do.'

In almost total silence, they rode back to Haddington Hall. As they turned up the drive, he said musingly, 'That's why the helpmate of a man who presides over the most destructive force on earth shows such compassion for a fox.'

'I don't know what you mean,' she said, watching the groom hurry out to meet them and take their reins. Then she dismounted and walked to her car.

'When you find out what I mean,' he said, following her, 'I'll be here. I'll be waiting.'

He shut the car door behind her. She was halfway back to the Base before she realised she hadn't thanked him or made her apologies to his mother, and at the guard-house before she realised she didn't give a damn.

She thought the corporal guard looked at her strangely, but the need to get home was too pressing to trouble about him. Her mind was a jumble of problems and miseries. The fox no longer represented the miseries. The fox now was their wearying marriage, threatened by the Air Force and his devotion to it, women like Helen, by Sharon and by Maxine's own damned stupid attitude.

Like Charles had said he prayed for a frosty morning, Maxine now prayed that for once Cas would be home. And for once, her prayer was granted. His car stood outside. She pulled in eagerly right behind it, and ran up the short path. She had flung open the front door and rushed into the sitting room, before she realised that her jacket and shirt were still unbuttoned and that there were leaves and bracken in her hair.

Caspar's face told her. Like a man in a dream he put down the cup he was holding. Slowly she turned to look at her reflection in the oval wall mirror.

'Did you have a fall?' Cas asked her, his voice even, his expression icy but composed.

'No. Oh, *no*!' She ran her hand abstractedly through her hair, felt a small leaf crunch in her fingers. If he supposed she had had a fall, he showed no anxiety. 'I . . . er . . . it was . . . awful. The fox. It was torn apart. I hated it.'

'I guessed you would. I'll get Jarman to fix you some coffee. I've just had some.'

'You're early.'

'But I need to go back to Ops in a couple of hours.'

'Cas?' She perched on the edge of a chair, and stretched up her hand to him.

'Yes.'

'Can we talk? Can I go and shower and then us just talk?'

She searched his face for a sign. A sign that he still did care. That it wasn't too late. That the fox wasn't dead.

But his face revealed nothing. Only a chilly wariness.

'Sure. If that's what you'd like. Now I'll tell Jarman to fix that coffee.'

As she started for the stairs, she heard Cas talking to Jarman.

She was halfway up when the telephone rang. Jarman answered it. 'Of course, Major. I'll get him at once.' And then to Cas, 'Major Mansell, sir.'

'Helen!' Cas's voice was clearly audible. 'You have?' His tone changed from that of a stern stranger to that of a man speaking to a trusted confidante. 'Oh, good girl! I'll be right over.'

From the top of the staircase, Maxine heard Cas say to Jarman, 'Mrs Craddock will be showering. Tell her I'll be back within the hour.'

But he wasn't. The fox was dead.

Twenty

'So what did Samantha Ryan tell you, Helen?'

Ignoring the cup of coffee that Helen Mansell had immediately poured for him and put on her desk beside the waiting chair, Craddock sat down and came straight to the point.

'The usual things the young wives tell me when they first come over here. Married Quarter badly insulated. Poorly heated. Draughts everywhere. Tiny rooms. Brits are cold. And they're homesick.'

'Oh, so that's all!' With a sigh of relief, Craddock reached for the cup and began drinking the warm sweet coffee. 'Just the way I like it, Helen. How come you always manage to get things right?'

'I wish I did.' Particularly in the session with Mrs Ryan, she thought. She had done them both less than justice.

It had started to go wrong when Samantha had said she reckoned she'd married the wrong man. She hadn't said who the right one was, but the name of Jonathan Scott had hung unspoken in the air. And right then, Helen was the wrong person to listen to such a confession. She was surprised and disappointed in herself, that after all these years of training and experience, she could allow herself to get personally involved. All she hoped was that she hadn't shown her feelings to Samantha.

'And as far as Samantha Ryan is concerned, that isn't all.'

'There's something else?'

'Yes.'

'What?'

'Well—' she paused. 'Samantha's had everything she wanted, and sunshine too. Lots of parties. Lots of young men in her home. Everywhere she was the campus queen. She'd reckoned on the same here. But she didn't get it. The men are more interested in—'

—'airplanes.' He smiled. 'It happens all the time. I guess she'll just have to get used to it.'

She hesitated. Then she asked, 'Has Maxine gotten used to it?'

The smile left his face. The sudden directness of the question had taken him unawares. Right then, he just couldn't allow himself to think about Maxine's feelings. Nor could he contemplate what it was Maxine wanted to talk to him about.

He took such a long time to reply that at first she thought he was going to come the Wing Commander over her, and slap her down. But when he spoke, his voice was quiet and hesitant.

'I hope so. I think there are times—' he spread his hands —'but what can I do about it anyway? What can any airman do about it? Flying's his job. Part of him. Part of the man. She's got to take the whole man.'

'With this jet engine, I thee wed?'

'Helen, you're getting your tail out of line!'

'With my fuselage, I thee worship.'

A rare spasm of anger crossed his face, quickly quenched. 'I was never any good at riddles, Helen.'

'What I mean is . . . this is going to be difficult to explain, sir.'

'I'm listening.'

'Well, Samantha is a . . .' she hesitated for the right words '. . . has well developed physical appetites which her husband has difficulty satisfying.'

'Riddle solved, Helen. Message understood. No need to go on.'

'She reckons it's all this flying he's had to do.'

'They've all had a lot of flying to do. A lot of flying in the course of duty.'

'Why not give him back the rest of his interrupted honeymoon?'

'Ramstein won't wear any rest right now. I've tried it. There's a helluva big NATO exercise coming up. Any time now. Operation Sabretooth. General Vosper expects the Sixth Tactical Fighter Squadron to add to its Hammadaz laurels. Ryan was the star then, and you don't drop your best man for a big game.'

Helen said nothing. Wryly she remembered Lieutenant-Colonel Bates, her superior's remark, that if you grounded a jock for that, you'd paralyse NATO.

'Both General Vosper and Dief believe the more you fly 'em, the better they be . . . and there's a lot in that. And apart from Ryan's smartass performance when he arrived, he's kept his nose clean. He's done great things. Ace of the Base. Ace of the USAFE come to that.' He looked at her slyly, 'Wouldn't you say Jonny Scott would buy that?'

'Jocks stick together.'

There was, she had discovered, an unspoken freemasonry among the jocks, as tight as the contract which bound each AC to his wizzo. It was born of the personality of fliers, the training of them to survive by their balls and their buddies, the dangers they faced, their reliance on each other, and the mutual trust they generated. Even when they hated the guy, even when they mistrusted him, they'd glue together, go to the wall together.

She said thoughtfully, 'But there was that scrap at the dance.'

'Did you ever find out why?'

'No.'

'Who else was there?'

'Samantha.'

'Was it over her?'

Helen shook her head vigorously. 'Jonny would never fight over her!'

Craddock shot her a knowing little smile, then shrugged his shoulders. 'They'd got juiced and loosed. They'd be letting off steam.' He brushed the matter aside. 'Horseplay.'

At that point, the 'brick', the personal bleeper that all officers of his rank wore, started buzzing.

Craddock stood up and identified himself. 'Yes . . . yes? In Hard Ops. Be right over.'

He began to walk to the door. 'Thanks for telling me about Mrs Ryan, Helen. Glad it was nothing serious. She'll get used to life on the Base. Like we all do.'

'You're working too hard yourself, sir. Never mind Ryan. You need your rest too.'

'Always watching my medical well-being.'

'I was thinking of Mrs Craddock.'

'Don't worry, I'll be home within the hour.'

But once again, he wasn't.

Operation Sabretooth had been laid on for next morning, and the implementation of the orders from Ramstein and the finalisation of details kept him in Operations until the early hours. It was three o'clock before he slipped quietly into the big bed beside Maxine.

With relief, he saw that she seemed to be asleep.

'All aircraft at Battle Readiness. Concrete bombs will be carried except for two Mark 16 live two thousand pound bombs in positions one and twelve on the wing pylons. As you know, the new Mark 16s have not been calibrated ballistically, so at the end of the exercise, together with the concrete bombs they are to be dropped and photographed on Kilcreggan Rock, fifty miles north of the Faroes, where the RAF test their live bombs.'

Standing at the right side of the dais in Hard Operations, Colonel Craddock watched the Chief Intelligence Officer put his long black pointer just under the hem of the black sheet covering the big map on the easel – and then, as he had done for the Operation Grand Chasm briefing, he paused for effect. This was the time to show the Doves on the Hill they still needed the Forces.

Operation Sabretooth was to be the biggest NATO Air-Sea Operation ever. The Navies and Air Forces of America, Germany, Holland, Britain, and Italy would be simulating hostilities all round the vast Russian coastline. For the last three days, Haddington Base had been in the same state of frenzied activity as it had been before the raid.

For as the Intelligence officer pointed out, this was to be as near For Real as possible. And the Sixth Tactical Fighter Squadron, now world famous for its immaculate execution of the arch-terrorist, had been chosen to lead the principal exercise.

Watched by twenty-three pairs of anxious eyes, the pointer began slowly lifting the black sheet. The only eyes, Craddock noticed, which did not appear concerned belonged to the newly decorated recipient of the Air Force's highest award.

In the sudden grand gesture of a magician revealing his cleverest trick, Marshall swept the black cloth right over the back of the easel.

Gasps, whistling, groans. Only Ryan's face remained impassive.

Pinned on the huge map, ten long red ribbons fanned out from Haddington, all the way up to ten separate square search boxes right up in the Arctic Circle.

'Somewhere up there,' Marshall continued when the noise died down, 'is your target. A big Russian submarine depot ship, role taken by—' the pointer switched to a photograph of a warship being flashed on the screen beside the map —'the British frigate *Hampshire*. The Brass want to test the possibility of combining both the reconnaissance and the bombing role. As soon as one of the ten aircraft finds the target—'

A derisive laugh ran round the room.

—'you are immediately to review bombing check lists, complete your computer launch programming, fuse your bombs, both concrete and live, and proceed to the Initial Point, the start of your bomb run – and report. Repeat, report. You will then have completed your task – you will have "sunk" her. On the other hand, if the *Hampshire* has located you and held you in AAA and missile range for two minutes before you report, then it's you that's "dead"!'

The anxiety on the faces disappeared. Now they knew what they had to do, difficult though it was, they accepted it. Craddock was struck by the will-to-win absorption on the faces of the ten listening crews.

They were obsessed with the exercise, already locked on to it. For the purpose of identification, Enemy and Friend were called Red and Blue, but in the players' own minds, the Reds were the Bad Guys – the Russians – and the Blues were the Good Guys – the Yanks. On the many occasions on which he had commanded War Games, Craddock had seen officers identify so much with their roles – both Red and Blue – that they began weeping when they appeared to be losing, and some took it so seriously they had mental hang-ups.

'F-15 fighters of the Aggressor Squadron from Alconbury will be airborne to intercept you. They will bear Russian markings. AAA sites are on the alert to shoot you down from the "frontier" of the exercise, which is the Scottish border. So watch it! The Stratotankers will be in position at Latitude 70 North, Longitude 03 East.'

The aircraft commanders and wizzos went efficiently about their separate business – tracking the individual search areas, plotting the Stratotanker rendezvous position, collecting radio frequencies, weather, maps, prohibited zones, Notams (Notices to Airmen).

Already they had become part of Operation Sabretooth, their roles accepted and the Game begun.

None more than Ryan.

Craddock watched him narrowly. Maybe he'd figured him out wrong. Maybe he wasn't the spitting image of his father that he looked. Maybe he was his own man – and a brave one. Apart from the beat-up on arrival, and a sassiness to himself, Ryan had given him no real cause for complaint. On the contrary, he had brought credit to the wing, and to himself as its Commander. The Sixth TFS was the crack squadron in USAFE. Ryan was the sort of guy they needed.

Craddock's own conscience, his own gut feeling had misled him.

Ryan swaggered over to where Scott and Gorringe, his new wizzo, were studying intently, the Notices to Airmen. For a full minute, he stood there silently watching them.

The Ace of the Base still hadn't forgiven Scott for what happened at the dance, or for Samantha. Or for that tight-assed girlfriend of his and her offers of counselling. He couldn't help thinking that Samantha was maybe right now pouring out her marital difficulties into the Ice Maiden's ear. It made him that much more determined to beat the shit out of Scott, put him in his flying place. Second place.

'What's the hassle, Jonny?'

Scott turned. For a moment, he was taken aback by the hostility in Ryan's eyes. Then he said quietly, 'No easy gig . . . this.'

Ryan shrugged scornfully. 'Just an average basket of crabs. An exercise, not the real thing. We're not sweating, are we, Milt?' He called over to Ames, who was collecting their manuals and code books.

Ames came over reluctantly. 'Certainly aren't,' he said, though it was a lie and a big one. He didn't believe Ryan's throwaway carelessness about the exercise. He mistrusted Ryan on an exercise more than on the Real Thing. On the Real Thing, Ryan wanted them to survive. On an exercise, he wanted them to win.

Swinging his brain-bucket by the strap, Ryan jerked his head for Ames to follow him out of Operations.

First to climb into their aircraft, first to start up, Ryan dropped all pretence that this wasn't deadly serious.

As usual, they were last in the take-off order. When Ryan opened up the engines to maximum afterburners, he shouted across to Ames, 'We're goin' for the score! We're gonna get that fucking ship, so help me Jesus!'

Twenty One

'One . . . two . . . three . . . four . . .'

Arriving early at his office block that morning, deafened by sound, Squadron Leader Naylor counted the F-115s as one after the other they took off down the runway and screamed up into the sky.

'. . . five . . . six . . .'

Ever since Operation Grand Chasm, Steven Naylor had worked ceaselessly at what he called 'mending fences' between the village and the Base.

The dance had certainly had an effect. So had the football match he had arranged between the Sixth Tactical Fighter Squadron and the Haddington Rovers. He organised the connection between Buzz's parents and the Danns, and Mr and Mrs Barlow had come over to stay in Fenside Cottage, where they established an immediate accord with Jennie in their mutual grief. Mrs Barlow could not be separated from her grandson. And Mr Barlow could not be separated from the Fenland waterways. Fishing was his only relaxation from the giant Pittsburgh mill, and Jennie and Mrs Barlow were convulsed with laughter at the sight from the kitchen window of gnarled British poacher and huge American steel man stealthily slipping moorings every evening in the old rowboat to disappear together into the misty night.

In addition to his own efforts, nature had been kind to the RAF Liaison Officer. The wind changed direction, and for two whole weeks had blown from the east. So the F-115s had taken off in the opposite direction and not flown over Haddington village.

And time blurred everything. Two weeks in politics was a very long time. People forgot. But today they would remember. Today the wind had resumed its prevailing direction from the west. The whole serviceable strength of Number Six TFS were one by one skimming the roofs of the cottages.

'. . . seven . . . eight . . .'

Inside the office block, his telephone began indignantly ringing. 'Hope to God,' he thought to himself, 'they're not having another go at Hammadaz!'

Then, reluctantly, in he went to answer it. By so doing, he missed seeing the last two F-115s take off. In the first of those aircraft, a bell was ringing even louder than his telephone and in addition a red warning light was flashing.

'Fire in the starboard engine!' Scott's new wizzo shouted.

As Gorringe reached for the throttle to pull it back before pressing the extinguisher, Scott grabbed his hand.

'False alarm,' he said quietly. 'Look at the temperatures and pressures. All normal.'

Glenn wouldn't have made that mistake, Scott was thinking, as he continued his climb. But then Gorringe was young and comparatively inexperienced and like everybody else he had to be given a chance to learn. Pity Ryan hadn't agreed to part with Ames. Not just for himself, but Ames too. They still made an odd crew, he reckoned, in spite of their success. Ames, he was sure, would be easier with him.

Even as the thought went through his mind, from his side window close to his port wingtip, he saw the *Probe* zooming past him in a near vertical climb. The Ace of the Base couldn't stomach anyone in front of him! Had Glenn been sitting in the righthand seat, they would have exchanged a couple of cracks. But as it was, Scott kept silent.

Not so Ryan in the cockpit of the *Probe*. The Exercise Area did not start for four hundred miles and for most of the way to Scotland, out of his mouth streamed plans, instructions and tactics.

'. . . there'll be one hell of an echo from the "Russian" ship. Just as soon as it's on the radar, switch off!'

'Switch off?'

'Don't want 'em alerted by our emissions. At nought feet, we'll sneak right up to the IP. Then we got her!'

Ryan was crouched over his control column like a jockey over the neck of a champion racehorse, as though urging the *Probe* forward. He couldn't wait to get right up there and find the ship in their allotted area of the Arctic Circle.

'But what . . .' Ames hesitated about asking such a dangerous question '. . . what if the ship's not in our allotted area?'

'I have a feeling about this one. Like I had a feeling about

Akhbar's convoy. The ship *is* in our area. We'll sniff out the bastard like we sniffed out Akhbar.'

High above Northumberland, in a cloudless sky, carrying thirty thousand pounds of kerosene, ten concrete bombs, two two thousand-pound high drag Mark 16 iron live bombs and six practice Sidewinders, the *Probe* roared confidently northbound over Otterburn. Under its wings fled a patchwork of English fields and woods till up came the Cheviot Hills and the Scottish border.

Ryan throttled back for the descent into the Exercise Area.

'Watch out for Bogeys now!' Ryan warned. 'Those Aggressor guys have brass balls!'

Right down to the ground they went, skiing over the moors and twisting through valleys. There was not a sign of any other aircraft, and Ryan was jubilant when he saw ahead of them sea mist forming over the Atlantic beyond the Caithness coast.

'Won't find us in this shit!'

Down into the middle of it he dived. Damp cotton wool covered the windscreen. Glancing across at the radar altimeter, Ames saw the needle flickering around fifty feet.

Then in the scopes, suddenly a tiny speck.

'Airborne radar contact, twelve miles at six o'clock low.'

Ryan pushed the throttles forward. Up went the machmeter to .9, 1.0 . . . 1.2.

'There's two of them . . . no, three! Four miles. Closing.'

Ryan lit the afterburners. Shuddering and roaring, just above the sea, the *Probe* rocketed through almost nil visibility at nearly a thousand knots. 'We'll lose 'em in this!'

'Two miles now,' Ames shouted. 'They got search radar locked on us!'

Ryan switched on the jammers.

'They're still on to us! Gaining. Switched now to Sidewinder target track.'

Suddenly, Ryan chopped the power, pulled hard back on the nose. Immediately the speed sagged in the steep climb. Air brakes went down. Then the undercarriage.

The *Probe* seemed to stop dead and hang in mid-air like a Goodyear blimp. Ames was thrown heavily against his straps, the G knocking all the air out of his lungs.

Seconds later, three F-15 fighters camouflaged Russian grey and marked with Red Stars, shot past their wings.

'That foxed them, Milt!'

Ryan cleaned up the aeroplane and, increasing the power, descended back into the mist.

'Keep your eyeballs skinned. They'll have another crack!'

But they didn't. Ames watched the specks on the radar get smaller, and disappear off the scope to the south.

'Aggressor Squadron my ass!' Ryan gave Ames a satisfied smile. 'What's ETA at the tanker?'

'11.06.'

The mist began clearing. Ames produced the flask of coffee, poured out two cups. Ryan drank his at one gulp, pushed the empty cup off the throttle box on to the floor, and looked into his HUP radar. Now there were heavy cumulus build-ups ahead. Interference and sea returns jittered across the scope.

On his Attack radar Ames managed to pick up the tanker beacon at ninety miles, but by that time the wind was gusting at seventy knots.

Even so, Ryan congratulated himself on reaching the tanker before anyone else.

'Request clearance to precontact, Booms.'

From her position prone on the floor of the tanker's tail, the girl Boomer answered. 'Firefly One, cleared to precontact.'

'Stick your boom out there. I'll go underneath and you plug us!'

Motoring out of the tail of the Stratotanker came the nozzle-ended pipe.

'Proceed with caution.'

'I'm always cautious, Booms.' Ryan neatly centred the *Probe* in the green of the tanker's belly lights. 'Moving in!'

The bomber was bumping and rolling in heavy turbulence as the Boomer 'flew' the boom towards it. The lighted nozzle came wobbling over the top of the *Probe*'s canopy.

'Stabilised precontact!' Ryan reported.

A scraping clatter behind their heads indicated that the boom had fouled the bomber's receptacle.

Ryan yelled 'Jesus! What the—'

'You got out of position!'

'Did I hell!'

'There's ice on your receptacle.'

'More like ice on yours, sister.'

The woman was keeping her temper. 'I'll try again.'

'Try harder. And this time for chrissake, get it in!'

But it was not until the fourth attempt that contact was

established, and the Boomer started the fuel pumps. 'Fuel flowing. No leaks.'

By this time, Scott was circling the tanker, watching the performance as he waited for his own suck.

When refuelling was finally completed, as Ryan broke away, his farewell to the Boomer was 'Woman!' He made it sound like a swear-word. 'You oughta go back to training school.'

'Maybe she was cold,' Ames suggested, reading off their new fuel load.

'Sure! Frigid. Tight-assed.'

'Helluva job for a woman.'

'Sure, sure. Women shouldn't be allowed on combat aircraft. *Bed*. That's where they belong, huh?'

Ames said nothing, as they headed towards the search area three hundred miles away. 'Oh, I forgot, you wouldn't know, Milt.'

'Wouldn't know what?'

'About women. About their place.' Ryan looked across at him slyly. 'You've never had one, have you, Milt? Not even that little nurse I handed on to you?'

Ames shook his head. He felt sick with a sudden helpless anger. He wanted to protect the fragile but meaningful relationship he had with Harriet from Ryan's coarseness. But he couldn't.

'Jeez,' Ryan shook his head in mock sympathy. 'I'd've said she was a cert!'

Ames turned to him furiously.

Ryan held up his hand. He grinned. 'Only kidding, Milt!' Then added, 'My! So it's serious, huh?'

Then pleased with his own little joke, his good humour for the moment restored, he concentrated his attention on the HUD radar in front of him.

They were now a hundred miles north of the Arctic Circle. The gale force winds had dropped. The weather improved.

'Five minutes from allotted search area,' Ames reported.

'Then keep your eyeballs skinned!'

They were flying at two hundred feet to escape 'enemy' detection above a strange grey-green silent sea. No waves, no white-caps, the iridescent surface like the skin of a vast jelly-fish. Millions of miles above them in great green and silver searchlight beams glittered the *Aurora Borealis*, covering the sky with an eerie phosphorescence, and causing interference on both radio and radar.

Ames's Attack radar was speckled with jumping sparks, making the screen difficult to read.

'Bad clutter!' he reported. 'Can't wc go higher?'

Ryan shook his head. 'Nope. They'd spot us.'

Using all his skill, Ames struggled to separate real from false, eventually reporting, 'Contact at ten o'clock. Twenty-one miles.'

Ryan put up his thumb. 'That'll be it!' He turned the F-115 to starboard till the contact was centred. 'Before Initial Point Checklist!'

Ames demurred. 'Haven't identified yet.'

'No need.'

As Ames picked up the plastic-covered checklist, he took another look at the blip, adjusting the frequency and the brilliance. Altogether too tall for a ship, he decided. An odd shape, too – one he'd never seen on a scope before.

Just as he took his eyes away from the radar, he glanced through the windscreen. A sudden shaft of sunlight had glittered on a jagged white blob.

'Iceberg.'

Swinging the aircraft back on to their search track, silently Ryan swallowed his disappointment. Five minutes later, the wizzo reported another contact. This time at forty-one miles.

Another iceberg.

Twelve minutes after that, another one. Even such a sensitive set as this, Ames was beginning to realise, in these conditions couldn't produce the definition necessary to distinguish between a ship and an iceberg.

But he went on trying. The search continued in a silence that grew colder as time ticked by. North, west, south, east went the *Probe*.

Nothing but icebergs on the radar. Nothing but crackling and interference on their audio pick ups.

'That's the ninth time you've led me on to an iceberg,' Ryan exploded. 'Don't you funnyfoot me again!'

But the tenth exploration of a contact produced the same result.

'Jesus! What's the matter with you, Ames? You're like that dumb Boomer broad.'

Ames was driven to say what he'd reckoned all along, but hadn't dared to. 'The ship's in someone else's area. That's why we can't find it.'

'Don't give me that shit! It's here, man! I know that goddamned ship is *here*!'

Ames said nothing. Something far more important to him than a pseudo 'enemy' warship was beginning to concern him. They were up at Latitude 82 North now, flying over a sea steaming with cold.

The time was 14.35. The brief Arctic day was coming to an end with the beginnings of a purple twilight. In the west, the setting sun burst through a build-up of black cloud, briefly painting the *Probe*'s nose a lurid scarlet.

No other searching aircraft had reported a sighting. One by one came the signals. They were returning to their allotted tankers, dropping their load on Kilcreggan, and returning home.

'Scott's given up,' Ames reported.

'He would!'

'Time we did.'

'Jesus! I'll say when it's time.'

'Dief's returning.'

'What did I tell you? No one's got a sighting. It's *gotta* be here!'

The sun settled below the horizon. Darkness began rising from the shadowy sea.

'Look at the fuel gauges, Rod!'

'I've looked.'

'Only six thousand pounds! Gotta return to the tanker. Ice'll be worse now. We'll—'

'—stay here till we find the bastard!'

'If we don't turn south, we're not going to find anything ever again!'

'Chickenshit!'

'Rod! All the other guys have gone home!'

'Then we'll be the ones to find her!'

Ames looked across at his aircraft commander. Helmeted head down like a ball player. Hugging his control column like the ball. Jaw jutting out. Eyes fixated on his HUD like on a goal.

'Rod!'

Ryan didn't hear. He appeared hypnotised. Possessed. Locked on to the target of a ship that wasn't there.

'Rod!'

Ames felt a terrible sense of isolation. In the shimmering twilight, Ryan looked alien. A creature from another planet. Someone who didn't understand Ames's language, someone beyond communication. Here the two of them were, low down on these wastes of water, hundreds of miles from civilisation, trapped in a grey universe peopled only by white ghosts of icebergs, going further and further away from Base, flying fast as a bullet into gathering darkness.

A shiver of panic swept over him. He was utterly alone.

'Rod!'

The eyes never blinked. The man never moved. A wild idea came into Ames's head that his aircraft commander was dead. Had had a heart attack. A brain haemorrhage. Been paralysed. That a dead man was locked on to the stick.

'D'you hear me, Rod? Rod, what's up?'

No response. The only sound, the roar of the engines. The only sight from the windscreen, the icy sea melting into night.

Suddenly Ryan came to life. He shouted, 'There!'

He was pointing at his HUD. 'Contact!'

Ames switched his eyes to his own big Attack radar. 'Could be another iceberg.'

'She's moving!' He glanced exultantly at his wizzo, eyes glowing like blown-on coals. 'She's moving!'

So she was, or so she appeared to be. For a moment, relief washed over Ames. They had found the goddamned ship. Now they could do what they had to do, return to the tanker, have that strange physical release of dropping their live load on Kilcreggan Rock, and head for home. Before closing time, he and Harriet would be sitting by the log fire at the Riverside Inn.

He called out, 'Range thirty miles.'

'This sure is *it*!'

Ryan slipped in the auto-pilot controls, and started the Before Initial Point Checklist, arming bombs and missiles on the console. Up came a row of ten red and yellow lights. Checking each individual missile, Ames called, 'Bombs fused! Cameras on! Bombing system on auto!'

Now the bombing computers had control of the entire aircraft – auto-pilot, when to release the bombs, everything. All Ryan had to do was to keep the electronic cross-hairs on the aiming point displayed on the Flight Command Indicator in front of him.

'Four minutes to IP!' Ryan shouted. 'Climbing to three hundred feet. Bastards haven't spotted us! Slowing down for bomb release.'

In four minutes it would be all over, Ames was thinking. Exercise completed. Bombs defused. Ryan again victorious.

Suddenly through the gloom, Ames caught sight of a superstructure towering above the horizon. Far too big for any British frigate, of a strange, almost oriental pagoda shape.

'Hold on, Rod!'

Ames snatched up his night binoculars.

He saw a grey-green camouflaged bridge. Two funnels. Guns in triple turrets.

'It's not the *Hampshire*!'

Ryan took no notice. The *Probe* had become a kamikaze rocket locked on to the radar contact ahead. All that was stopping the release of the bombs, both concrete and live, was the Master Armament Safety Switch in the On position, mid-way on the instrument board, with a thick safety tape across it.

'Centering the target!' Ryan called out. 'Three minutes to IP.'

'Abort! Stop!' Ames shrieked. 'It's a real Russian! It's the heavy cruiser *Volvonov*!'

Suddenly, bright yellow flashes in the twilight. The gun turrets turning towards them and belching fire.

Ryan screamed. 'They're mad! They're firing at us!'

'Warning us to keep away!'

Up came a red and yellow curtain of cannon fire. Blast rocked the F-115 sideways.

'We'll teach the bastards! Two can play at this!'

Ames reached for the auto-pilot controls to disengage them, but Ryan pushed him away.

'Two minutes to IP.'

Ames yelled, 'You're crazy, Rod! Crazy!'

'Centered the T!' Ryan shouted. 'We got her! We got her!'

Ryan's voice was high and exultant. He lifted his right hand. Horrified, Ames saw him reach for the safety tape on the Master Armament Safety Switch to rip it away and turn the switch to Off.

He shot out both his arms, grabbed Ryan's hands, held them desperately.

Locked together like Siamese twins, swearing, elbowing, yelling, squirming within their straps, inches below the Armament Safety Switch, the two men rocked over the throttle box from side to side of the cockpit, fighting for mastery.

Little clicks, tiny movements in azimuth and altitude. Blindly, a slave to the computers, the auto-pilot was obediently taking them to bomb the ship now held automatically and irreversibly in the cross-hairs.

The bones in Ames's hand seemed like they were snapping. His fingers weakened, started to unclasp. He felt helpless, defeated. I'm giving up, he thought. This is the end of me. The end of everyone. Maybe the end of the world. His mind was shot through with the sharp painful memory of that first time he met Harriet, his stupid, callow words to her outside the Base: 'If *I* promise not to start the Third World War, will you promise to see me again?'

Jesus Christ, and here they were maybe doing just that! Starting the Third World War, The Third Contingency, The Big One.

Unconcerned, impassive as a manmade God, the electric clock in front of him ticked five seconds . . . ten seconds . . . fifteen seconds . . .

Ryan saw nothing, heard nothing, was aware of nothing but the need to free himself of the panicking son-of-a-bitch Ames. He knew what he had to do. This was For Real again. Real bullets. Real cannon. Real bombs.

And only he could do it. He was possessed of the greatest power on God's earth. Like his father, he was in the right place at the right time. Tear off that tape, and he changed the whole world. Tipped the earth on its axis. Blasted the Evil Empire. Touched the hem of God's garment again. Executed once more the Hammadaz raid. His father had led his wingmen through a curtain of cannon fire like this into the muzzles of the Vietcong guns. And here he was, his father's son, poised to sink that Commie ship single-handed.

He heard the chickenshit Ames yell, shrill as a woman, 'Ryan! You're mad! Mad!'

The word echoed tinnily around the cockpit. With a sudden violent jerk, Ryan twisted his hands free, shoved Ames away, toppled him aside and grasped the tape.

Ames was flung at an angle over Ryan, his arms flailing. Tossed like that, he saw a little gleam of light. The glow from the phosphorescent instruments glinted on the hilt of Lieutenant Ryan's knife projecting from the sheath on Ryan's hip.

He remembered reaching for it, grabbing it out. He remembered the wild triumph on Ryan's face as he began to rip off the safety tape. Then the whole world exploded inside his head. There was a nightmare of noise and shouting and screaming and dancing lights.

And then like waking from a dream, he heard a voice that was shouting and recognised that it was his. There wasn't any other voice. The knife was in his hand and he was plunging it into Ryan.

Again! And again! And again!

And when his head cleared, there was blood all over his hand—

And Ryan was dead.

Book Three

16 December
The Court Martial

'This is a goddamned moxie, Cas!' General Vosper tossed his cap on to the table in the court martial ante-room, hooked out a chair with his foot, subsided into it, and resting his elbows on the table, cupped his jowls in his clenched fists. 'Jesus-Christ-on-a-crutch, Cas, we're all in the shit!'

On the way over from the helicopter landing pad, where Craddock had dutifully met him, General Vosper and he had exchanged distant but polite pleasantries. Now the General was into business.

His angry eyes gleamed up at Craddock, still standing. 'Sit down, for chrissake, Cas! We gotta sort things out! Like I told you before, we gonna take that motherfucker to the goddamned cleaners!'

Craddock said nothing. The General had certainly told him several times in the last month what was going to happen to Ames. And he had hinted, not very subtly, at what might happen to Craddock if the General's way did not prevail.

It was close on eleven o'clock. From the other side of the brown-painted door to the courtroom came the sound of measured feet, the scraping of chairs, clipped voices, as the court assembled.

'It's an open and shut case, Cas! The son-of-a-bitch is yellow! He panicked. Murdered his AC. The best jock we got! Jesus, I'd shoot the bastard!'

He unclenched his hands to slap them, palms down, on the table. Then he got up and began pacing the room. 'I guess you know the damage? To you and me, Cas? Oh, sure it's recoverable from! Just! But we gotta minimise!'

He stood for a moment, staring out through the small high window at the concrete skyline of the Base and the wintergreen landscape beyond. The Jacob's ladder of effortless promotion, up through NATO to the real smooth highlife of the Hill that he usually saw when he gazed into his future landscape, had for the present retreated.

'I jest can't figure out, Cas, why you didn't spot that rotten apple. Or your psy – chiatrist friend, the good-looking Major.'

'Major Mansell, sir.'

'Yeah, *her*! Why didn't she spot the bastard?'

'She did suggest the crew should be changed.'

'Suggest! Suggest! That's no goddamned good! And from what I hear tell, you were all barking up the wrong tree! You all had it in for Ryan!'

'According to Ames's deposition, Ryan had a brainstorm.'

'Brainstorm my backside! No one's going to put it on record that the finest pilot in the USAF had a brainstorm!'

'That will be Ames's plea. That Ryan was going to bomb the Russian ship. That he had to stop him.'

'Jeezus! A decorated hero! Son of a Nam hero. Now you hear this, Cas Craddock! I want a clean clear verdict. No ifs and buts and fancy psy – chiatry. Sure a rotten apple got through! Your fault, Cas! And Major Mansell's! And Dief's! But we're all human. An' Ames'll pay the price. It'd look a goddamned lot worse if the bloody Brits and the Krauts and the Frogs and the Ruskies reckon two fucking madmen were up top and one of 'em was going to hose a Russian ship! It's not on, Cas! The USAF will not tolerate it!'

At that point, the hammering of the President's gavel on the court table could clearly be heard.

The General moved to the brown-painted door. 'I'll go in for my watching brief, Cas. And I sure will be watching! Tell Walton to pick me up at one for lunch.'

He opened the door and closed it quietly behind him. A court orderly had a seat ready for him, and the General tiptoed towards it respectfully, though the President was a mere colonel – an ex-pilot called Standish, now in Administration, long nosed, intense eyed. Reassuringly severe.

General Vosper sat down close to the Judge Advocate, Colonel Horder, and there, too, the General found reassurance. The bullet-headed, square-jawed Horder was a prosecutor who would surely press for the maximum sentence. General Vosper settled himself in his seat with confidence and stared darkly at the prisoner.

Ames didn't try to meet his eyes. He didn't try to meet anyone's. He fixed his eyes on the flag behind his seven judges, as he whispered hoarsely, 'I do swear by Almighty God . . .'

'You are charged that while on active service on 18 November, contrary to Section 9, paragraph 8, you did murder Captain Roderick Ryan, your aircraft commander. How do you plead?'

The hot air vents in the wall lightly stirred the flag. It seemed to Ames that all the stars turned away from him and only the thick red bars remained.

'Not guilty, sir.'

The President put his hand to his ear. 'I can't hear you.'

'Not guilty.'

'Not guilty.' The President squinted disapprovingly down his nose. 'I see.' He turned his beaky profile to the Judge Advocate. 'Is the prosecution ready to present its case?'

One after the other, Ames watched them take the stand. Not the real people. Figures in a strange, unfamiliar landscape. Figures in a play, figures in a TV box, figures in a marionette show.

Not hostile figures. Just unknown, bloodless. And in their own marionette-ish way, doing their best.

Dief – Major Diefenbaker now, crisp in best uniform, new cropped high and tight haircut, polished shoes, fresh shaved jowls, gave his account of the de-briefing after Operation Sabretooth. What Ames had said. Ames's description of taking out the auto-pilot, nursing the *Probe* back to the tanker, jettisoning his bombs and heading for home. Was he coherent? In command of himself? In a state of panic? The lawyers tangling about the word 'panic'. Christ, Ames could have told them!

'You say the defendant reported heavy firing from the Russian ship?'

'Yes, sir.'

'Was there any damage to the aircraft?'

'No, sir.'

Then the crunch question. 'Colonel, did you believe the defendant's account?'

A moment's silence. Then, quietly, 'Yes.'

The President of the court fell on Diefenbaker's single hesitant word. He leaned forward. 'The court will interrogate the witness.'

More questions, phrased and rephrased. And then the single word 'Yes', had become 'maybe', 'in part' and eventually gotten itself changed to, 'I believed Ames believed it was necessary to kill his AC.'

A different ball-game altogether. Ames was no lawyer. But he knew that.

Major Mansell did better. Precisely and coolly, the Ice Maiden affirmed that Ryan was in her opinion an over-aggressive, over-motivated, father-fixated pilot with marital and sexual difficulties, who possibly could have had a mental breakdown triggered off by manic depressive tendencies. Yes, this she agreed was with hindsight. Otherwise she should, *would* have taken steps. Did she accept then that some of the responsibility might be hers?

She did.

Yes, she knew that Ames had this last week been examined at the USAF Department of Psychiatry and found fit and sane.

Had she any comment?

None. She agreed.

So there were no medically extenuating circumstances?

Not in so far as the accused was concerned.

The calm precise tones were those of a friend, not a foe. But Ames longed for Harriet's warm, out-going friendship. He'd had several letters from her, but he had not been allowed visits. He'd have given ten years of his life to talk to Harriet. Then the thought leapt into his mind that if the verdict went against him, he might not have ten years left, maybe not any of his life left at all. And his mind couldn't focus on the rest of Major Mansell's evidence.

When she was dismissed, Captain Scott was called. Ames saw him hold the door open for her, exchange a look and touch her hand as they passed. The small gesture seemed immensely portentous to him, made Scottie and Major Mansell infinitely further removed, creatures in a landscape where happiness was possible.

Then Scottie was talking about an incident at the Base dance. Ryan had pulled a knife on him.

'Is this the knife – exhibit A? The murder weapon?' the Judge Advocate asked, bringing Major Danby, the defending officer, to his feet, demanding that the word 'murder' be extrapolated from the record.

Ames didn't listen. The sight of the knife made his stomach turn. He didn't care what they called it. Didn't they know he asked himself every bloody second of every bloody minute of every bloody hour of every bloody day, if it was murder?

He had been right, hadn't he? He'd saved everyone else, hadn't he? He'd stopped a terrible international incident, maybe a war, hadn't he? He seemed to have been split down the middle. His head was sliced in two like a pumpkin. Half of it said yes, half of it said no. He'd like to have got up and asked these seven judges what they'd have done. Let Ryan sink the Russian ship? Or not? And if not, how else to stop him?

Distantly he was aware that Scott was having a hard time. Why had Ryan pulled the knife? He was bigger than Captain Ryan, wasn't he? Had Captain Scott threatened him? Why hadn't he reported the incident? Was it true that Captain Scott had been embracing Captain Ryan's wife?

As Scottie left the stand, Defense Counsel shot his client a commiserating glance. He leaned over. 'You'll be taking the stand after lunch.'

Jesus, lunch! How could anyone eat lunch? Defense Counsel and Ames were led by the court orderly into one of the small rooms off the Main Assembly Hall, which was used as a changing room for entertainments and concerts. The orderly brought them hamburgers and Cokes from the Hamburger Heaven across the road. Defense Counsel ate with nervous voracity, finished up Ames's hamburger for him, and told him not to be nervous.

'I'm past it,' he said. 'I don't feel anything at all.'

Ames had reached that high, high point in flying where you get what's known as 'cut-off'. He was floating, disembodied, hydrogen-filled, a balloon glued to the ceiling that none of them could catch.

Physically he was aware of the greasy garlicy taste of those mouthfuls of hamburger in his mouth, as he took the stand.

From the ceiling, he gave his deadpan account. Defense Counsel led him gently. The Judge Advocate figuratively reached out a long pin and tried to bust him.

Ames simply repeated, 'I did what I had to.'

Over and over again, he said that to every question.

'Did you feel remorse?'

Ames said nothing.

'Shall I rephrase that? Did you feel any remorse or sorrow at having killed your aircraft commander?'

Ames felt that all right. That reached him. The ceiling wasn't high enough. The pain shot through his gut. In anguish, he shouted, 'You bastard, what'd you have done?'

And then he was down from the ceiling, down from the witness stand. Defense Counsel was mopping his brow. The seven judges were conferring. He could feel their hatred of him.

And then Colonel Craddock was called.

There were, Caspar Craddock counted them, fifteen paces from the Assembly Hall door to the witness stand. At the tenth, one came directly facing General Vosper, and for the last five, turned slightly to the left.

On that tenth pace, Vosper's eyes caught and held his. Craddock got the message. He could sense the atmosphere in the court, as he marched the last five and lifted the Bible in his hand. If you were the accused, it was going badly, if you were General Vosper, it was going well.

'. . . to tell the truth, the whole truth and nothing but the truth, so help me God!'

And when, he wondered wryly, as he carefully laid down the Bible, did God ever help those who told the truth? Not very often, he'd guess.

Well, one would see.

'Will you tell the court,' Defense Counsel began, 'your opinion of the defendant's account of the stabbing of Captain Ryan?'

Colonel Craddock took a deep breath. This he had rehearsed in his mind many times. He had rehearsed it aloud last night. When, for the first time, he had told Maxine about Ryan and his father.

They had sat together till the early hours, like they used to do when they were first married. There had been no question in his mind what he had to do – this time. He just wanted to know that he had her loving support for it.

Now he was aware of Vosper's eyes boring into his back. He cleared his throat. 'I accept his account as truthful.'

A faint whisper round the court, hastily subdued.

'Without question?'

'Not without question. But having asked those questions, that is my conclusion.'

'What opinion did you form of Captain Ryan?'

'He was a first-class pilot. A courageous officer. At times over-aggressive. At times headstrong.' He paused. 'Like his father.'

'What is the relevance of that remark?'

Craddock drew a deep breath, like someone plunging into an icy pool. Here he stepped over the brink, crossed the Rubicon, gambled his career to exorcise his ghost.

'Lieutenant Rory Ryan, Captain Roderick Ryan's father, served under my command in Vietnam. On several occasions, he showed a disregard for orders. The most flagrant example was on 29 August, 1968.'

'What happened then, Colonel?'

In a quiet deadpan voice, Craddock continued. 'We were flying the new wonder aircraft Starstreak. We'd lost three already. Causes unknown. That day we were flying Offensive Patrol towards Hanoi. Two vics behind me, Lieutenant Ryan leading the port, Lieutenant Hartley the starboard. We had orders not to proceed beyond the 20th parallel. Enemy and friendly lines and positions were confused. Having reached 20 South, I ordered a return to Base. We were all in the process of turning when Ryan reckoned he'd spotted movements down below. Against my orders, he dived, together with his wingmen. Sporadic fire came up from the jungle. Again, I ordered him to return, but he steepened his dive. Then up came a curtain of cannon fire and Sam 7 rockets. I saw their bombs explode on a village.' Craddock paused. 'None of the Starstreaks pulled out.'

There was dead silence in the court now.

Then the President said, 'They showed great courage, Colonel.'

'And great disobedience. Three days later, the news filtered through that the village they wiped out was a Vietnam Army Advance post. The three Starstreaks were lost for worse than nothing. For severe losses inflicted on the people we were fighting for.'

'Yet I understand Lieutenant Ryan was awarded the Medal of Honour?'

'Yes, sir. An Immediate Award.'

'So presumably you approved it?'

'I didn't block it.'

'All the time knowing what you did?'

'There had been great publicity. HQ had to justify the loss of three more of their wonder planes. It would have been impossible to rescind the award.'

'And in your opinion, Captain Ryan was a chip off the old block? Liable to do the same?'

'That was not only my opinion. That was my experience of him.'

The President again. 'But you did nothing?'

'I tried to have him rested. I was over-ruled.'

'And as far as Lieutenant Ryan was concerned, you did nothing to put the record straight?'

'No. At the time, things were going very badly. Widespread protests against the war at home. Good publicity was essential.' Craddock looked the President in the eye. 'It won't be the first or the last time, that truth is sacrificed to expediency.'

At least he had the satisfaction of seeing that barb go home.

He was fed to the Judge Advocate then. 'Are you telling the truth now, Colonel?'

'On oath.'

'Did you not ever feel you should have taken firmer action on Captain Ryan earlier?'

'Looking back on it, I do.'

'Do you feel there is any action you should have taken as regards the accused?'

'On that, no. Lieutenant Ames has always shown himself to be a skilful and conscientious officer.' Craddock cleared his throat and addressed the President. 'Faced with the situation that he finally found himself in, I cannot see what else he could have done.'

The President almost rose out of his chair. 'I am inclined to order those words to be struck from the record.'

Colonel Craddock was invited to step down. He walked through into the ante-room, knowing as he did, that Vosper would follow him.

'You've blown it, Cas!' The General shut the door quietly behind him. He was strangely, deadly quiet-voiced. 'You're finished! Washed up! What made you do it? For a chickenshit like Ames? Isn't worth you wiping your feet on. He's a born loser. Jesus, you're mad!'

'We're all mad, General. Some a bit less than others.'

'You'll be back to the States and retirement. No star!'

'Maybe, General, I've found my star.'

'Jesus! What sort of talk is that? What's got into you? What's Maud . . . Millicent . . .'

'Maxine.'

'. . . going to say? You throw away Ramstein, Brussels, maybe the Pentagon. An' you don't make life any easier for me! An' for what? For bloody what?'

'For me. For being me, I guess.'

'Christ, what sort of shit is that? What's so great about being a goddamned colonel retired? When you could've been enjoying the good life with me? Well, are you gonna wait for the verdict?'

'Yes.'

'I'm going back in to hear the summing up. Coming?'

Craddock shook his head. 'I'll wait here.'

'Tell yourself what you've done, huh? Tell yourself loud and clear.' The General paused with his hand on the door. 'I'm real sorry, Cas! Real goddamned sorry! I liked you. I liked Maud.'

He shut the door.

Craddock sat with his arms folded over his chest as another hour ticked away. The sky behind the window became that exquisite pinky violet of a Fenland evening, then faded swiftly into dark velvety blue. The lights came on all over the Base. The blood red drops of the obstruction lights, the acid white of engineering workshops, the blue of the hard hangars, the golden buttery blobs of the main camp roadways.

He stood up and looked out. He loved it all. The big, bustling, tumultuous dangerous Cage. A Cage of Eagles. From which he had let one dangerous eagle escape. At least he had faced that fact head-on. Life, he thought, kept presenting you with the same problem till you got it right.

Maybe now he had.

Through the door, he heard the sound of the seven judges retiring to consider their verdict. Twenty minutes later, the orderly put his head round the door to tell him they had returned.

As he closed the door behind him, Ames was already on his feet – white faced and trembling – to hear their verdict.

It seemed a long time before the President spoke.

Ames closed his eyes. The words seemed to come to him from a long way away.

'. . . not guilty of murder . . . guilty of manslaughter . . . sentence three years at Fort Leavenworth Prison, followed by dishonourable discharge . . .'

The powers-that-be could allow no less, Craddock thought. At least it wasn't murder. And maybe he had done something for the poor bastard. Maybe none of them would be standing here right now if Ames hadn't done what he had done. But that was a fact too hot for any of them to handle.

Craddock left General Vosper talking to the President of the court and walked outside. The air was cool and sharp with frost. His car was drawn up by the kerb.

Maxine was at the wheel. She leaned over and opened the passenger door, looking him over, minutely and anxiously. 'What was the verdict?'

'Manslaughter.'

'How long?'

'Three years.'

'How did he take it?'

Craddock shook his head and shrugged helplessly. 'Christ knows!'

Maxine started up the engine and accelerated the car away from the kerb.

'What about you?'

'The General opened the prison door.'

'Or maybe you opened it yourself?'

'Maybe I did.'

'So you told them?'

'I sure did.'

She let out her breath in a long sigh, not looking at him, concentrating on the road ahead. Past the pizza parlour, the bowling alley, the amenities store, then up Dowding Avenue to the officers' houses and the slight rise that led to their own.

The lights were all on. He could see Jarman bustling about in the dining room, setting the table for the evening meal.

'And the General told me—' Craddock smiled a small, grim smile —'I'm as good as finished. We'll lose all this. You've lost out on Brussels. Ramstein. On being a General's wife. On all that high life on the Hill.'

'We'll survive.' She took his hand. In a low voice she said, 'I've found something better than all that. I've found you.'

He suddenly wanted to say, what more could anyone expect of life than to find one other person? But he didn't know how. And even if he had known, he doubted he could have brought himself to say it.

Instead he put his arms round her, held her tight and kissed her on the lips.

As they walked towards their door, a heavy mist was rolling in from the sea, ringing the yellow street lamps of the Base with fuzzy haloes, softening the blues and greens and reds, blurring the lines of hardened hangars and bomb dumps, melting the whole Base away.

While in the sky above pricked the first few stars of evening.